I0602382

COLD STONE & IVY 3

The Seventh House

H. Leighton Dickson

Copyright © 2024 H. Leighton Dickson

All rights reserved.

ISBN: 978-0-9938865-5-3

DEDICATION

To Karen & Krista
Who, like Ivy, never gave up hope.

Also,
To Mary Wollstonecraft Shelley, the Mother of Science Fiction.
Bless her and bless her monsters.

ACKNOWLEDGMENTS

I think this series, COLD STONE & IVY, is a fanciful amalgam of so many influences from my youth. From Verne, Wells, Christie and Doyle, to Penelope Pitstop and Scooby-Doo, from PBS' 'Mystery!' with its Edward Gorey credits to Carolyn Keene's more sensible Nancy Drew, these creations inspired a very young me. Archetypes, stereotypes, cliches and tropes fired my imagination and channelled an insatiable thirst for mysteries and answers. Ivy is very much rooted here in my geeky teenage soul.

CONTENTS

"Like one who, on a lonely road,

Doth walk in fear and dread,

And, having once turned round, walks on,

And turns no more his head;

Because he knows a frightful fiend

Doth close behind him tread."

\- Simon Taylor Coleridge

The Rime of the Ancient Mariner

Prologue

Of Chocolate, Goggles, and Those Who Walk Again

"We are fashioned creatures, but half made up."
- Mary Shelley, Frankenstein: The Modern Prometheus

Feb 15, 1889

Veste Oberhaus Fortress/Observatory, Passau

Empire of Blood and Iron, *Germany*

"Do you see them?"

"Nein," said Karl.

"I can't see them either," said Emil, and he juggled the goggles over his eyes.

"Those are too big for you, *Dumme,"* said Karl. "They're as old as your Oma."

"And just as cracked," said Georg with a grin.

Emil shrugged and tugged at the straps that held the lenses in place.

"Keep looking," said Georg.

Karl leaned back from the edge of the window. "It's just a news story, Georg. Your sister is pulling your nose again."

Emil laughed, but Georg shook his head. There was a chocolate smudge on his bottom lip.

"It's in the broadsheets," Georg said. "They can't lie in the broadsheets. It's forbidden."

"It's forbidden for us to be up here too," said Karl. "Yet here we are."

"Thanks to my father," said Georg. "He likes us to keep watch."

The three boys squinted in the late afternoon sun, their breath hanging like fog in front of their faces. They squeezed their shoulders through the open window, the high tower of the observatory giving them an unprecedented view of the confluence of the Three Rivers. The *Ils*, the *Inn*, and the mighty *Danube* joined in Passau like the threads of a braid, carrying on through the snowy foothills to Vienna and beyond.

"Besides, there's no such thing as *Wiedergänger,*" Karl muttered under his breath.

"What about revenants?" asked Emil. He looked like a mad owl with his goggles and straps. "My Oma used to tell me stories about them before bed."

Karl laughed.

"Exactly! Revenants, undead, *Wiedergänger,* vampyres. Stories for children!"

"My father has been a guard here for five years," said Georg. "He isn't a child. He says there's a bone army coming from the Gilded Empire, and I believe him."

"A *bone* army?"

"That's what he says…"

The three boys fell silent, breathed deeply the cold winter air. Night would fall soon as it did on winter days in Germany, and they needed to take advantage of the remaining light. Classes had ended early that day, so the boys had made their way to the fortress of *Veste Oberhaus* for hot chocolate and a visit with the unit stationed there. There was always hot chocolate when the boys were pressed into service. It made the hours spent in the tower passable. That, and the pride of aiding King Wilhelm and the glorious *Empire of Blood and Iron*. They were sure they'd seen his airships sailing over Passau the other day.

"Nothing," said Karl after a long while, and he wiggled his shoulders to free himself from the others. "Besides, even if there **were** *Wiedergänger*, they couldn't travel on the river. It's not frozen."

"It never freezes," said Emil. "I wish it would. Then, we could skate."

"If it froze, the *Wiedergänger* could walk," said Georg. "That's the easiest way to get from Vienna. At least, that what my father says."

"But it's not frozen. It's water."

"Still…"

"Has your father talked about the *Wiedergänger* swimming with their rotting hands or missing feet?" asked Karl. "Or maybe they're using boats? Emil, has your Oma ever talked about the revenants using boats?"

"Maybe it's a bone navy?" Emil said with a grin.

Georg grumbled but said nothing, and the boys turned back to watch the river.

"Wait," said Emil.

"What?"

Emil pointed to the horizon. The boys leaned out, gripping the window ledge, and narrowing their eyes.

In the distance, the snowy hills converged where the three rivers became one. But something was happening to the surface of the Danube, changing the way it sparkled in the fading light.

Karl leaned out as far as he could, raised his hand over his eyes.

"Ice…"

"What?" said Georg.

"Ice," he said. "The river is freezing…"

From a dark river of glittering grey, white fingers of ice stretched across it, crackling and spreading, reaching from the east and the Austrian borderlands and Vienna.

"I have to tell my father," said Georg.

Together, he and Karl bolted from the observatory tower, their boots echoing as they raced down the stairs. That left Emil. He leaned out as far as he could, twisted tiny gears on the goggles as lenses slid into place.

"The Danube is freezing," he breathed. "The bone army is coming…"

Chapter 1

Of Men: Undead, Engaged, and Iron

"Nothing is so painful to the human mind as a great and sudden change."
— Mary Shelley, Frankenstein: The Modern Prometheus

It was a dark morning when the carriage rolled out from under the Lasingstoke arch on the road to Lancaster. Inside, Rupert St. John struck a match to light a French cigarette and settled back in the blankets. It was early, it was cold, and he'd barely had time for a cup of coffee. Mary Jane had refused to speak to him. So had Cookie for that matter, but then again, Cookie rarely talked to him in the morning. She was a cantankerous woman and he a cantankerous man. Their conversations were little more than sparring matches, with never a clear victor. It didn't bother him, her condemning silence.

Mary Jane was another matter entirely.

The carriage lurched to a halt under the west gate that marked the edge of the property. St. John sighed, blowing a thin river of smoke through his lips, waiting for the coach to resume its northwesterly course. It was a four-hour ride at the best of times but in this hail-dump of snow and rain, he couldn't afford any delays. Bertie had not answered his telegraphs and the dread he'd felt reading the London Illustrated Times had only grown worse.

"Ah, Mr. St. John, sir," came the voice from the dickey and a young face peered down through the trap.

"What the bloody hell is wrong, Davis?" he growled. "I've a train to catch. Surely the drifts aren't so bad that a pair of Warmbloods can't plow through?"

"Aw, no sir, it's not that." Davis Savage made a face. "Just, well…best come take a look, sir."

St. John clenched the cigarette between his teeth and pushed open the door.

Something was blocking the Lasingstoke gate.

"What the hell?"

He stepped out now and Davis joined him, leaping from the dickey to the snow-covered road. Behind the gate, two iron pillars blocked the way, making it impossible to continue by coach.

"What the *bloody* hell…?"

"Are those legs, sir?" asked Davis.

"Legs? By God, boy…"

Snatching the carriage lantern, he stepped forward and raised it up, up, up.

"It's the Milling Sentinel, sir!" gasped the boy. *"Cor,* I didn't think it could even move!"

St. John growled.

"On the orders of Her Majesty, Queen Victoria, and the War Office of Steam," boomed a voice from above. *"All residents of Lasingstoke are to return to the Hall until further notice."*

"What's going on, sir?" asked Davis, eyes wide. "Why can't we leave?"

"Damnation," he growled again. "It seems we're under House Arrest."

"Because of the Mad Lord, sir?"

"Aye, Davis." He threw the cigarette into the snow, crushed it under his shoe. "Because of the bloody Mad Lord."

***

White, upon white, grey upon grey. The view from the airship's porthole was a study in monochromes, and Ivy leaned her forehead against the glass. The pilot had announced that they were leaving the airspace of the Gilded Empire and entering that of Blood and Iron, but it all looked the same to her. Hills, forests, rivers, fields. Towns with freckles of gold from lanterns and Edison lamps. She found no warmth in those lamps, no life in the hills or forests, rivers or towns. But then again, she had died awhile back. It was only the Mad Lord de Lacey who'd brought her to life.

She choked back the tightening of her throat. It was mid-day but grey, as grey as the fields below, and she narrowed her eyes, trying to spy him moving on his dead horse along the river. He froze the Danube as he went. He was a creature of frost, a child of ice. The snow was his landscape. He'd never needed the sun.

"Excuse me, *Fräulein,*" came a voice, and she turned to see a man in airship uniform. "We are approaching the Imperial Airship *HMAS Royal Carolina.* I understand you will be disembarking, along with *Herr* de Lacey?"

She nodded woodenly.

"Very good. We dock via corvus. It's cold and unnerving at first, but quite safe."

She nodded again. He tried to smile.

"If you need anything, please let me know."

She smiled back but it felt strange, forced, like rubber.

And then he was gone, leaving a waft of cold air in his wake. She released the smile and straightened, risked a glance around the airship's cabin. It was tight for a *Gilded* frigate, likely meant for transporting a small entourage of ambassadors and royal courtiers, but she had to admit it was beautiful. Archduke Rudolf, Crown Prince of Austria, had spared no expense to ferry them away from Vienna. Polished mahogany, white curved ceiling, burgundy velvet, gold trim. No cold in here, unless you counted her heart.

Officers and ambassadors sat cross-legged, holding elegant cigarettes and meaty cigars, sipping sherry and whisky and port. It was a picture of sublime opulence, but the tension was as thick as the smoke. Eyes darted toward her, then quickly away, and she scanned the faces until she found Christien in the crowd.

He was seated at a far window, holding a cigarettello in his mechanical hand and a folded broadsheet in the other. But his eyes weren't moving as they stared at the paper, and she knew he was deep in thought. *We stop him,* he had told her days ago. Just like that. But that was far easier said than done, and she knew his remarkable mind was running scenarios like a kinetoscope, trying to solve this biggest riddle.

How did one stop the end of the world?

Three bosun's pips sounded and she turned back to the window. The *HMAS Royal Carolina* hovered to starboard, sails of black and gold, hull of polished brass. She watched the propellers spinning as they marshalled the airship's flight, not forward, not back, not skyward, not down. The *Carolina* hovered far above the Danube at the border between Austria and Germany, and if she stared long enough, she could see the river undulating like a serpent. But it wasn't a serpent, and it wasn't the river. It was an army of bones – re-animated corpses and skeletons pulled from the earth to follow their Crown Prince, the Mad Lord of Lasingstoke.

She heard the rustle of cloth and the tick of copper piping as Christien lowered himself into the seat next to her.

"Ready?" he asked.

Slowly, she shook her head.

He said nothing, merely sat beside her as the diplomats rose to their feet. The *Royal Carolina* was close now and she could see the hands work to secure the corvus that would serve as a gangway between the ships. She heard the shouts of the airshipmen, the pips and whistles and the rumble of docking. Closer now, she leaned forward to watch ropes tossed and hatches swung. Great, geared handles winched as the corvus clanked across the gap between ships. It hung like a bridge across a chasm. Which it effectively was – a sky bridge made of iron.

She turned. He was staring at her, eyes dull, brow arched. Patient. Condescending. His mechanical fingers held the stub of the cigarettello, and smoke rose like a twisting adder. Not for the first time, he looked like Rupert.

"Ready?" he asked again.

She began to answer, but her throat tightened, and tears welled up behind her lashes. She nodded. A mechanical cap sprang out, snuffing the cigarettello with a click. He rose, then, and helped her to her feet. The airshipman reappeared and held up a fur coat.

"It's a cold crossing," he said.

Yes, she thought to herself. Death was a very cold crossing.

Christien took the coat and slid it over her shoulders. Like a child, she thought darkly. Like a bloody dependent child.

They followed the diplomats and ambassadors down the galley to the docking bay, and the temperature dropped with each step. Winds whipped through the bay, and she was as grateful for the fur as she was for Christien's arm. They hung back while the other passengers crossed, a hand on each articulated railing, each footfall eliciting a shudder in the deck of the ship. One gentleman barked as his topper was plucked from his head and sent whipping through the skies. It became a dark speck in moments. They all watched it go.

"Ivy?"

She nodded and Christien helped her to the hatch.

"Don't look down," said the airshipman.

She took a deep breath, reached for the railing, and stepped out onto the corvus. It wobbled under her boot.

"One foot in front of the other," said Christien behind her.

Reached, took another step. Another wobble, and again.

It was blisteringly cold, and her lashes immediately stuck together. The wind blasted her hair, her coat, her tattered skirt. It was sharp and bitter and strong, and she realized that if she let loose the railing, it would easily push her over the side. Then, she'd be like the ambassador's top hat, twisting and tumbling on her way down.

Don't look down.

Step by step, she made her way; reach, step and wobble, reach step and wobble. She was halfway across before she looked down.

Down.

Down to the Danube, where shapes moved in an undead wave. Down, where Sebastien rode on his singular mission to end the world. Down to his great coat and his pale horse and his clockwork eyes. He had saved her life at the cost of his own. Even now, icy fingers called her back to the emptiness and the dark.

"Ivy."

If she looked hard enough, she could see him. She leaned over the side. If she really looked…

"Ivy!"

She could just lean. She could just fall. She'd be with Sebastien forever if she did just that.

She didn't even notice the rattle of the walk before Christien's hand was on her shoulders.

"Ivy. Walk."

She glanced around, disoriented.

"*Now.*"

Prince Edward was standing in the dark hatch of the *HMAS Royal*

Carolina, his large frame all but filling the space. He gestured with his bear-like hand, waving her on. Waving her in.

Little cymry, he'd called her.

Horrible accent. Complicated man.

She stumbled into his arms as she finished her trek, and he lifted her off her feet and carried her like a bundle of wheat into the docking bay. He set her down and held her out at arm's length.

"What was all that rot, m'dear?" he chortled. "Why, you could've been snatched away! Right away! And that—" He leaned in close. "—would have been problematic. Problematic, indeed, wot?"

"I'm sorry, sir," she muttered. "I don't know what I'm thinking."

He looked up.

"She's all wire and nerves, m'boy," he said to Christien over her shoulder. "Take her up to Cabin Two. It's reserved for Mummie, but she ain't aboard, is she? Ah HA!"

With that, he turned and thundered up the gangway steps, a swath of diplomats in his wake.

Christien grabbed her hand, almost yanking her off her feet as he moved to follow.

Ivy said nothing, let him drag her down the *Royal Carolina's* opulent hallways until they reached Cabin Two. The door was locked, but Christien held up his mechanical arm, and a skeleton key buzzed out. Within moments, they were inside. He closed the door and spun around.

"What the bloody hell, Ivy?"

"I'm sorry, Christien. I just can't. I don't know what to do. I don't know what to say. This is nothing I've ever known. It's nothing I've ever even imagined. I wish we hadn't left Lasingstoke."

"I told you."

"You did. You did." She wiped her eyes and sank to the plush mattress of Victoria's bed. Good God, she was in Queen Victoria's cabin, sitting on her very bed. "But he was determined to go, and I had to go with him—"

"Why?"

"To help him. To keep him safe."

"From?"

"From himself?"

"Well, you did a bang-up job of that, now, didn't you? Were you seriously going to make up for it by throwing yourself over the rail?"

She released a breath, then another and another.

"This isn't some horror broadsheet, Ivy, and it's not some tragic love story. Star crossed lovers, fated never to be together, *Romeo and Juliet* bollocks."

How did he know? Was she a book so easily read?

"Romeo and Juliet ended, Ivy. Their story ended. If they had lived, who knows what they could have done together, who they may have been."

She blinked slowly as his words found home.

"You're the writer of your own story, Ivy. Do you seriously want to end it that way? '*She threw herself off an airship bridge. The end.*' I may be miserable, but even I don't want to end like that. And if there's one thing I've learned from you, it's to fight for what you want."

She looked up now.

"I need your help, Ivy," he growled. "God, the world needs your help. And you know what? Bastien needs your help. His story shouldn't end like this either. So, give yourself a good cry, blub it out all over Old

Vic's pillows, and let's get on with it."

He shook his mechanical arm, growled again.

"Damnations. I'm out of cigarettes."

"Well, it *is* the end of the world," she offered meekly.

"Bloody comedienne, you are," he said. "Right. I have some ideas, but first, I'll round us up some tea."

"Coffee?"

"Rupert would be proud."

As he rung for the service, she flung herself into Victoria's linens, breathing deeply the scent of lavender and roses, ghosts and ash.

She was asleep in minutes.

***

The Passau Presser, February 20, 1889

Der Apokalypse Comes to Germany

With scenes from the Book of Revelations, the dread convoy from Vienna has been sighted making its way along the frozen Danube. It is said that they have been summoned by the fourth horseman of Der Apokalypse, and witnesses have confirmed that, among the hideous walkers, there is indeed a man riding a pale horse. It is rumoured to be the same Englishman alleged to have killed Rudolf, Crown Prince of the Gilded Empire of Austria, but since Rudolf himself is now confirmed to be very much alive, this must remain in the realm of speculation.

Fr. Antione of St. Stephen's has commissioned a special Exorcism Symphony to be played by the cathedral's impressive pipe organ in hopes of dissuading the Wiedergänger from setting up an encampment. Tickets to the Symphony will be available at the Veste Oberhaus, the Cathedral and City Hall.

Chapter 2
Of Pearls, Pins, and Projectiles from the Sky

"All men hate the wretched; how then must I be hated, who am miserable beyond all living things!"

- Mary Shelley, Frankenstein: The Modern Prometheus

He had never minded the cold.

In fact, for as long as he could remember, he had welcomed it. It made his skin tingle, made his fingers ache, and reminded him that he was still alive. He had always leaned into the drum of his heart and marvelled at its beating. Life had always been precious, fleeting, precarious. And now, gone.

Funny thing, life.

He didn't need to stop. The horse he had named Ash walked tirelessly, for in fact, he too was dead. Through the snow and across the ice, the pale hooves maintained a steady pace, their rhythm more home to him now than the stride of dear Gus at Lasingstoke. *Lasingstoke.* Like breath on a foggy morning, he remembered it. Two wings, four great corners, seven distinct houses. They called him home. They called him.

No, he corrected himself. One did.

Seventh.

Seventh, where he'd lived and died and lived again. Over and over until death became him. Soon, he would enter its shuttered doors and bring peace to the howling spirits confined there, including his own. In fact, he'd bring that peace to the entire suffering world. But first, he would go to Lonsdale and see his creator one last time. The man who created him. The man he'd loved.

The man who had killed him over and over and over again at Seventh.

It was dark but the sky was full of stars. A lifetime ago, he would have lain under the blanket that was night, arms crossed beneath his head, and try to number them. He always lost count, but he never minded. The stars were his companions, the night his guardian. Now, he saw them differently, and he swept his clockwork eyes along the banks of the river.

The Danube? Was he in Austria still or had he crossed some invisible line into Bavaria? Borders had meant little to him before, and nothing now. No fence or wire could keep him out, no guard or bayonet, no *Eisenmänner* or Sentinel or dog. *Dogs.* He loved dogs. They had loved him too, once.

But yes, this was surely the Danube. He had been on the river for the most part, freezing it as he went to give Ash fair footing. He studied the riverbanks, the mounds of snow and the bare trees that lined the shore. Black branches reached for the sky like skeleton hands.

Or maybe, that was the skeletons.

As if in a dream, he looked around. He'd seen the dead for as long as he could remember, but those were spirits, begging for vengeance. These were literal dead, undead and walking, skeletal and dry. Some with all their bones, others missing arms, ribs, heads, vertebrae. Most had legs, save those that dragged themselves for a time by their arms. But some couldn't keep up, and he wouldn't stop. He couldn't count the stragglers that he'd left behind.

This had started in Vienna. In the courtyard of the Hofburg when he'd risen from the dead. Quite biblical, he thought, though he was no saviour nor saint. All the rules were different now, and there was only the horse, the river, the ice and the end.

There was a fork in the river. Three forks, actually, and he leaned left, letting Ash take him and the shuffling mob westward.

Music floated like snowflakes down the Danube, and he cocked his head. It was church music from a pipe organ. It was sad and sweet, and he narrowed his eyes to look for a cathedral's spire along the bank. In the starlight, he could see the walls of a city, but of all the many cities he'd visited at night, this was a peculiar sight. It was completely dark, with no lights from windows, streetlamps, or candles, and he knew it was intentional. He had seen few living people during the days since the Hofburg, but now, he could see through those walls to the bodies within. They were living, as opposed to his current company, and they crowded together to watch from dark windows and darker roofs.

Were they watching him? Were they afraid?

Was he?

He could see through the walls of the city, thanks to the lockets that were his eyes, and everything flickered with ghostly light. Ghostlight? Or was it Arclight? He couldn't tell anymore. Alone in a high tower, a figure rolled a contraption toward a window. With his new eyes, he could see that it had three wheels, and he knew it was a Gatling rifle. It looked like a small cannon but could fire rounds repeatedly. Bavarian invention. He'd read of them in Rupert's journals. He knew it was being trained on him now.

Would it matter if he were already dead?

Still, he raised a hand and called Arclight. She was the locket of time and place, and she created orbs of intersection with merely a thought. He sent one of those orbs rippling through the walls and through the tower toward the mounted rifle. The figure leapt back as the orb swallowed it whole, disappearing in a flash of light. Arclight. Ghostlight. His family. His friends.

Almost immediately, the orb appeared above the ice of the river, and the Gatling rifle hovered a moment before dropping like a stone. The ice cracked, the surface split, and the river opened like a gaping mouth, taking some of the bone army with it into the water. In a heartbeat, the ice closed back up with barely a trace of either rifle nor hole nor half dozen dead that had accompanied it.

Ghostlight. Arclight. Lostlight.

Then, Frankow.

Immediately, he forgot about the orb and the rifle and the city altogether, and he followed the left fork of the river toward Paris.

***

Dearest and Most Darling Ivy,

We can't begin to tell you the uproar that is currently wreaking havoc upon our little hamlet of Over Milling. Since your debacle in Vienna, and the death and subsequent resurrection of the Crown Prince of the Gilded Empire, neither Franny nor myself can be seen out in public without a swarm of unwarranted, unwelcome questions regarding your scandalous disappearance! To his credit, my dearest Liddell Ninny has been a staunch defender of yours (and the Mad Lord's, to be sure) and the wedding plans are proceeding swimmingly. I do hope you will be in attendance. I simply cannot imagine such a fête without you at my side.

In other (likely related) news, the temper in Over Milling is also heightened due to the sudden disappearance of the Sentinel from the Milling Square! Add to that the fact that it has turned up at the Mad Lord's estate of Lasingstoke, settling its imposing self at the gate and allowing no one in or out. Gadzooks! Not even milk deliveries are allowed in. Fortunately, Lasingstoke has a healthy farm on the property, else your poor brother would be wasting away by now! I daresay the Scourge himself is furious, but as for Franny and myself, we've heard nothing from him.

And lastly, dearest, bravest heart, we hope all this kerfufflery hasn't knocked you off your writing game. You are most gifted in this regard, most gifted indeed, and it would be a terrible pity if the wildness of your life had tamed your writing habits. For dear Franny's sake, please do NOT let this happen. Next to her infatuation with the Duke of Clarence, your scribbles are the things that bring her most joy! Why, she has even sent said Duke some of your scribbles, and she's sure he's most keen! Why, you shall be as famous as Austen by Sunday!

In conclusion, we do hope you are well and indeed, alive, to read this and remember to kiss your own cheek for us. With hopes to see you very soon,

> *Fanny Helmsly-Wimpoll (soon to be Liddell)*
>
> *Franny Helmsly-Wimpoll (one day to be Saxe-Coburg Windsor)*

***

Penny Dreadful and the End of the World

Chapter 1

...

...

...

...

For the first time in her life, Ivy had no heart for stories.

She sat on the edge of the deep, wide, royal bed, breathing the strange scents. Medicine, machine oil, rose oil, lavender. The florals were overpowering, yet soothing in an oddly maternal way. The *Carolina* was the royal airship, and this, Victoria's private cabin. While she was a clockwork queen with rolling crinoline and an iron lung for a corset, she was still an English woman. She adored her gardens.

Ivy looked down at her boots. She remembered when she'd bought them in Lancaster with Fanny and Franny. The oxblood leather was scuffed and worn, but they fit like gloves over the stockings and the breeches. Her skirt was in tatters over them all, little more than a muddy ruffle after the events of the last two weeks, and she studied the fabrics that made up the skirt. Wool and lace, contrasts in meaning, opposite in worth.

She glanced over her shoulder at the Queen's small boudoir. There was a keyhole dresser complete with gilded mirror, and she almost didn't recognize the reflection that stared back at her. She looked wild, she thought to herself. Completely feral, a girl with only the faintest trappings of society. Her hair was matted, her cheek bruised, and she was not surprised to see her blouse splattered with blood. She had lived a lifetime these past weeks. She had even lived a death, and she wondered if 'deathtime' was something that would hold meaning in this End of the World. There was surely a story in that, had she the heart to tell it.

She rose to her feet and approached the mirror, slowly scrying the objects on the dresser's burled surface. Hairbrush, pearls, cameo earrings, *eau de parfum.* Each one a story in the making. Almost like an automaton, she picked up the hairbrush, studied it for a moment, before running it through her dark mane once, twice, three times. How could there be stories when the world was crashing all around her? There were snags in her hair, along with sticks and mats, bent pins and leaves. Her world *had* crashed all around her, and in an airship no less. The *Chevalier*, airship of the House de Lacey, shot down by an ironclad in the fields of Alsace-Lorraine. She narrowed her eyes, studying her face as she dragged the brush fiercely through her hair. But she had survived that crash. She and Christien and Sebastien, they had all made it out alive. And dear, dear Castlewaite with his gap-toothed smile. They had survived and they had overcome and found a way to revive the prince. If that wasn't a story, what was?

She laid down the brush, shook out her hair. Dry strands lifted to the ceiling with static electricity. She'd read about it in a journal from the Stepney Library Rooms. *Electricity.* What a marvel. She twisted the hair into a knot at the nape of her neck, filched a few royal pins to finish the job.

She had survived.

She picked up a string of pearls and held them against her neck. Her mother had owned pearls like this, much smaller to be sure. Her father couldn't afford much as a police constable. She laid them down.

She didn't need pearls.

The world needs your help, Christien had said.

She looked down at the tattered skirt, hovering like a cloud over her breeches. She reached down, grabbed the hem with both hands, and, with a deep breath, she tore the fabric up to the waist. Carefully, methodically, she ripped the skirt away from her hips and dropped the woollen bolts to the floor.

Bastien needs your help.

She turned back to the room, spied a small wardrobe, pulled open the doors. Frills, lace, ribbons, silk.

His story shouldn't end like this either.

Hiding behind the pomp, a blouse.

Sebastien *was* the story. The only story.

Three bosun's pips sounded through the pipes and she glanced out the porthole, where a trio of German airships rolled into view.

***

"What the hell are they doing?" Christien asked. The prince looked up from his map.

"Oh, I suspect they'll drop a bomb or two, wot?" Edward said.

"Where? On what?"

The Crown Prince of Steam said nothing. There was a cigarette at the end of his mechanical arm, and he lifted it, took a long, deep puff.

"Oh *whom?"*

Edward released a breath of smoke and arched a bushy brow.

"Oh god," said Christien. "Not on Sebastien…"

"What d'you expect them to do, boy?" asked the prince. "Let him run amok through Bavaria, rotting the food and raising the dead? It's madness, boy. The Mad Lord is finally living up to his name."

"That won't stop him," said Christien.

"Tell that to the Kaiser. He's bloody furious about that withered arm!"

Christien peered out the porthole. Propellers whirring, the *Blood and Iron* airships floated closer, their eagle-headed canvases blurred in the grey skies. It was a very grey morning. The land below was blanketed in snow and stitched together by stands of black trees. He could see the river winding through the fields. He didn't think it was the Danube anymore, but he'd be damned if he remembered his geography. Didn't matter. The river below was rippling with the bone army, and it was all because of his brother.

"What are they doing?" came a voice and he turned to see Ivy slipping into the main. Gads, she was a sight. White blouse under a red corset, riding breeches tucked into oxblood boots, no skirt. Boy's peacoat, cloak of fur. She was only missing the bowler. She'd had one, once. Her hair was pinned back, and she hadn't bothered cleaning the mud from her face. But it was all Ivy, he realized. Unconventional and odd, a force as free as his own brother, and it took all his wits not to smile.

"Morning, wee *Cymry,"* boomed the prince. "Did mummie's bed suit?"

"It did, sir. Thank you, sir," said Ivy, with the hint of a curtsey.

"Say! That's one of mummie's old blouses! She couldn't fit an arm into it anymore, but it fits you right smart! Ah HA! Ah *HA!"*

"Please, sir, tell me what's the plan with the airships?"

"They plan to bomb him, Ivy," said Christien.

"Smoke the revenants to smithereens," said Edward.

"What? No!" She turned. "Christien, bombing him won't help. It won't stop him."

"I've told him, Ivy. This is the Kaiser's doing."

A steward appeared at the prince's side.

"Excuse me, Your Highness," he said. "Teslagraph from the *Walküre Eins,* sir."

"That's the big one," said Edward. He took the paper and slipped his pince-nez to the bridge of his nose.

"This isn't the end of the world, sir," said Ivy.

"Rotting food, rising dead, earthquakes and pestilence?" Edward guffawed as he read. "Sounds damned apocalyptic to me, wot?"

Through the porthole, Christien could see men on the lead airship, *Walküre Eins,* rushing about the open deck. Of course, an airship could bomb a city from its position in the skies. A line of walking people, whether dead or not, would be little trouble at all.

"Is the food still rotting?" Ivy asked.

The prince narrowed his eyes.

"Is the food still rotting, sir? I mean…" She peered out the window. "Look at the river. The ice thaws after he's passed. After the dead have passed. Maybe the food stops rotting too?"

Christien moved beside her, peered down to the dark ribbon that was the river. The girl was right. He could see the convey of revenants moving along the river like an undead wave, bobbing and rippling in the grey morning, but he could also see that, where they had passed, the river opened back up again.

"He hasn't hurt anyone in this strange procession, has he?" she asked.

"Doesn't matter," said Edward. "You were there in the Hofburg. He's a risk to all of Europe."

"This can be stopped, sir," said Christien.

"Yes, I'm afraid it can," said the prince, and he held up the teslagraph. "And it will. Right now."

Christien growled and spun on his heel, marched through the narrow airship passages until he came to the open deck. The wind almost blew him backwards and it gave him the briefest moment of hesitation. The last time he'd been on the open deck of an airship had been over Alsace-Lorraine when the *Stahl Mädchen* had shot down the *Chevalier*. It had been an utterly terrifying experience, and he wasn't sure how any of them had survived.

He steadied himself over the roar of the engines. The three airships were dreadfully close, with the *Walküre Eins* nearly parallel to the *Royal Carolina*. He could see the crew, the bridge, the cabins, but not the bomb. He had no clue if they'd be dropping it from over the side, from a porthole in the hull, or from a hatch in the keel. It eluded him.

Wait! *There!* He spied a small porthole opening in the belly of the gondola. He looked down to the river, then back up to the *Walküre Eins*. With a deep breath, he rolled his shoulder, and a clockwork rifle clicked into place.

"Why didn't you just leave it alone, Bastien?" he grumbled to himself. There was no answer. There never had been.

In one smooth motion, he swung his arm up and fired.

***

Sebastien looked up. Four airships blocked the faint grey sun.

"*Walküre Eins,*" he said to the dead.

Then he, too, raised his hand and his forehead began to throb.

But from his eyes, Arclight began to sing.

***

The impact shook the deck of the *Royal Carolina* as the *Walküre Eins'* balloon exploded outward. *Not again,* Ivy moaned as she pitched through the deck door and slid toward the side rail of the main. She hit the bulwark hard as the deck bucked again and she dropped to her knees, flung a hand to grab the rail before she slid any more. She wasn't certain she could survive another airship crash over snowy German fields, and she definitely didn't want to give it another try.

The wind whipped her hair and her fur cloak, and she cast her eyes across the deck. Christien was tackled by the *Carolina*'s airshipsmen, and she saw his clockwork rifle as they pulled his arms behind his back. He had shot the balloon of a *Blood and Iron* ship, she realized, practically an act of war. There was no way out of it for any of them now.

The *Walküre Eins* lurched awkwardly toward them. Her propellers and flapping canvas caused wind to gust at frantic speeds across both decks. As she pulled herself up to lean over the rail, she watched in horror as the German ship released her cargo, and many large, black cylinders dropped from the sky.

***

Orbs spun from his fingers, colours bleeding across their smooth surfaces like oil in a puddle.

"*Walküre Eins*," he said. "God forgive me."

The orbs spread out as the bombs fell, swallowing them in a flash of light. Ash shook his maned head and Sebastien nodded.

"Yes," he said. "I understand."

And he raised his arm. Orbs spun into life above him and before.

***

Like a handful of pebbles dropped into a pool, the sky burst open above the German airship. Ivy recognized them immediately as Arclight's time-and-place bending orbs, and she screamed for the crewmen to get down. It was too late, however, as bombs materialized directly over the *Walküre Eins*, falling onto the airship that had dropped them. The canvas and rigging burst with explosions, and the *Carolina* rocked leeward, buffeted by blast after hot blast. She reeled in midair, her own propellers hit by flying debris, and Ivy clung to the rail as the *Walküre Eins* became a roaring ball of flame, spinning slowly, desperately downward. Airshipsmen leapt from her decks to theirs, and a few more sailed earthward, carried on the wings of great parachutes.

But the other two ships were not deterred, and Ivy watched in horror as bombs were released from their rocking hulls. This time, however, no orbs miraculously appeared, and far below, the snowy river erupted with fire, water, ice, and earth. Soon, the *Walküre Eins* followed, shattering herself in thousands of pieces across the fields. Ivy huddled against the bulwark until the roars quieted and the smoke began to clear. When she peered over the rail, the river was open as far as she could see.

Of the bone army, the horse, or the Mad Lord of Lasingstoke, there was no sign.

Chapter 3

Of Towers, Trains, and a Surprising Carriage Ride

"She is tossed by the waves but does not sink."
Motto of Paris

The Bavarian Bulletin, February 21, 1889

Pale Rider and Caravan of the Dead Defeated

In a show of Blood and Iron's power, the dreaded 'Caravan of the Dead' has been declared eradicated by Chancellor Bismark himself. A swift bombing campaign was conducted outside the city of of Passau with four of the Empire's most decorated airships dropping almost one dozen AE-50s across the banks of the Danube River.

"There is no longer a need for fear or public hysteria," says Bismark. "The threat has been dealt with in proud Blood and Iron fashion with only minor damage to one of our fleet. The Empire shall sleep soundly tonight."

Forensics teams have confirmed the destruction of the biological anomalies, commonly known as Wiedergänger, *and over a hundred skeletal remains require identification and reburial in the days ahead.*

***

Paris, Industrial Republique of France

Paris, City of Light, sparkled in the early morning—haughty, defiant and proud. The river Seine wound its way through her streets like the arms of a lover, glittering like a bejeweled necklace under the rising sun. The Sorbonne was in Paris, she remembered. World famous and progressive, the Sorbonne was a university that had a criminology program open to women students. It had been her dream, once upon a time.

Once upon a time. That's how stories began.

Ivy sighed and leaned over the rail, watching the city open before her. She knew little of its layout, likely couldn't distinguish the Sorbonne from the Louvre, Notre Dame from Versailles. Not from the air and most definitely not in the dawn, even though they were low-flying and slow. But a gleaming structure rose from the golden streets, and it took her breath away to know that they were headed straight for it.

"La Tour Eiffel," said Christien, and he stepped to the rail beside her, cigarette smoking in his mechanical hand. "They say it's the most progressive docking station in all the world."

"Even better than Big Ben?"

He nodded.

"That's what they say."

"I didn't think it was opening until next month," she said.

"I believe they're making an exception for the *Carolina,*" he said. "After the madness over the Hofburg, she needs maintenance and clearly, Bertie has some pull."

The early morning air was cool, the wind biting, and she tugged the fur a little tighter around her shoulders.

"I'm glad they're not arresting you," she said finally.

"They can't prove anything," he said. "Did I shoot the canvas or was it one of the bombs? Again, it seems Bertie has pull, and this time, I'm grateful for it."

He took a long draw of the cigarette.

"No, they're putting this square on Bastien where it belongs."

"He's not dead," said Ivy.

"Oh, I know it," he said. "Likely disappeared into one of them damn orbs. So, here's the plan."

"We split up," she said.

"We split up," he said.

The *Carolina* bumped and they grabbed the rail as the airship made ready for docking. Clangs and whistles, pips and roars. It was second-hand now, old hat, and she cast her eyes over the city below.

"Edward says he'll help me get back to London," she said. "I think a train to Calais, then a boat across the Channel. As much as I'd love to go home, I'm not sure I can afford the time."

"Straight up to Lasingstoke," said Christien. "Rupert will help you figure things out. *If* you can get in, that is."

"Bloody Sentinels," she growled, and he grinned.

"Spoken like a mol from Stepney."

He turned to her.

"Do try to get into my parents' room, if you can. It hasn't been touched in years. There's bound to be information in there somewhere. Information, secrets, answers, something."

"I will," she said. "Then, Lonsdale. I'm not looking forward to that." Christien grunted.

"Do your best to keep the old bugger alive," he said. "But honestly, I wouldn't blame Bastien if he does kill him. Frankow's done some horrible things. Remember Sophie?"

She tightened her lips and looked down at the city. The lights were bedazzling, the tower formidable.

"Anyway, I'll go to Normandy, to our estate outside Caen," said Christien. "It's still running a profitable stud farm. Bastien always talked about the horses."

"French Warmbloods," said Ivy, with the first smile in days that didn't feel strange. "But why there?"

"I'd like to snoop around a bit. After all, the lockets came from Normandy, commissioned for my family by an Elias Ashmole, if my memory serves. And *if* Williams and Crookes are to be believed."

"And if they've been commissioned," said Ivy, "Then it stands to reason that they can be *de*commissioned."

"Exactly."

He flicked the cigarette over the side and leaned forward on his elbows, the wind plucking at the dark hair on his forehead. His cheeks were red from the cold, his lashes edged with frost, and once again, she thought he was a very handsome man.

He caught her looking at him.

"We could have made a crackerjack team," he said quietly.

"We still do," she said, and he smiled.

She leaned next to him, swept her eyes across the city below.

"What about Marie Valerie?"

"What about her?"

"Never mind, then," she said. "I'm sorry. She was dodgy, but I thought you fit."

"We're both dodgy, so perhaps we did."

"We'll stop Sebastien. Maybe you'll get another crack?"

"Bastien brought her brother back from the dead," he said. "I'm sure they'd make me a duke and give me a duchy in Bohemia if I wanted. No, it's not that."

"What is it, then?"

He grinned sadly, clearly about to say something but stopped when the *Carolina* bumped again. Her crew began to assemble on the main, grabbing ropes and battening hatches. The Eiffel Tower was less than two hundred yards ahead now, and Ivy cast her eyes over the iron girders and steep stairways, the steam lanterns and the steady blink, blink, blink of the telegraph rod. Science and marvels, she thought. The things people could create when given the chance.

"Another time," said Christien, and he pushed off the rail.

Still, it was several minutes more until an automaton waved them in.

***

He had lost most of the dead in the river.

He wasn't sad. They were dead, after all, merely animated by his presence and power. The bombs that had been dropped had shattered the corpses and scattered the skeleton bones, but he hadn't seen any of it. Arclight had created an orb, and he and Ash had ridden straight through.

He should have given it more thought, he realized, rather than simply let it open somewhere on the road ahead. In fact, he wondered if Arclight could take him directly to Lonsdale if he willed it to do so. Or if it could take him somewhere else, perhaps in time. He still didn't know how it worked, and here it was, a part of him, firmly spinning away in the sockets where his eyes had been.

He slid from the horse's back and looked around. They were in a forest, with old spruce and pines covered in snow. He could see a light in the distance and for a fleeting moment, it made him feel warm. Warm. He remembered that feeling, and for some reason, he thought of Ivy.

He left Ash and trudged through the snow toward the light.

It was a cottage with a low, thatched roof and rough timbers for a frame. The windows were thin and without shutters, and he stood at a distance, peering in. There was a family sitting by the fire – an old man, a young man and two women, one fair and one dark. It was the very picture of familial affection, and he found it warmed him more than the light. Their clothing was old, the furnishings historic, and it seemed Arclight had taken him somewhere in time other than 1889. Curse the locket. He'd been careless with its use.

He glanced around. At least there were no dead.

No, that was not true, and he turned slowly to see several vapours floating in the shadows. They flickered and flowed, and he counted seven distinct spirits. They didn't beckon like most spirits did, they merely hovered, watching until he felt a breath on the nape of his neck. Slowly, his fingers wrapped around the tri-barreled pistol at his waist and spun around.

There was no one there.

He stepped back and turned. The spirits were gone too.

Curse the lockets. He couldn't tell what was real anymore.

With a final glance at the warm house and warmer family, he made his way back into the forest, where Ash was waiting.

***

As he stepped off the steel-plated base, Christien couldn't resist a glance up at the huge, cog and piston system that made up the hydraulic lifts. Copper wheels larger than a man, cables stronger than ten elephants, and a steam engine that squealed and smoked. The lifts made scaling the Tower that much easier for the public but, much like Big Ben, the airship docks at the top were accessed primarily by hundreds and hundreds of narrow, open steps. Still, the lifts were remarkable feats of engineering, and he couldn't help but be impressed. They were all the rage in London now, where there was the money and the will to build them.

The view that greeted him at the base of the Tower, however, took his breath away.

"An exposition to end all expositions!" barked the Prince of Wales. "At least, that's what ol' Boney is saying. It's supposed to open in May but they're terribly behind in schedule. Typical of the French, wot? Fashionably late to their own party! Ah HA! Ah HA!"

With the river on the north, he cast his eyes south to the vast *Champ de Mars*. He'd seen it years before when it was little more than a public square. Now it was a construction site, and even at this early hour, workers were beginning to arrive. Half-finished buildings had been erected around the square, some stone, others glass. It was clear that this would be a grand exhibition indeed, despite Edward's views on the matter.

"Gads, the pavilions," said the Crown Prince. "Bolivia, Nicaragua, Gas. Why, I hear they're going to run a demonstration on the powers of electric lights! Can you imagine? No more candles, no more coal?"

"This is the *Industrial Republique of France*, sir," said Ivy. "Their very name is a claim to progress."

"But whatever shall happen to our *Empire of Steam?* " he said. "I can't say I'm in favour of progress if it renders steam redundant."

"Where is the station, sir?" Christien asked. "I'll need to get Ivy a berth as soon as possible."

"Quite right. Quite right." The bear of a man swung around, hands gripping his ebony cane and thumping it on the ground. "There! *La Gare Lisch.* Should take you to *la Gare du Nord,* and that'll get her on her way to Calais."

He began to rifle through his pockets.

"From there, a passenger ferry to Dover, train to King's Cross, carry on up to Lancaster, etc, etc. You know the drill, girl. Damnations, why have I no notes?"

He swung around to the cloud of attendants, nervously hovering behind him.

"Money, goddammit! Get me some money! The girl has to get to England to stop the end of the world, wot?"

The attendants began to dig through their own pockets.

"Right," he said, and stuffed a wad of pound notes into Ivy's hands. "That should be enough?"

"More than enough, sir," said Ivy. "What I don't use—"

"Rubbish. Use it all." He turned, clapped a mechanical hand on Christien's shoulder. "As for you, m'boy, you're practically a lord yourself. No need for this pocket change! You're quite sufficient! Besides, I think the War Office gave you a bloody garrison in that arm, wot? Pistols and lockpicks and cautery iron nonsense! Ah ha! Ah HA!"

Christien offered a thin smile.

"I am quite sufficient," he said.

"Now, where's the carriage?" The prince swung around. "Boney said he was sending a carriage to fetch me for tea and French kippers. *French kippers*, wot? Who'd have thunk it? Now, maybe I could lay m'paws on a fine, French croissant, I would be a very happy man. I do love m'self a fine French croissant!"

And he stomped off, followed by his cloud of attendants, leaving Christien and Ivy under the Tower. She looked up at him, the pound notes clutched tightly in her hands.

"Good thing you have pockets, now," he said.

"You're not helpful."

"Come on," he grinned. "Your train to Calais awaits."

Together, they set off across the *Champ de Mars* towards the trains.

***

The Paris Morning Times, February 21, 1889

Early Test or Royal Guest?

An airship has been seen docking weeks ahead of schedule at the Tour d'Eiffel, according to a source on the grounds of the Champs de Mars and the soon-to-be-open Exposition Universelle. Rumoured to be the

HMAS Royal Carolina, flagship of the Empire of Steam and frequent conveyance of His Majesty, Albert Edward Prince of Wales. In fact, it is widely believed that His Royal Highness is, in fact, attending a secret meeting with IRF president, Louis-Napoleon Bonapart, to brief him on events surrounding the death, funeral and subsequent resurrection of Crown Prince Rudolf of Austria.

While there have been no reports regarding the Caravan of the Dead since the German bombing raid yesterday, French troops have already begun amassing at the Bavarian border, and our very own French Gardiens have been put on alert in case the mysterious Pale Rider and his army make their own resurrection and attempt to cross into France.

"We are prepared to defend our great country from all manner of enemies," Pres. Bonapart is recorded as saying. "If this army is indeed of the Devil, then we shall surely send them back to Hell."

Stay tuned for more updates on the Pale Rider, the deployment of the Gardiens and the latest fashion tips from the Prince of Wales.

***

It took several hours to square the trains that would take Ivy from *la Gare Lisch* to *la Gare du Nord*, and ultimately to Calais. From Calais, she was on her own, for there was no way to book passage across the Channel from Paris, despite the Republique's progressive reputation.

He was grateful that Ivy had, indeed, given him half the notes. While he was 'practically a lord', in fact he was quite broke. Penniless, insolvent, skint. There had been no way in hell Marie-Valerie would ever have considered him. It had been a pleasant delusion, however; a vain attempt at reclaiming childhood fancies, a faerie dream. If they had been different people with different parents, different duties, different expectations and demands…

Then again, if any one thing had been different, the son of a minor English baron would never have met the daughter of an Austrian Emperor, never have dared hope, never have lost his heart in so reckless a manner.

Life was strange and fickle and cruel.

He stood on the platform, hands in pockets, as the great, black steam train pulled away with clouds of smoke billowing in her wake. He watched her go, all seven cars of her, and stayed for a moment longer on the bustling platform void of train. Slowly, he turned and made his way passed the passengers and tourists, automatons and shops, to the steps of the station, and the streets of Paris at noon.

It was beautiful, busy, loud, and alive. Once again, he thought about slipping away, getting lost in a lifestyle both bohemian and free. There was no chance in hell they were able to stop the end of the world if Sebastien was set on it, so may as well make the last days his own. He shrugged his shoulder and a cigarette popped out of his hand, its supply replenished thanks to Bertie. He brought it to his lips and snapped mechanical fingers. A light was produced instantly, and he puffed once, twice, three times, ignoring the looks from the passers-by. Complete and whole, with arms of flesh. They didn't know the half. They didn't have a clue.

He let out a long, smoky breath.

He'd need a coach to Caen.

He spied horses across the bridge on the far side of the Seine, so he stepped down to the street, when suddenly, a carriage rattled up in front of him, almost running over his shoes. He jumped back and swore in French, as the carriage door swung open, and an elegant, high-heeled boot slid out.

"Get in," said Marie-Valerie von Habsburg.

Chapter 4

Of Trains, Teslagraphs, and a Teacher Named Wells

"I shall commit my thoughts to paper, it is true; but that is a poor medium for the communication of feeling."

– Mary Shelley, Frankenstein: The Modern Prometheus

Bertie flicked his mechanical wrist and a cigar popped out.

"Bloody hell," he grumbled. "I wanted m'pen. Abercrombie! Abercrombie, come here!"

He lit the cigar, regardless, and stood at the balcony window overlooking the manicured gardens. It was early spring, and a grey fog hovered over the ground. Élysée Palace was as ornate as the Hofburg or Buckingham or any other European palace, and he grunted at the irony. While the French had denounced royalty of all kinds, their president, Louis-Napoléon Bonaparte, still lived in golden rooms with velvet curtains.

"Abercrombie!"

"Your Highness," said a man behind him.

"Bloody hell, Abercrombie! Sneaking up on a body like that!"

"Apologies, your Highness. I have a quiet step."

"Make a fine intelligencer, you would," said the Crown Prince, and he turned from the window. "I need you to send a note to the War Office. It must get there before tea."

"We do have a Teslagraph on the airship, Your Highness," said Abercrombie.

"Bully!" said Bertie. "I do love me a new-fangled Teslagraph, almost as much as a French kipper, wot?"

"Will you be dictating the message yourself or shall I trot it over?"

Bertie chewed the butt of his cigar a long moment, swept his deep-set eyes over the foggy palace grounds.

"Trot it over, Abercrombie," he grumbled. "I have a parlay with Boney in a half hour. This may be the very thing to get this damnedable new alliance started."

"Of course, Your Highness," said the secretary. "Allow me to ready my finger press."

Abercrombie shuffled over to a desk, slid up a velvet chair, and pulled a small device from his pocket. It was a clockwork finger press, all the rage with the cryptographers in the War Office. It slid over both hands like mechanical gloves and produced an encrypted symbol for each letter tapped. The Crown Prince stepped over, trailing smoke like a veil.

"Bloody marvellous, wot?" he muttered. "What will those boys in the War Office think of next?"

"Cypher key, sir?" asked Abercrombie.

Bertie thought a moment.

"Sunday Tea," he said.

"Sunday Tea," Abercrombie repeated, and twisted a dial on one hand. "Ready, Your Highness."

The Crown Prince puffed a few good puffs, before clearing his throat.

"Subject: *Vanguard & Place Setting to Lasingstoke Hall, Lancashire*"

***

Penny Dreadful and the End of the World
Penny Dreadful and the Mad Viscount
Penny Dreadful and the French Train of Despair
Ivy sighed.

Trains were as much of her life as tea and fountain pens, but there was simply something disconcerting about being the only Englishwoman on a train full of French. She tried to squeeze against the window, not for the first time wishing she'd learned more than a few phrases somewhere along her life's short journey. It would have been helpful, she reckoned as she stared out the glass. It would have been smart. But there had been so many other subjects vying for time while raising her brother in the little rowhouse in Stepney. Surely, she could be excused for not making languages a priority.

Still, she felt oddly alone.

There was a girl with her mother sitting next to her, and a young man sitting across. With thin brown hair and a large forehead, he looked like a banker. She swept her gaze around the train carriage. Old and young, men and women, families and financiers, all heading to Calais. Calais, the city of beaches, with mountains of chalk and cliffs as white as those in Dover. She wondered how many travellers might be staying on for a holiday and how many would be crossing the Channel. She'd be wise to make some acquaintances. She needed a ferry crossing, and while she now had the funds, she really didn't have the tongue. A companion who knew a phrase or two in French would be an immense help.

But she didn't have the heart for connections. Not yet.

She turned away and leaned her forehead against the smoky glass, watching her reflection as a big fat tear rolled down her cheek.

She threw herself off an airship bridge. The end.

Gads, Christien was right. She was a maudlin creature now, all woe and sighs and sloth. Had she really given up on life? If so, how easily it had been lost. It's what her mother had done so many years ago, closed off the world, day by day and person by person, until she was as dead as a living woman could be. Strange that her daughter would be courting the same thing.

She felt a nudge at her right arm. It was the girl. She held up a handkerchief and smiled.

"Pour tes larmes," she said.

Ivy took the handkerchief, wiped the single tear away.

"C'est bien," she lied. *"Merci."*

"English?" the girl asked, and Ivy laughed.

"Oui. English," she said but paused. "No. Welsh."

The young eyes grew round but her mother yanked her close and whispered words unfamiliar to Ivy. The girl shrugged and looked back at her, eyes darting down to her breeches and boots.

"No skirt," she said in English. "Maman says it's shocking. I say it's free."

"Free," Ivy repeated. *"Libre. Oui."*

"Féministe?"

"Oui." She smiled and leaned in, raising a brow. *"Et autere."*

"Emmaline!" snapped the mother. She grabbed her hand and dragged her to another seat. Ivy watched them go.

She wiped her cheeks once more, and turned back to the window, the rolling hills, and fallow fields.

"An *autere*?" came a voice and she looked up. It was the man with the thin brown hair. He was smirking, but in a way that didn't cause Ivy to bristle. There was no contempt in that smirk, and his eyes were eager. She nodded.

"Of broadsheets," she said. "Penny Dreadfuls."

"Exceptional," he said. "I've always fancied myself a writer, but I fear I must first put food on the table."

"There's no money in it, to be sure," she said. "Are you a banker, sir?"

"Gads, no!" he laughed, and he turned in his seat, showing her the patches in his elbows. "I'm set to be a science teacher once I graduate."

"Oh, well done," she said.

"I was taking a class at the Sorbonne when we got the call."

"The call?"

"To come home, because of the, you know…"

He nodded to the window and Ivy felt a cold wash up from her boots.

"They're calling this phenomenon the Pale Rider, aren't they?" he went on, "Like in the Bible. Apparently, he started in Vienna, and is sweeping across the continent. The War Office has called us all back, although I'd much rather stay and learn what he is. He can't be natural, so he must be supernatural, or supranatural, or perhaps even extraterrestrial."

"Extraterrestrial?" she gasped. "Whatever does that mean?"

"Why, out of this world!" And he sat forward, eyes dancing. "Who knows what may come from the Moon or even Mars one day. I'm dreadfully curious about it all, which is why I suppose I'm drawn to science. Is it a single man or a horde of man-like creatures? Why is he raising the dead? Is he sent from God, or is he a servant of the devil? Perhaps a bit of both? Or is he an alien, bound on conquering our fair planet for the resources?"

He sat back and grunted.

"Man is not the only chapter in the story of humanity, miss. Oh no, not in the least."

She took a deep breath and thrust out her hand.

"Ivy Savage," she said.

"Herbert George Wells," he said, taking it. "Call me Bertie."

"I know another Bertie and it's very complicated," she said. "May I please call you Herbert?"

"Gads, no," he said. "How about H.G., then? That sounds terribly collegiate!"

"H.G. it is," she said.

He slid across the seat, directly in front of her now.

"No, Miss Savage, I would very much wish to stay and investigate. There's a story here, I know, because with all that's going on, I can virtually assure you that war is on the horizon. A war of the very worlds."

And he nodded to the window again. This time, Ivy followed his gaze.

On the swiftly rushing horizon, Sentinels were gathering.

***

Christien tore his eyes from the window. There was nothing wrong with the view. It was a perfectly admirable panorama of the Norman countryside – winter hills dotted with farms, stands of bare trees lining the fields, grey clouds hanging low in the sky. No, it wasn't the lack of scenery that caused him to look away. It was the subject in the seat across the carriage.

Marie Valerie Mathilde Amalie von Habsburg, Archduchess of Austria, Princess of Tuscany, and daughter of the Gilded Emperor himself.

Her hazel eyes bored holes into his. He was certain she had looked at nothing else since he climbed into the carriage at the station, while he had settled for anything else. Her sandy hair was piled beneath a striped fascinator, and a gilded feather waved jauntily with the rhythm of the coach. She sat perfectly straight, gloved hands folded in her lap, and she looked as though she could slay him with a word.

He knew better now. She was a mistress of illusion.

"What do you want, Valerie?" he asked.

"To take you to Caen, of course," she said.

"I am perfectly able to arrange my own transportation."

"This is much better."

"Is it?"

"Are you hungry?"

He was, in fact. It was a miracle that his stomach hadn't begun to grumble.

"No."

"You lie," she said. "You have been deprived of comfort for some time."

"Thank your family for that, then, will you?"

She didn't smile. Her eyes stayed locked.

"It's two days by coach to Caen," he said.

"We will stop in Évreux," she said. "There's a respectable inn—"

"Respectable inn?" he blurted out. "*Respectable inn? Am I to share your bed again?*"

"If you wish." Now, she did look away, her gaze fixing on the grey outside the window. "You have never protested before."

God, he wanted another cigarette.

"You're engaged, Valerie. Set to marry that buffoon, Franz."

"What has that got to do with sharing my bed?"

She turned those steely eyes on him once more and be damned if he almost fell. She set every fibre of his being aflame.

"I am not an emotional woman," she said. "And I have a duty to my country which I will honour with my dying breath. But if I could choose whom to marry, I would choose you, Christien Jeremie St. John de Lacey. I would choose you."

Part of him believed her, but then, part of him *wanted* to believe her. Illusion was stock in trade for the Black Swans, desire their currency. Still, she had a mind as steely as her eyes, with resources as vast and deep as the sea.

"If we aim to stop Bastien at all," he said. "We'll need an airship to meet us at the estate, take us across the Channel to London."

"London?" she asked. "Not Lasingstoke?"

"The Ghost Club," he said. "I need a word with Williams and Crookes."

"To stop the end of the world?"

"You make it sound so dramatic."

"It is the Habsburg way."

She studied him and arched an elegant brow.

"So, you are adamant you will not share my bed tonight."

"Not tonight. Not any night. Not even if this were the very last night we would ever spend on this sorry earth." He leaned forward. "In fact, I will never share your bed again, Valerie. Not ever."

She reached up to rap on the ebony wall behind her.

"Then we should make haste to the end of the world."

Suddenly, the carriage echoed with a loud clang. Struts squealed, horses whinnied, and the cabin rocked forward, then roughly back. The coachmen shouted in High German, and outside the window, the grey panorama of the countryside began to fall away. He pressed his forehead against the glass. The ground itself was falling away, and they were rising above the sad, grey, rural landscape of Normandy. He could see the horses carry on down the road, pulling wheels and axle, dickey and driver, but it was a carriage stripped of its car. Higher and higher they rose over the ground, and he turned his eyes upward to see cords and pulleys and gears. Beyond those, the gondola of an airship and the great gilded canvas of the House Habsburg.

He leaned back in his seat and Marie Valerie smiled.

"The Habsburg way."

And she reached for a cigarette.

***

As soon as the horse stepped a hoof through the orb, the bones began to rise.

His life had always been odd. It stood to reason that his death would be as well.

Sebastien sighed and looked around at the fog.

Fields, a road, a stand of black, branchy trees. It could be the road to Paris, but then again, nothing was certain. He had willed the lockets to take him to Paris, but, despite the fact that they were a part of him, he still had no clue as to how they worked. Perhaps, he would understand once he had the third locket. Perhaps, it would make sense.

But then again, he would likely be ending the world once he had the third locket, so travel would be the least of his worries.

There was motion in the fields, and he looked to see a small flock of sheep moving restlessly in the winter grass. He smiled. It was close to lambing season, and he knew that most of the ewes were likely pregnant. He liked sheep. They were peaceful and placid and reminded him of home.

Home. Would he ever see it again? Would it be as he remembered, or would it be cursed as most of the world?

The flock grew agitated, and he could see them start off in one direction, then turn to skitter in another. Nervous bleats carried over the quiet morning air. A ewe bolted but her front legs buckled, and she went down in a heap. One by one, the others began to collapse, necks thrashing, hind ends twitching. Soon, the entire flock was down, nothing more than grey mounds in a grey field.

"Me?" he whispered aloud. "Did I do that?"

His heart ached at the simple loss.

The army of bones simply stared ahead, wavering on fragile limbs. They had no will. They had no goal. They were simply drawn to him like the relics of Melk.

He cursed himself and kicked his heels into Ash's flank. The pale horse leapt forward in a gallop, leaving the dead behind on the road to Calais.

***

"A Teslagraph arrived this afternoon, sir," said Charles Neville. "From the Bulldog."

Elliot Makepeace, the Empire of Steam's Secretary of War, glanced up from his desk, a pair of spectacles making his eyes look very large.

"Are we certain it's from the Bulldog?"

"Cypher code Sunday Tea, sir," said Neville.

"And it's been deciphered, Charles?"

"It has, sir."

Neville passed the paper to his superior.

"Good lord," said Makepeace as he read.

"Sir?"

"God damn the Ghost Club and their little toys."

"Sir?" Neville repeated.

Makepeace dropped the paper.

"Alert the MOD and summon the ministers," he said. "And Neville, what's the latest on the Place Setting?"

"We have twelve Sentinels in the North, with more at the ready if called upon."

"Call upon."

"And where shall the table be set?"

"Lasingstoke Hall, Lancashire."

"A bit remote, sir," said Neville. "One is already there, if I remember correctly. Five can be there within twenty-four hours, and all twelve within forty-eight."

"Make the call. And the Vanguard?"

"Highly sensitive, sir. There is an ironclad airship moored to a dreadnought patrolling the Channel. She is manned by the Alliance, with Anton Boudin at the helm. A bit of a Rogue's Gallery, sir, but quite proficient."

"She could cause a bit of an international incident were she not proficient, Neville."

"Indeed, sir. She could."

"Very well. Carry on and keep me posted."

Neville nodded and quietly slipped from the Secretary's office.

Makepeace leaned back in his chair.

"If it's a fight that Mad Lord's a-wanting, we'll give it to him," he muttered. "Sunday Tea, indeed. The Empire of Steam will bring out the fine china for this. Damnations, we'll bloody well break out the crystal."

With a satisfied grunt, he reached for a cigar.

***

The French Morning Press
Pale Rider Spotted in Reims

In a cruel twist of fate, it appears that the much-lauded bombing campaign of Chancellor Otto von Bismark has not, in fact, succeeded in ridding Europe of the dreaded Pale Rider and his undead hordes. A plague on livestock follows the Rider wherever he goes, and farmers from across the region have reported incalculable losses of sheep, hogs, cattle and poultry. The Ministere de l'Agriculture *has assured farmers that they will receive government assistance to recoup these losses, and they have joined with other French ministries in pressuring the office of the President to take decisive action on this most debilitating of phenomena.*

Livestock losses seem to be concentrated along the direct path of the Rider, and farms several miles away report no ill effects. Currently, the Rider's projected route takes him and his horde to Paris, and plans are underway to evacuate the city. The Conseil Supérieur de la Guerre *has ordered all available Central Gardiens to the city, and, in case of a change in route, all Northern Gardiens toward Calais.*

The French Morning Press will continue with updates as they come in.

Chapter 5

Of French Towns, French Sherry, and les Gardiens

"There is something at work in my soul, which I do not understand."

    – Mary Shelley, Frankenstein: The Modern Prometheus

The fog was still heavy, so he slowed Ash from his tireless trot to read the sign at the side of the road.

Reims, Grand Est.

Well, that was not even remotely close to Paris, if remembered his French geography correctly. Rather, farther east and north. He'd never been to Reims before, but he knew the northern provinces because of Caen and the de Lacey estate in the northwest. But he'd realized that he didn't need to get to Paris at all. It was actually Calais he needed to reach, and from here, it would take him less than twenty-four hours to get to the port city on a horse that could canter forever. Crossing the Channel was another matter entirely, and hoped he could be skilled enough with Arclight before he reached the sea.

In the distance, he could see the town, but could barely make out the surrounding wall because of the blanket of fog. Spires and steeples hovered above it, however, as grey as the rest of the world, and the air was eerie and still. There was something odd on the road before him, rippling the fog like a dark wave. It wasn't the dead, for the earth around him had only begun to tremble and heave. No, this was different, and he began to think that they were living.

The bone army began to push up from the frosty ground. He wished it were harder for them. He wished the earth was more frozen, more like a prison to keep them in, to keep them under, beneath and therefore, unseen. But it wasn't, and their skeletal hands pushed up through the dirt like grotesque flowers reaching for the sun. Except there was no sun and they were reaching for him, their Crown Prince. They were drawn to him now, just like the relics in the Abbey of Melk. He could know each of them intimately, if he wished. Names, families, even manner of death. They were his people now. His realm, his court. And he hated the crown he wore to rule them.

A familiar sound floated above the fog, and he looked up. There was indeed a crowd approaching from the city, but behind them, a huge metal behemoth clanked, its red beam slicing through the grey like a rapier. It was a *Gardien*, a French Sentinel that was closer to the English kind than the German, and this one walked on iron legs, each footfall booming like thunder. He'd been so cavalier about the one in Over Milling, taking it for granted as if it were a bridge or a steeple. He'd never thought it could work, had never imagined it pulling its great boot from the little garden in the square. He would look at it with new eyes from now on.

Given that his eyes were now lockets, that would be an easy thing.

The bone army pushed up around him, waiting on unsteady legs, silent and frail, as the crowd materialized from the fog. There were roughly two dozen men with pitchforks and muskets, axes and pistols, and they fanned out on the road before him.

"Leave us, creature!" shouted one man in French. "Go back to hell with your demons!"

"I'll leave," he said, also in French. "Just let me pass and I'll be gone."

"You kill the sheep," shouted another. "You rot the bread!"

"This is the Province of Champagne," said another. "But the grapes are rotting, and the wine is rancid!"

"I'm sorry," he said, casting his clockwork eyes across them, watching their hearts beat and the blood pump through their veins. "I will go quickly, then, if you let me pass."

One man stepped forward. He held a pistol and Sebastien noticed that his hand was shaking. Not surprising, really, when considering the circumstance.

"In the name of the Father, the Son and the Holy Spirit," he said, his voice breaking. "I sentence you to Hell."

And he fired, the sound echoing across the quiet road.

Ash startled beneath him, and Sebastien looked down to see the tiny lead ball had pierced the horse's sickly chest.

"You shot my horse," he said.

He could see the ball embedded in the layers of muscle and he reached down, laid a hand over the wound. The ball slid through the tissue and out into his hand. He remembered that his own three-barrelled pistol currently had no bullets, so he slipped it into his pocket for later.

"You can't send a horse to Hell," he said abstractedly. "It has no soul, or did they not teach you that in your church?"

Suddenly, a second shot rocked the quiet and his head snapped back at the impact, almost sending him from Ash's back. He pushed forward to lay himself against the horse's pale neck, waiting as the waves of pain became mere dizziness. Shot in the head. Shot in the head. *The Crown Prince is Dead. Shot in the head. War is coming on iron feet.*

Sophie has shot him in the head, but it was her finger and a much different thing.

Slowly, he righted himself, reached into the mass of damp curls at the back of his head, and pulled the second ball out. This one, he held in his palm. There was no blood, there were no brains. Just a leaden bullet from a rusty gun.

"You can't kill me," he said. "I'm afraid it doesn't take. It never has."

The crowd murmured and exchanged glances.

"I'm going to ride through your town," he said. "The dead will follow me, but they won't hurt you. Then, I'll be gone, and you can live your lives. While you can, that is. I'm afraid things may get thorny once I reach England."

"Then you shall not reach England," said the man with the pistol.

Sebastien pocketed the second bullet and urged Ash to walk on with a squeeze of his heels. Both horse and dead pushed forward, but the crowd did not move. So, the dead flowed around, between, and through them like water around pebbles. The *Gardien's* red eye sliced across them all as if trying to determine a target, but Sebastien kept moving forward, Ash keeping a steady pace. They were almost through the crowd when one of the men whirled.

"No," he growled. "You will all go to hell!"

And he lunged forward, swinging his axe and a revenant exploded in a shower of bones. Another stabbed a pitchfork through the torso of another and swung the corpse around to knock several others over and apart. The crowd rushed the bone army, harvesting the revenants like stale wheat and bones scattered across the road.

Sebastien urged his horse into a trot when a man snagged his boot.

"Got him!" he cried, and he grabbed the hem of the great coat, began to pull the Mad Lord from his horse. Sebastien reached down and grasped the man's wrist, and immediately, everything changed.

The man froze, his eyes and mouth grew wide, and the scent of burnt flesh filled the air. He released the boot and staggered back, holding the twisted bones that used to be his arm. It was several heartbeats before he dropped to his knees and his screams drowned out everything in the world.

The crowd turned.

Horrified, Sebastien looked down at his own hand, pulsing with Ghostlight's deathly cold and Arclight's unearthly power.

The *Gardien* began to whine, and the red light fixed on him.

"Anywhere," he said aloud.

Arclight summoned an orb and Ash stepped through.

***

Valerie lifted the cracker to her mouth, watching him with eyes of steel. She bit, her teeth white pearls against the peach-kissed gloss of her lips. She was daring him, he knew it. Taunting him, teasing him with her beauty, but it was wasted on him. Right now, all he wanted was the cracker.

She chewed slowly, exaggerating the pleasure of eating, when the growls of his belly were barely deafened by the growl of the airship engines above them. She licked the tips of her fingers, one by one by one, then turned to the basket at her side. A small bottle of sherry, a wheel of Brie, a bunch of red grapes and a jar of sweet chutney. Slowly, she picked up the chutney, dipped a finger and put it to her tongue.

"Delicious," she said. "I'm quite filled."

His mouth watered but he said nothing.

"It's too bad you do not want what I have to give," she said. "I only wish to help you."

She packed up the basket, reached over and pushed open the carriage door. A blast of cold air struck like a fist, but swiftly, she leaned over and dropped the basket out into the skies. She pulled the door closed and sat back.

"I do hope that does not strike the roof of a house," she said after a moment.

Still, he said nothing.

"But at least, I kept the sherry," she said. "Forgive me for being indecorous. It seems I've lost my glass over the side."

And, eyes locked with his, she lifted the bottle to her lips.

***

Le Petit Journal
February 20, 1889
Évreux, Normandy

Évreux Church Punched by Plunging Picnic

In an unexplained occurrence, a strange object has crashed through the roof of Église Saint-Taurin in downtown Évreux during the celebration of afternoon mass.

"It is a sign from God," says Fr. Gilbert d'Angle. "A blessing of His bounty and provision."

But not all worshippers agree.

"It nearly took my head clean off," says member of the congregation, Serge Dufour. "Smashed right through the tiles in the roof when the good Father said Amen!"

Early investigations point to refuse tossed from an overhead airship, prompting calls for sweeping airship reforms regarding both waste disposal and flight logs.

***

They were in a forest, with old spruce and pines covered in snow. He could see a light in the distance and for a fleeting moment, it made him feel warm. Warm. He remembered that feeling, and for some reason, he thought of Ivy.

He frowned. He'd been here before. Damn Arclight and her double-damned orbs.

He left Ash and trudged through the snow on the forest floor toward the light.

It was the cottage, the same cottage with low, thatched roof and rough timbers for a frame. The one with the thin windows and no shutters, and the family sitting by the fire. The old man, the young man and the two women, one fair and one dark. Once more, he cursed the locket. He'd not asked to come here.

Then again, he'd said 'anywhere,' so, to be fair, no fault given.

He stepped back and turned, only to see the seven spirits once again.

"What do you want?" he asked.

They said nothing. Spirits rarely did. But spirits could communicate effectively when they had the need. Once again, he felt the breath on his neck.

"What do you want?" he repeated.

"Laisse-les," said a voice.

It was French, and his mind adjusted once again.

"Who are you?" he asked. "And why do you keep bringing me here?"

"They are *mine,"* said the voice.

He turned slowly, this time to see a figure behind him. It was unnaturally tall and cloaked in darkness. The seven dead swooped to him, hovered around him like smoke from a smouldering fire.

"I don't want them," said Sebastien.

"Then leave us and never return."

There was something odd about the voice, raspy and edged, as if pasted together from many tongues.

"I'm trying," said Sebastien. "Something has brought me back."

"If you return, I will kill you."

"Too late," he said.

"Just leave."

The figure called the spirits into himself and stepped back, disappearing in the shadows of the night.

Sebastien sighed, surprised at the feeling of breath leaving his lips. Was he breathing? Could he still breathe? What did that mean for him as Crown Prince of Death?

He looked down at the snowy ground and frowned.

Calais, he thought to himself. Or perhaps he thought it to Arclight, Mistress and Creator of Orbs. Regardless, he needed to get to Calais. He would ask the next orb to take him there.

He turned back to the forest, where Ash was waiting for him. But he did pause to reload the three-chambered pistol with the bullets from Reims, just in case.

***

It was 3:00pm by the time the train rattled into *Les Fontinettes* station in Calais and Ivy was tired. Bertie Wells had talked her ear off about his theories both scientific and otherworldly, and she couldn't help but think that Sebastien would have enjoyed talking with him. She divulged nothing, of course. Not the fact that she knew the source of this Pale Rider, nor the fact that she knew him before he had been known as such. Certainly not that she had been killed because of him and then brought back.

"Oh gads, look," said Wells as the brakes squealed to a lurching stop. "More Sentinels. They call them *Gardiens* here, though, don't they? I prefer the term *mechanic-hommes*, but that's me and I'm no *auteur*. Not like you, Miss Savage. Although I'd love to put my pen to paper one day. I love a good book. That's why I came to Paris, isn't it? To fetch a first-edition copy of M. Vernes' *Le Tour de Monde en Quatre-Vingt Jours.* A bookseller near Notre Dame secured it for me, although I should never have bought it. It was almost a month's wage, and me, but a poor university student. But some books are worth every penny, don't you agree, Miss Savage? Have you read M. Verne? I'm certain he'd love to see these *Gardiens,* if in fact, he sees anything, for he is rather old now, I'm told."

Ivy shook herself from her reverie.

"How do we get to the docks?" she asked.

"Oh, you can follow me once we disembark. Perhaps we could catch a closer look at those Sentinels before we sail. Have you ever seen a Sentinel up close, Miss Savage?"

A Sentinel thundering down on them in the fields of Alsace-Lorraine. The Sentinel on TANC track wheels rolling across the River Ill in Strasbourg. Sentinels blasting holes into airships in the Hofburg courtyard.

"Never," she said.

"Bloody marvels, they are. The next war will be waged by mechanical beings, I guarantee it. Men will win or lose on the backs of the Sentinels."

The train whistled and Ivy rose to her feet, along with the entire train car.

"To the docks, Miss Savage," said Wells. "Then to the ships. You have a ticket, yes?"

"Not yet," she said. "I need to make the purchase here but I'm afraid I have no idea how or where."

"Come with me, then," said Wells. "The War Office gave us specific instructions. I've been ticketed on a steamer called *Tully Shepherd.*"

She followed him through the crush of bodies as they exited the train and stepped onto the smoky platform. The smell of cigars, steam and oil wafted along on the chill fog that had settled over the station. People rushed in every direction and there was an air of quiet panic as news of the 'Pale Rider' had reached the port city. She struggled to keep Wells in her sights as he wove in and out of the crowd.

He snatched a broadsheet from a newsboy and scanned the headline.

"They've been sighted just outside of Calais," he said. "Gads, that's quick. How *are* they moving?"

Don't let him get on that horse…

She swallowed her racing heart as they stepped out onto the streets, and she almost ran into a pair of iron legs. She froze.

"Blimey," said Wells. He stared up at the mechanical creation, eyes wide, mouth agape. "*Un Gardien.*"

"Please, Mr. Wells," she said. "The docks."

"They're so big…"

And he reached his hand out to touch the cold metal.

The great head swung down, its red eye flashing, and Ivy felt her heart stop.

She grabbed his tattered sleeve and dragged him around the iron giant. Its red eye watched her go.

***

L'Express

Du Nord and du Pas-de-Calais

February 19, 1889

Pale Rider Makes Calais!

All citizens of Calais are urged to evacuate the city in preparation for the arrival of the Pale Rider and his ungodly hordes. Citizens are urged NOT to engage said army and to avoid any altercations with any of the creatures. Reports are being circulated of mass casualties in the city of Reims, in which many citizens braved the terrors to protect their town and were direly wounded in the attempt. The Mayor of Calais has issued a strict warning against such actions, and instead has insisted that evacuation or encampment are the only options for those who value life and limb.

Les Gardiens *have been dispatched and a fleet of six are already in position at the gates of the city proper. Tourists and foreign nationals have been recalled to their home countries and all sea-going vessels, both commercial, personal and military, have been ordered to assist with the evacuations.*

L'Express will continue to report on conditions as they arise.

Chapter 6

Of Mecha-Men, Ironclads, and a War of the Worlds

"Beware; for I am fearless, and therefore powerful."

- Mary Shelley, Frankenstein: The Modern Prometheus

It was an odd sensation stepping out of an orb and on to solid ground, and it took a few moments for his head to clear. Evening, clearly, and, from the salt scent on the air, near the ocean. His heart swelled at the thought that maybe, just maybe, this time Arclight had taken him where he'd wanted to go.

It was late afternoon, he was on a road, and the city of Calais lay before him.

He knew it was Calais. He'd been here before. It was remarkably similar to Dover, with the white cliffs, the low tides, grassy sand dunes and skies that stretched as far as the eye could see. The city itself was vastly different, however, with low limestone houses, red tile roofs, and a wall that had served its citizens well over the centuries. But this evening, a very different wall protected Calais. Six Sentinels stood shoulder to mechanical shoulder, towering over the grassy dunes to defend against him and his bone army.

He shook his head, even as the ground at Ash's hoofs began to heave.

Damn the dead. How he wished he could be rid of them. His life would be so much easier. But then again, that had been his problem all along.

He could see the beams sweeping the air from their deadly eyes. He was a good half mile away and wondered if their beams could reach him at this distance. He also realized that these were not just red beams this time. No, these were French Sentinels. Beams were blue, white and red. How very patriotic. How very lethal. He wasn't convinced he'd survive a blast, given how they turned everything in their path to char. He might end up like one of his undead companions, no flesh, all bone, with only a stone cold will that drove him onward.

Sad, really. It wasn't at all how he thought he'd end up.

"Attention, Pale Rider," boomed a mechanical voice over the road and the fields. *"You are denied entry to the city of Calais. If you proceed, we will turn you to ash."*

He reached down and patted Ash's neck.

"One more time, my friend," he said to the horse. "Let's see if we can avoid these giants and cross the Channel without a boat."

The horse tossed its pale head, and Sebastien closed his eyes.

"Dover," he said aloud. "Dover. Arclight, take me to Dover."

An orb appeared from nothing. They always did. Like an eerie, otherworldly soap bubble, it spun and swelled into existence, low to the ground, beckoning. He nudged Ash forward, prepared this time for the blast of cold and blackness that accompanied the trip, and the moment a hoof touched the orb's oily surface, they were gone, sucked into the void of time and space that was Arclight's realm. With Ghostlight, he saw things. Faces, shapes, wisps of silver, shades of grey, reflections of colour, echoes of sound, shadows of life. The Deadworld. With Arclight, he saw stars, planets, a warping, bending blanket of space. But in the orbs, Arclight and Ghostlight met.

He wondered how that would change once Lostlight was in the mix.

It was barely a heartbeat, but it seemed as long as a lifetime, then he was out, back in the cool, ocean-soaked evening of the coast. Dover.

Not Dover. Calais. Legs of iron, monsters of metal.

He was directly at the feet of the *Gardiens*, and six beams sliced down toward him.

***

The stable compound was quiet, and the evening shadows were long. A lone gas lamp flickered by the courtyard door. It was a large square compound, with rows of stalls on three sides and a long, two-story house on the fourth. The moon gleamed over a row of leafless trees and a mist had settled over the cobblestones. It was the very picture of serenity and peace. But the horses knew better, and the whinnies rose to fever pitch within moments.

Whup whup whup whup

Along with the whinnies, the sound of a motor carried over the fields, and soon, a wind picked up in the courtyard, swirling bits of hay across the stone.

Whup whup whup whup

A courtyard door opened, and man peered out, silhouetted in kitchen light. He watched as a great shape darkened the clouds.

"Merde," he said under his breath.

It was an airship, large and glorious, flying a Gilded flag at her prow. As her gondola cruised over the stable roofs, her canvas blocked out the sky, and her carriage swung low across the cobbled ground.

Groaning and squealing, the carriage slid against the stones before coming to a stop by a copper water pump. The man watched in awe as the airship hovered in place, until a door swung open from the gondola. A dark-haired man with a clockwork arm stepped out, followed by a very fine lady.

The couple stepped back, grabbing their hats as the airship lifted into the twilight sky. They all watched as it *whup whup whupped* away.

After a long moment, the man at the door stepped forward.

"Monsieur Christien?"

"Oui, Geraud," said Christien, and he led the woman forward. "This is Arch—"

"Valerie," said the woman, interrupting. "I am honoured to meet you, *monsieur."*

"We were not expecting you, *monsieur, mademoiselle,"* said Geraud.

"And we were not expecting to come, Geraud," said Christien. "But we have some work to do in the library before we head back to London. If there's a bit of broth and bread from dinner…"

"There is more than broth and bread, *monsieur,"* said Geraud. "There is some cold duckling, stewed apples, and a wheel of very fine

Camembert."

"That sounds wonderful," said Christien. "We've a very long night ahead of us."

"Bien sur," said Geraud, and he held out an arm for them to go inside. "And welcome, Mademoiselle, to '*L'ecurie de Lacey.*'"

***

Sebastien leapt from Ash's back as a blue beam sliced through the pale horse, cutting him in two. There was no spray of blood, merely a buckling of legs and a thrashing of the neck as the two parts crumpled and went down. Sebastien ducked behind an iron leg and pressed his back against it, feeling the heat as a second beam sprayed across the metal. The *Gardien* lurched to the side, and memories of the field in Alsace-Lorraine came flooding back.

"Cease and surrender," boomed a voice.

He clung to the side of the leg and closed his eyes, calling the dead this time, willing them to his side. Almost immediately, the ground began to heave.

"By the order of President Bonaparte—"

He released the leg and sprinted between the mecha-men, drawing their attention around and around and around. Beams flashed at all angles, slicing great gashes in metal chests and cabled arms, domed heads and reticulated torsos, but the ground was crumbling now as the dead pushed through. One *Gardien* tried to step over a pit of assembling bones, but his iron foot sank deep and slowly, he pitched awkwardly off balance and careened into the *Gardien* at his side. In turn, that giant lurched backward into the *Gardien* behind him. The roar and squeal were deafening as, one by one, the *Gardiens* began to fall.

Beyond the wall, buildings burst with flame, struck by beams that were sent in wild directions, and smoke billowed into the darkening sky. The dead kept coming, however, not slowed by collapsing metal, and they crawled up and into the *Gardiens* as they split, sliced open by each other's beams. The utter chaos of skeletal creatures moving inside them, disrupting circuits, blocking gears, caused two more Sentinels to shudder and seize up, throwing sparks far across the field.

The fifth had both feet firmly planted and its torso spun wildly as it fought for control. But its eye beams flashed across the sky, carving the ground and the nearby buildings and the dead, setting fires in the winter fields, despite the dusting of snow.

"Ghostlight," cried Sebastien. *"Liberabo antimonii!"*

A wave flung out from the sparks in his hands. A beautiful, rippling wave of colour that struck the fifth and immediately, antimony in the locket began to spin it into gold. Gold like the sunset, gold like a fire. Soon, the *Gardien* itself was entirely gold, gleaming from helm to boot as if it were forged by the Gilded Emperor, Franz Joseph himself. All motion ceased, save for the beam which was locked and raining destruction the direction of the Calais docks.

Sebastien slipped around the debris and pulled his pistol, grateful for the bullets of Reims, and he fired directly into that menacing eye. The head shuddered as the mechanism imploded, buckling and howling, collapsing upon itself in a cacophony of rent metal. Suddenly, it exploded outward, and the Mad Lord was thrown off his feet by the force of the blast.

Slowly, the great gold giant crashed to the ground, shaking the skeletons off their feet and raining dirt and metal into the sky.

Sebastien groaned from his place in the grass. He wanted to sleep. Just close his eyes and let it all be done. Forget his plan and forgo the end of the world. The world would end on its own, regardless of his assist. He could sleep for just a little time. He could perhaps dream…

There was a thundering step, then another.

Head spinning, Sebastien pushed himself to his knees. One iron giant remained, an arm swinging by cables and cords, its abdomen sparking from the gears within. The dead clung to its legs like ants, and it took another thundering step toward him, crossing the ground with an amazing stride. He glanced around. The blast had blown the pistol from his hand. The white eye searched the rubble for signs of life.

He closed his eyes and willed an orb, sent it directly in the path of the oncoming *Gardien*. It was small but he knew by now that size did not matter to the orbs. Unmindful, the giant strode directly into it, brushing it with an iron shin, and Sebastien watched in fascination as the orb expanded. Within seconds, it engulfed the mecha-man in its oily embrace. The great helm jerked in confusion, trying to decode its new situation, when immediately the orb contracted into nothing, taking the *Gardien* along with it.

He didn't know where it went. He hoped it wasn't beautiful.

He pushed himself to his feet and looked around. Bodies and bones struggled beneath smouldering metal, and sirens wailed in the city beyond. Flames reached orange fingers to the sky and smoke filled the evening with grim shadows.

"I want to go home," he said to no one in particular.

The earth rumbled beneath him, and he stepped back as a large shape pushed from the loamy soil. It was Ash, pale but in one piece. He shook the soot from his sticky mane and turned his long nose to the Mad Lord.

Sebastien smiled, surprised at the swell of emotion. He reached forward and laid a hand on the horse's forehead.

"I'm happy to see you," he said. "I'm so happy you're ali—"

His voice caught. He couldn't finish, for in fact, it wasn't true, and his eyes stung for the first time in years. Tears? Could the dead weep? Could he? He wrapped his arms around Ash's pale neck and buried his face in the mane. He ached. Everything ached. Everything was wrong – he'd made it wrong, but how in the world could he ever make it right?

Could he? Could Ivy? Could Christien? Rupert St. John and his scathing wit?

No. Frankow.

He took a deep breath, marvelling that his chest still worked that way.

Frankow couldn't make it right but perhaps, he could make it stop.

He would make everything stop.

Over the grinding of the gears and the roaring of the flames, Sebastien could hear voices shouting in the distance. He released the horse and wiped his cheeks. He looked down at his hands. Dirt and oil, sand and blood.

He still had blood.

He took another breath, filled his chest with the pretence of air, and glanced around. The pistol was only yards away, it's tri-barrelled hilt embedded in snow. He grabbed it and returned to swing onto the horse's back.

"To the beach," he said. "We're going home."

The horse sprang forward like a ghost.

***

The docks were at once similar yet different to St. Katharine's Docks in London – flat, dense and low, with the salt smell of the ocean heavy on the breeze. Panic had only increased as they made their way to the shipyard, and the frenzied crush of civilians rushing for safety made the walk as difficult as swimming against a riptide. *Bassin Ouest* was a long, low-slung canal that led to the boats that were serving as ferries for tourists and travellers to cross. Those ferries were packed now as terrified citizens of the *Empire of Steam* tried to secure passage across the Channel. Some were arguing with dockmen; others leapt across the gangways onto the ships. But *Gardiens* were out in force, striding through the narrow streets with grinding gears and thundering metal, somehow avoiding the tides of people that flowed around their iron feet. Ivy swallowed the dread rising in her throat, rose on tiptoe to scry the grey horizon. Indeed, there was smoke in the distance, along with flashes of light, and she shook her head. She had travelled by airships and trains, whereas Sebastien was on a dead horse. There was no way he could have arrived in Calais at the same time as her.

No, she stopped herself. There was just no *earthly* way.

"That's simply not acceptable!" came Wells' voice behind her. "She's a citizen of Steam! We cannot abandon her. We must leave for England now!"

She turned to see him at the water's edge. He had been pressing a longshoreman for an extra place for her on the steamer, *Tully Shepherd*, but truth be told, she hadn't been paying attention. The steamer was sitting low in the water, full to splitting with anxious passengers, and the noise from the ships was deafening.

"Sorry, sir," cried the longshoreman over the din. "The *Tully Shepherd* is full. With the War Office's recall orders, all the ships are commandeered. I've got your name here, but you'll need to find a berth for your friend somewhere else."

"But, but, but…" Wells swung around to look. "Where?"

The docks were swiftly being emptied as boats of all sizes left for Dover, Folkstone and Newhaven.

"*Any*where," the longshoreman said. "Just get out of France now. The Pale Rider is coming and there aren't enough ships."

"Look!" shouted a voice from the ship. "An ironclad!"

All eyes turned to see.

Cutting through the grey waters was an Empire of Steam destroyer, the name painted across her iron bow.

"*Thunder Child*," breathed Wells. "By the gods, that's a name…"

"She'll take him out," said the longshoreman. "The *Thunder Child* will sink them all if he tries to cross the Channel."

"I'm sorry, Miss Savage," cried Wells as he clambered over the rail onto the *Tully Shepherd*, the longshoreman at his heels. "I truly am! I wish there was another way—"

Suddenly, the ground shook and Ivy swung around to look at the fields far beyond the docks. Black clouds billowed and the grey sky flashed with blue, white and red lights. She could only imagine the chaos caused by Ghostlight and Arclight working in tandem. She'd seen it first hand on the deck of the *HMAS Carolina*. Add the bone army and you'd have a recipe for anarchy unrivalled in modern times.

The ground shook once again, but this time, Ivy realized it wasn't the ground.

It was the dock.

All around the piers and jetties, the waters of the Channel were bubbling, bringing with it flashes of white.

Screams rose from the ships as spray blasted from the waters, and the rancid smell of rotting flesh burst from the sea. The dead came with it, in bits and pieces of varying decay. Some flesh, some mere bone, all rising against the sea to greet their Crown Prince and make way for his coming. Skeletal hands clawed at ships' hulls, rocking the closest boats in a dangerous attempt to free themselves of their watery graves. The living were forced to grab axes and paddles to smash the sinister fingers before any ship was pulled under. As one of the last departing, the *Tully Shepherd* heaved deep in the water, it's crowded decks frantic and filling with the dead.

Beneath her boots, the dock shuddered, and Ivy hit the planks, straining with her fingers to catch hold as it lurched to one side. Corpses in all states pulled themselves to its oily surface and water splashed over the frame. Another post buckled beneath their mad, scrabbling weight.

All the docks were filled with dead, and on the shore, cobblestones burst as dead pushed up from beneath. He was here, she knew it; closer than was possible, but with Sebastien, all things were possible and there was the rub. He was as innocent as he was dangerous, currently a child of no world, and as such, a destroyer of all.

A part skeleton pulled itself past her on the slanted deck, only skull and spine, ribs and arms, trailing seaweed as it went. Tiny crabs clung to the bones, and slicks of silt filled its cavities. Behind it, a hand. Just a hand, itself moving like a creature of the sea, scurrying on the tips of boney fingers.

He was so close now, she knew it. She could feel it in her own bones. She could sense him like a spectre, like a person standing too close, causing every nerve in her body to tingle and call.

The dock lurched again. Saltwater splashed into her face.

Sebastien, her dear sweet childlike Mad Lord, had to be stopped. She also knew *that* in her bones. But more than that, he might have to be killed and she might have to be the one to do it.

She pushed to her feet and spun on the tilted dock. The *Tully Shepherd* had pulled away, now a good five feet from what was left of the pier. She took a deep breath, curled her fingers into fists, and backed up a few steps. Six feet away now. Seven.

"She threw herself off an airship bridge, the end," she muttered to herself. "Bollocks, Remy. You're right. It's not going to end this way. I'll make sure of it. I promise."

And with one last, good, deep breath for luck, she put one very fine boot in front of the other and ran.

She ran and ran, hurtled over the crawling corpses and scraping bones, fought the tipping, slipping, soaked deck boards toward the water's edge and the end of the dock and the expanse of sea between her and the *Tully Shepherd* and when she got there, she launched herself high and far, over the roiling, boiling sea toward the steamer. It was as if time had slowed, for perhaps it had, and she saw the *Tully Shepherd* lose the last of its clamouring dead. She saw Wells in the midst, watched him turn, watched his eyes grow wide at the sight of her, watched him push through the crowd toward the rail. Felt the sickening lurch of her belly as she began to descend, toward the hull or the sea, but then she hit, and all the air rushed from her chest. Her boots kicked, and her hands flailed, but the hull was too slick, and she couldn't hold. She fell backwards into the sea.

Wells caught her wrist, and she struck the side again, stars popping behind her eyes.

"Come on, Miss Savage!" he cried, and her arms felt the strain as more passengers reached to grab her.

Finally, they hauled her over the rail and onto the ship's deck. Wells dragged her over to the steamer's cabin where they both sank to the floor. Fog rolled in as the little steamer chugged into the Channel. Soon, *Bassin Ouest*, then all of Calais, faded on the horizon. An unnatural quiet fell like a cloak, with only the sound of the waves and the occasional bell carrying over the waters.

"Well done," said Wells after a long moment. "Couldn't have done *that* in a skirt."

It hurt too much to smile, so she didn't, and together they sat, backs pressed against the rough cabin wall, watching with dull eyes as the blue, white and red shores of the *Industrial Republique of France* disappeared from view.

***

Calais was silent. The people were in hiding, the city's remaining *Gardiens* distracted and searching for him in distant fields. There were no ships in the dockyards, no steamers or ferries or even longboats left at *Bassin Ouest*. There was only him, his horse, a circus of quiet, waiting bones, and dead fish floating on the surface of the sea.

They arrived at land's end, the furthermost tip of the *Industrial Republique of France*. It was a stone embankment; not a dock, not a pier, but still a boat launch regardless, a slipway ramp that led directly into the waters. The fog was settling, the breeze smelled of smoke, fish, oil and decay. The end of all things was coming. It would not smell like gardens.

He slid from the back of the horse, patted the sticky neck. Ash was a good horse, he thought to himself. Not ever living, to be certain. But still.

The fog was rolling in, but he didn't need clear skies. This time, he just knew what to do. He raised his arms, and the sea bubbled to respond. Soon, the bubbles turned to spray, and a shape burst forth from the grey. It was an old fishing troller, worn by time, almost consumed by the ocean. It bobbed for a moment on the surface, spinning slowly, before it began to float toward him. It bumped quietly against the edge of the stone embankment, water pouring from every fissure.

He turned to Ash.

"I'll call," he said. "You'll find me."

Ash tossed his head and turned toward the sea, making his way down the slipway ramp where the waters lapped an iron beach. The horse didn't hesitate, simply sloshed into the water until he was gone.

The Crown Prince turned back to the troller, settled quietly as it was at the side of the stone embankment and took a step. Once his feet left the land, the bone army crumbled, animated no more.

"From dust you came," he said to no one in particular. "To dust you shall return. Or maybe water. Either or."

The troller rode low in the water, but he didn't care. Water sloshed all over his boots and great coat, but he didn't care. There was only one thing on his mind. Arvin Frankow. Arvin Frankow, his doctor, his mentor, his killer, his friend.

Arvin Frankow was at Lonsdale, so he was going to Lonsdale.

He was going home.

Chapter 7

Of Friends, Family, and a Photo in a Frame

"I'm a creature of fine sensations."
– Mary Shelley, Frankenstein: The Modern Prometheus

The morning was grey, and a fog had settled over the vast fields of Lasingstoke Hall. In the middle of one of those fields, Rupert St. John stood, in a woollen coat and riding boots, holding a cold cigarette and studying the Sentinels as they rumbled around the distant gate.

"How many is that, then?" asked Davis at his side. He held the reins of two horses, who snorted and pawed at the winter grass.

"Six," said Rupert. "But I suspect that very soon, there will be twelve. It's what the War Office calls a Place Setting."

"A Place Setting? Are we on the menu, sir?"

"Looks like it."

"But why? Do they think Sentinels can stop the Mad Lord?"

"Perhaps they can," he said. "But I suspect it's more for us than for him. Keep us in and unable to assist."

"They've cut the Teslagraphs, too," said Davis. "Ain't no message getting in or out."

"They'll set up a perimeter using the four corners as anchors," he said. "I'm not sure how they'll do it, some form of mad science I suppose. Lasers, electricity, hydraulic blasts…"

"Hydraulic blasts," muttered the boy. "Sounds like one of Ivy's stories."

"It does indeed." The Scourge chewed on the butt of his cigarette, deep in thought. "But however, they do it, they'll make sure no one can get in or out over that wall. Ah, here we go. Watch."

With remarkable precision, the Sentinels began to split up, two staying at the gate, two thundering down the south wall toward Fourth, and eventually Fifth, while the other two clanked their way north to the corner at Sixth House, and then Seventh. Lasingstoke was a large barony, almost six hundred acres of fields and forests, paddocks and pastures, and the six-foot stone wall ran along its entirety, keeping horses in and wildlife out.

"Soon, there'll be a Sentinel at each corner, with more on the way."

"A Place Setting," said Davis.

Rupert threw a side glance at the boy. Freckle-faced and young, there was the beginnings of stubble growing on the ruddy cheeks. He was a clever lad, full of imagination and skill, and he was falling hopelessly for the cook's ginger daughter.

"A Place Setting. Indeed."

Davis pulled his cap from his head, ran a hand through his hair, then popped it back on. Tugging it tight.

"What about…" He pursed his lips. "What about us folk, like you and Mrs. Mary Jane, and Lottie?"

"I won't lie to you," Rupert said. "If it does look like Laury is headed here, they may well choose to destroy the Hall and all the houses, just to remove the incentive. Create chaos and change the calculus."

"Gads," said Davis. "And us?"

"Collateral damage, I'm afraid."

Rupert dropped the cigarette to the ground, crushed it under his boot.

"But if he does come back, they'll aim to take him out anyway they can," he said. "And they most certainly can."

"If it were up t'me," said Davis. "I'd fight 'em."

The Scourge bit back a smile.

"You'd fight them, Davis? How?"

"Well…" He looked down, scuffed the ground with his boot. "I been working in the airship docks since the *Chevalier* left home…"

"And?"

"And the War Office may not be the only ones with 'Hydraulic Blasts.'"

"Oh, well done," said Rupert. "Let's go take a look, shall we? Perhaps we need to prepare the Hall for guests?"

"Make a plan," said the boy.

"Change the calculus."

And together, they grabbed the reins, swung into their saddles, and wheeled the horses back to Lasingstoke.

***

He wasn't sure how the boat managed the Channel. The night had been dark, the waves high, and the seas had been rough even for February. The boat had no sail nor motor to guide it, having recently been a wreck on the ocean floor, and he was certain it had something to do with the lockets. They wanted home as much as he did. He trusted that they'd lead him to their sister, Lostlight, wherever she was.

Now, he stood at the top of Dover's white cliffs, casting his eyes over the shoreline below him. There were many lights on the westerly horizon, and he knew that it was the official Port Harbour. Most of the vessels that had left Calais would be docking and disembarking there, so he had willed the wreck to tack west, toward the cliffs themselves. There, he'd scuppered it on a pebbled beach, and had hiked the grassy dunes up the escarpment in the dead of night. Fortunately, he had the moon and the lockets to light his path.

His great coat flapped in the ocean breeze, and he breathed in the scent of the salt air. It reminded him of the nights he and Arvin would walk the hills overlooking Wharcombe Bay, discussing life, death and the things in between. Those were good memories of a time when he'd believed his life served a greater purpose. Now, all his memories were suspect, tainted by the revelations of the past few weeks. He should have left it alone, he realized. He should have stayed in Lasingstoke with his horses and his dogs and the singular companionship of Miss Ivy Savage.

She'd died because of him. And so, to bring her back, he'd died.

Strange, the bargains one made in the name of love.

He turned and walked across the wet sea grass. It frosted as his approach, crunched under his step. Ash was waiting for him, glimmering in the faint moonlight, and it was then that the earth began to tremble beneath his boots.

"No!" he snapped. "No dead. I'm tired of this! I forbid it."

The earth did not heed, and soon, the grass was nothing more than churned soil, producing an army of corpses that stood, silent and frail, all around him. He pushed past them all and swung up onto Ash's back, but he took one last look to the sea, and the shimmering waters where the sun was rising in the blood red sky.

Over the cliffs, an airship hovered silently. He narrowed his eyes, recognizing the canvas as War Office. It made sense. They were following him, likely hoping he wouldn't head for London, but unsure on how to stop him. He'd already taken on *Eisenmanner* and *Gardiens*. He wondered when he'd meet a Sentinel of Steam. Given the condition of the one in Over Milling, they shouldn't present a problem.

He wheeled the pale horse and headed down the grass.

The bone army followed him, as did the airship.

However, he was not looking to see the second airship – an ironclad dreadnought – glide in over the Cliffs, following them all.

***

The Times News, London

Pale Rider Arrives in Empire of Steam

The Pale Rider has been spotted in Dover, *complete with bone army in tow. It is unclear how they managed to decimate the Sentinels (known as les Gardiens) in Calais and cross the English Channel, but the phenomenon is clearly on its way to London. City mayor, Sir Alfred Newton, Baronet, has called for citizens to hunker down and wait out the caravan, citing*

unfounded panic in other major European cities.

"We all know Paris was prepared," says Newton. "But that in fact,

the Pale Rider and his caravan completely bypassed the city in favour of

Calais. We don't want to succumb to the same hysteria that gripped the

French capital. We are citizens of Steam, after all."

Nonetheless, automabobs are being made ready with evacuation

plans and ration outlets in case of emergencies. Reporters for the Times

News will continue to update our readers as to the progress.

***

While some of the ships, boats, ferries and steamers made their way directly along the Thames to London, the *Tully Shepherd* was not one of them, and Ivy was forced to catch a train from Dover Priory to King's Cross. Fortunately, she still had Prince Edward's wad of notes in her pockets, so the fare hadn't been a problem. The sheer volume of terrified travellers had been, however, and it had taken hours to get to King's Cross.

Wells had abandoned her once there, citing a need to return post-haste to his fiancée in Kensington to await the end of the world. Alone once again, she stood under the large platform sign, mind racing, heart heavy and torn.

She could go directly into London to see her father and mother, let them know she was still alive and on the case. She hadn't seen them for months, and in truth, it might the be last time for all of them. She could easily snag a cab to the neat little rowhouse by the factory in Stepney. Blimey, she could even walk.

Or she could head straight to the War Office at Whitehall, speak to Henry Babbage and Ninian Liddell and his compatriots, get their remarkable minds on the problem. But no, the answer to this problem could not be found in the War Office. No, she had to go north, but to Lasingstoke or Lonsdale? She had no clue.

"Pale Rider spotted in Dover!" cried a young voice, and Ivy turned to see a newsie, flogging broadsheets under a black arch. She waved him over, and he promptly came, expertly weaving between the feverish travellers.

"It's only a ha'penny, miss," he said as she stuffed a pound note into his fingerless glove.

"It's all I have," she said. "Grab a custard before things go mad."

His eyes grew round.

"Fog custard," he laughed. "It's cig and gin for me!"

And he disappeared, scattering the broadsheets as he went. She turned her eyes down to the paper.

"Dover," she murmured. "How, Laury? How did you cross the Channel? How ever are you doing this?"

She looked up at the sign. There were destination platforms for all cities in the country but suddenly, she knew. There was only one place she had to go right now. One place that had what she needed. All the resources. All the heart.

With broadsheet in hand, she stepped on to the platform.

***

Christien awoke with a start to the sound of a rooster, crowing in the yard. He lifted his head from the desk and looked around the room.

The library at *'l'ecurie de Lacey.'*

From stone floor to vaulted ceilings, shelves filled with books lined the walls, and every nook was stuffed with papers. Three antique desks, that normally sat elegant and bare, were now littered with documents, a testament to how late they'd worked into the night. Indeed, every bone in his body ached, and while he knew that there were countless rooms with soft beds and clean linens just waiting for him, he knew he wouldn't get what he wanted today. He never got what he wanted and always because of Sebastien.

A shot to the head wouldn't take him out, he thought abstractly. But a shot to the heart?

Valerie was curled up in a highbacked chair, feet tucked under her like a cat. Her eyes were closed, her breathing soft, and she clutched a leather dossier to her chest. He was glad that she at least had stolen a moment of sleep. She had been dogged in her search, going through the paperwork like a detective, and he had to admit he was proud of her diligence. Black Swan or no, she was a remarkable woman.

He rose from his chair, careful not to disturb her, and left the library to wander the halls toward the kitchen. The walls were whitewashed limestone, and most bare, but portraits of horses and landscapes dotted the space. There were leaded glass windows as well, and he could see the courtyard where the horses were being exercised in the morning light. Their breath fogged as they moved in wide circles, and he admitted they were an elegant breed. French Warmbloods. He had no idea what that meant. All mammals were warm-blooded, so it seemed a bit redundant. Still, both Sebastien and now Ivy talked about them like they were the pinnacle of the equestrian world. Then again, his family was so odd that perhaps they were.

Otherwise, it seemed like any other morning at *l'ecurie de Lacey,* and it warmed his own blood, just a little. Routine, like ignorance, was bliss.

He followed his nose to the kitchen, where the smell of freshly baked bread and coffee lured him in. Like most French farmhouses, it was stone with a low ceiling and dark beams. Copper pots hung next to dried herbs from a rack high over the oven. Two people stood at the cooktop, and they turned at his approach.

"Monsieur," said Geraud. "This is Sidonie Nédélec, the head cook and house matron."

The woman nodded and held up a French press. *"Café au lait, monsieur?"*

"Oui, merci," said Christien. Geraud gestured to a table spread with biscuits and jam, apples and cheese, and once again, Christien found his belly grumbling.

"Did you find what you were looking for, *monsieur,*" asked Geraud.

"I did not," said Christien, settling at the table and grabbing a biscuit. "There's simply so much to go through and so little time to do it in."

"I was asking Sidonie if she had any information," said the groundskeeper. "And she thinks she remembers something after the death of Madame de Lacey."

The woman named Sidonie passed him a cup. Aromatic French roast with more than a splash of cream. It was heaven on his tongue, and he sighed. He was such a creature of appetites.

"Forgive me, *monsieur,*" said Sidonie. "But I remember M. Rupert coming the summer after your dear mother's passing. He cleaned out the *chambre principal…*"

"Master bedroom," said Geraud.

"Oui, master bedroom," said Sidonie. "He said he wanted to remove all traces of M. Renaud from the estate, which is, you know, *difficile,* because M. Renaud was proprietor."

Christien picked at the seeds in a slice of apple before taking a bite. He closed his eyes, savoured the sweet juice as it ran down his throat. He would never take breakfast for granted again.

"He also went through the library and boxed many, many things, including books, journals, ledgers and photochromes."

Christien nodded.

"Did he leave them here or take them back with him to England?"

"He left many boxes in the attic, *monsieur,*" the cook said. "And even more in the cellar, but he did take several to London. To a, to a…"

She looked at Geraud.

"Un société des fantômes."

"Oui. Ah, a Society for Ghosts, *monsieur.*"

Christien's heart sank.

"The Ghost Club," he said quietly.

"Oui," said Sidonie. "A Ghost Club."

"I didn't think Rupert had anything to do with the Ghost Club," said Christien, and he pushed back from the table. His mind was engaged, so his stomach could wait. "But it stands to reason, I suppose."

"Will you wish to examine the attics, *monsieur?* "

"Yes, I think we must. Williams and Crookes made such a fuss over Ghostlight. I think it stands to reason that I would have known if they were in possession of another locket."

"Maybe they don't," came another voice, and he turned as Valerie entered the kitchen. Her hair was dishevelled, and she had circles under her eyes. But she had something in her hands. It was a small wooden frame, and she passed it to Christien.

"I found it behind a set of encyclopaedias."

It was a photochrome of a man and woman.

"Your parents," she said, and he nodded. "You look like him. Your brother looks like her."

"I know," he said, and ran his finger across the cloudy glass. "She was sun to his moon. Wait—"

He sat forward.

"You see it?" asked Valerie.

"Yes…"

In the photochrome, it was clear. Around Jane de Lacey's graceful neck was a locket.

***

While Ivy had booked a sleeping compartment on the long train north, she did not sleep. Rather, she wrote, working her pencil to the nub to write out theories and possibilities, answers and more questions. She must have dozed, however, for she woke with a start when the train pulled into the station at dawn. To her surprise, the stationhouse was empty.

Her breath fogged in front of her face as she stepped outside, breathed deep the sweet cold country air. Grey and green, she thought to herself. This place was always grey and green. Cold stone and ivy. Nature and human nature. There had to be a way to save it. She had to find a way.

She hailed a cab with a red horse under harness. No steam cabs here. Horses were still the rage. She was content, then, as they rattled down the rutty road through the little town, finally pulling up to a grand house with a long, low wall surrounding the garden. She paid the cabbie with another pound note and trotted up to the great green door. Her heart thudded in her chest even as her belly loudly rejoiced, and she smiled at the realization that her body knew this place intimately. Even nerve in her body just knew.

The door swung open, and the shrieks threatened to wake the dead long before the Mad Lord ever could.

Fanny and Franny Helmsly-Wimpoll grabbed Ivy by the arms and yanked her inside, slamming the door of Wimpolldon behind them.

***

The Milling Magazette

In other news, the temper in Over Milling is also heightened due to the sudden presence of the Empire's Sentinels. Indeed, INVASION is a more apropos term! It is believed that six have so far assembled at the estate of Lasingstoke, settling their imposing selves at each gate and corner, allowing no one in or out. It is likely due to the unconventional behaviour of its Baron, Sebastien Laurent St. John Lord de Lacey, and reports of serious conflicts in Vienna. Connections to the Pale Rider are pure speculation, although it does confirm what locals might suspect from his customary odd behaviour.

Stay tuned, readers, for the next issue of the Milling Magazette to find out what happens next!

Chapter 8

Of Teamwork, Steamwork, and a Stag in the Trees

"Of what a strange nature is knowledge! It clings to a mind when it has once seized on it like a lichen on a rock."

– Mary Shelley, Frankenstein: The Modern Prometheus

He could barely tear his eyes from the photochrome.

"Are you certain that this isn't Arclight?" he asked. His throat was dry, his voice barely a whisper.

"No, that is not *der Archelicht*," said Marie Valerie. "Similar, but not."

They were back in the library, having pulled all the books from the shelves in search of hidden photochromes. There were none, and the library was now in chaos, with old books and papers scattered across the floors. Geraud had begun the work of diligently gathering everything into piles along the walls, but it was clear he'd have work for days, if not weeks, putting them back.

"Well, it's not Ghostlight," said Christien as he studied the chrome. "I wore her around my neck for half a year. I know every ring, every pin, and every facet of that damned locket now."

"Did your father give this Lostlight to her?"

"I assume so," he said. "For their wedding, maybe?"

"Do you remember her wearing it?"

"No. But I remember so little of her."

"Did he take it when he…when she…?" She stopped, threw a quick glance at Geraud's bent back, and Christien shook his head.

"It's alright, Valerie. We need to talk about it. My father was a violent man, and he met a violent end. I'm not surprised there are still echoes of that violence in both Bastien and I."

She put her hand over his, but it was his clockwork hand, driving the point even farther home.

He pulled it away, popped a cigarette from it instead.

"Besides, my family commissioned these damned lockets once upon a time so in reality we're responsible for setting Bastien on this path. We need to be free to talk about it."

"But *are* you free, Remy?" she asked. "*Can* you talk about the things you've gone through?"

He stared at her. *Guilt, shame, fear, regret.* Fury at the injustice, heartbreak at the loss. An entire family ruined, stained in blood.

Could he talk about it? Could he ever?

"Monsieur?"

Geraud turned to face them, a pile of books in his arms.

"Forgive me, *monsieur,* but it is well known in these regions about tempers of the de Lacey men. In fact…"

He paused.

"Go on," said Christien. "Speak, please."

"Sidonie has sent for her mother, Sylvette. She is very old and knows the history of this place. She has a story."

"A story?"

"A local legend, really. But it may shed some light."

"On the lockets?"

"On the brothers."

"Brothers," Christien grunted. "It's always the bloody brothers."

"Sisters are no better," said Valerie.

"Families, then," said Christien, and he looked up at Geraud. "When is she coming?"

"Soon," said the man. "She is very old, so it takes time."

"Exactly what we don't have."

From the kitchen, a servant's bell chimed.

"That may be her," said Geraud. *"Un moment, monsieur."*

He laid the books in a teetering pile and quietly left the library. Christien inhaled the cigarette smoke, rolled it in his mouth for a long moment, before letting it out in a tight stream through his lips.

"We don't have time for stories and legends," said Valerie.

"I don't think we have time for anything, to be honest," said Christien. "But we don't have much to go on. It's a bloody puzzle with so many pieces missing."

"We could run away to the ocean and make mad, passionate love until the world ends."

She could wrap him around her little finger with a word. One crook and he would be slain.

He deliberately didn't look at her.

"My father threw Sebastien out the window that night," he said. "Maybe the locket went with him."

"Surely a servant would have found it," she said. "Would one of your servants keep it?"

"The servants at Lasingstoke are an odd sort," he said. "Loyal and odd. It's just as easy to think a magpie stole it."

"Perhaps it was buried along with her?"

"Hm," he said, and he cocked his head. "In that case, it could still be in the graveyard at Seventh."

"Seventh House is the one that is haunted, yes?"

Under normal circumstances, he would have laughed. He would have dismissed her comment as the superstitions of a fool. But now, everything was changed, anything was possible, and Marie Valerie von Habsburg was no fool.

"We need to get to Lasingstoke," he said. "But first, we need to go to London and talk to Williams and Crookes. Find out what the hell they know about this damned third locket."

"Who are Williams and Crookes?"

He grunted, took a long drag of his cigarette.

"The Ghost Club."

She reached over and plucked the cigarette from his fingers, brought it to her lips, and inhaled. Then, she smiled.

"The Ghost Club," she said. "How daunting."

"Monsieur?"

It was Geraud.

"Sylvette is here."

"Time for a legend," said Christien.

And he rose to his feet.

***

He'd barely been riding for an hour when he saw the first evidence of the War Office.

He and the bone army had crossed field and forest and had just come to the road that would lead them northwest. It was clearly a highway, as it was wider than a regular road, and flanked by low stone walls. They were traveling through Kent Downs, and the horizon was low, green and hilly. Perfect for a gallop on Gus' grey back. But he wasn't on Gus, and his heart twisted at the fact. Would Gus recognize him if he returned? Would anyone?

He was heading into the town of Brabourne now, a few miles south of Ashford. At least, that's what the sign had read. Another road, another town, another churning of the ground as the dead pushed forth. Hands, skulls, ribs, femurs. An undead harvest destroying the earth. That was his legacy. Not justice, not duty. Death.

Castlewaite had once called him the Avenger of Blood.

Maybe he had been wrong, all along.

He urged Ash forward along the road toward the town. It was a winding road, some parts cobbled, other parts dirt, and the buildings on either side seemed checkered with history. Victoria's rowhouses with Georgian townhouses, Tudor pubs butted up to Jacobean manors. There was likely a Gothic cathedral at the centre of town, maybe Roman ruins on the outskirts. There would also be a castle somewhere. History flourished in towns like Ashford, her roads travelled for as long as time itself. Shrubs and small oaks lined the road, buds only beginning to peak out in search of bleak February sun.

But it was a ghost town, he realized. There was no one visible. No one on the street, no one in the windows. Hiding, most likely. Or evacuated. Carriages had been abandoned at the sides of the road, carts of apples overturned and untouched. No birds, he noticed, and he wondered if they, like the sheep in France, were dead because of him.

He hadn't thought it through.

The emptiness began to weigh upon him, then, as Ash plodded through the barren town. Sophie had insisted he was the Crown Prince of Death, that it was his destiny to end all things and take up his throne in the ashes. He had believed it readily, for it just made sense given his fractured, broken, death-filled life. But was it the truth, or was it the lockets? All the world was laid open under their spin. Did he serve them, or could they, in fact, serve him?

Standing in the middle of the high street was a man in Royal Army blue, hands tucked smartly behind his back. Sebastien slowed Ash to stop. The bone army stopped too.

"Your Lordship," said the man.

"You know me?"

"Aye, milord."

"To be expected I suppose," said Sebastien. "I'm sure the broadsheets are having a heyday. Corporal, yes?"

"Aye, milord."

"Are you with the War Office?"

"Aye, milord," said the man. "They've asked…"

His voice caught in his throat, and it suddenly occurred to him that the corporal was terrified.

"They've asked that you stay out of London, milord."

"I have no desire to go through London, Corporal."

"Are you…" He cleared his throat. "Are you going to Lasingstoke, milord?"

Sebastien swept his eyes along the buildings and the lockets could see everything. There was a small unit hiding around the corner of a pub up ahead. No Sentinel, but cannons and heavy artillery and a row of cavalry horses waiting for the word.

"I have no quarrel with you," he said. "Nor with the War Office."

"I know that, milord," said the man and he nodded. "Are you going to Lasingstoke?"

"The Seat of my Barony, yes," said Sebastien. "Is there a problem with that, Corporal? I have broken no laws."

"No, milord," he said. "The War Office would like to escort you and your…"

The man glanced at the skeletons, swaying on decayed and missing feet.

"Your…"

"I don't know how to get rid of them," said Sebastien.

The corporal nodded again.

"Perhaps you could ask your supervisor to pass that on to the MoD? Put some very fine minds to the task of ridding one of unwanted corpses. The spirits I can handle, but these walking dead are a bloody nuisance. Very bad for the landscape and the soil. Although I suppose it is like a good tilling."

He looked down at the torn-up road.

"A very deep, thorough tilling."

"I, ah, I'll do that, milord." The corporal nodded swiftly. "The War Office would like to escort you to Lasingstoke, to help you stay away from populated areas, so that…"

"So that people won't panic."

"Aye, milord. So that people won't panic."

"Is that what you've done here?" he asked. "Evacuated the town?"

"Aye, milord. We've done that."

He thought a moment.

"It doesn't seem much like a request," Sebastien said. "Considering there is a unit with cannons waiting for me behind the pub."

"In case you decline the offer, milord," said the corporal.

The Mad Lord looked up at the skies. The War Office airship was still following, playing hide and seek among the clouds. He looked back at the corporal.

"Do you think you can do what neither the *Gilded Empire, Blood and Iron* and the *Industrial Republic* have not?"

The man swallowed.

"I didn't ask for this," Sebastien said. "I am a creation of the War Office. And Arvin Frankow. And maybe Death herself. Unless that's me."

The man nodded a third time. Clearly, he was out of his depth and simply trying to follow orders.

Sebastien sighed.

"I shall do my best, however," he said. "I'm not in control of very much at the moment, but I shall do my very best."

"Thank you, milord," said the corporal. He stepped aside and held out an arm, and several yards away, another man stepped out from a doorway to take his place on the road ahead.

"Remember to ask," said the Mad Lord.

"I will, milord. And thank you."

As Sebastien urged the pale horse forward, he noticed the corporal closed his eyes tightly as the dead flowed around him. Like a rock in a river, he thought to himself. How utterly strange his life had become. How much stranger his death.

He turned his face to the wind and followed the road, and the men of the War Office, out of Brabourne and onward to Lasingstoke.

***

"But we cannot, dearest," said Fanny. "Lasingstoke is surrounded by Sentinels."

"Under house arrest," said Franny, and she buttered another piece of toast. "Impossible to breach."

"But why?" asked Ivy, eagerly accepting her third croissant of the morning. "Do they think Sebastien is going to Lasingstoke?"

"I don't think *they* think anything, dearest," said Fanny. "They just know he's outrunning and outwitting all of them, so best shore up the one resource they do have."

"I need to get there," said Ivy, and she sat back with her tea. "Remy wanted me to check out his parents' bedroom."

"For clues?" asked Franny.

"Exactly," said Ivy. "For clues."

"Your cup is empty," said Fanny. "Granny! More tea!"

The old woman shuffled over, grumbling the entire time. But Ivy was used to it and made no mention, not even as the china pot trembled while she poured, and tea splashed over the sides. Granny was both granny and housekeeper. It was simply the Helmsly-Wimpoll way.

"Do you need to get to Lasingstoke?" asked Fanny.

"Or do you need to get to Lonsdale?" asked Franny.

"Well, both," said Ivy. "I need to speak to Frankow—"

"*Save* Frankow," said Franny.

"Yes, save Frankow and to find Lostlight, the third locket, before Laury does. But do we go to Frankow before Lasingstoke? Or after? Which is Laury headed for first, Frankow or Lostlight? Is Lostlight at Lonsdale or Lasingstoke? Or is it somewhere else and I must keep looking?"

She sighed and sipped her tea.

"So many questions. I'm at my wits' end."

"Tsk tsk, dearest," said Fanny. "You? Of all people? You're never at your wits' end."

"Never run out of wits," said Franny. "*Im*possible."

"Let's think this through, dear hearts," said Fanny, and she leaned forward. "All we can do is what *we* can do. We need to get into Lasingstoke, but we can't because of the Sentinels."

"Nasty Sentinels," said Franny.

"We need to get into Lonsdale, and we can, as far as we know."

"As far as we know," repeated Franny.

"As far as *we* know." Ivy sat forward now. "And we do know some things…"

"That others may not," said Fanny.

"Oh, they don't," said Franny.

"So, what do we know that we can act upon?" said Ivy.

"Does the War Office know the Mad Lord is heading for Frankow?" asked Fanny.

"Does Bertie?" asked Franny. "Does anyone?"

"No," said Ivy. "As far as I know, only Remy and I know Sebastien's plan."

"Well then," said Fanny. "No one should be trying to protect Dr. Frankow so there should be no Sentinels or guard posted."

"Therefore, Lonsdale is accessible," said Ivy.

"I have a steam car," said Franny.

"And they have resources," said Ivy.

"Many crazy resources," said Fanny, and she smiled at the thought.

"They may have answers," said Ivy.

"All the answers," said Franny.

"And maybe the locket?" asked Ivy

"Lostlight the locket in the Lonsdale loony bin?" said Franny.

"What a delightfully odd place to store it," said Fanny.

"Maybe…" Ivy breathed. "Well, it's a start."

And she sat back, her heart swelling with the way their conversations tumbled all over the map, but inevitably led to greater, more wonderful places. She was so glad she'd chosen to come here first of all. The sisters Helmsly-Wimpoll were investigative gold.

"That's what *we* can do, dear heart," said Fanny, reaching forward and taking Ivy's hand in hers. "That is all that is on our plate. Speaking of plates…"

She turned in her chair.

"*Granny*! We're going on an escapade and are in need of a basket!"

Ivy smiled to herself. With Fanny and Franny Helmsly-Wimpoll on the case, perhaps the world did stand a chance. If not, well, there was no better company to end it with.

Ivy pushed up from her chair.

***

The men of the War Office were stationed several hundred yards apart like posts along an invisible fence and he followed their direction without dispute, considering it the path of least resistance. They had directed him through another empty town and had likely blocked the roads to travellers for safety and surveillance. It was less than an hour later, however, when an officer directed him off the highway toward a gulley.

"City coming up, milord," said the man. "War Office suggests a detour."

"Not evacuated?" asked the Mad Lord.

"Not in full, milord."

"Which city is it?"

"I can't say, milord."

"Hm," he said, but he obliged, shifting his weight so that Ash left the road, exchanging dirt for grass. Sebastien didn't mind terribly. It was a beautiful view with rolling green and hedgerows for miles, with the path taking them up hills and down deep vales surrounded by trees. The dead continued to meet him, rising up and tilling up the green, churning it into brown soil, while he painted it white with frost. He wondered how long it might take for the minds of the MoD to come up with a plan. He wasn't convinced anyone could, but he was at a loss. This journey would be much more pleasant had it not been accompanied by the army of bones, but then again, rather less apocalyptic.

He looked around now. They had been on a steady downgrade for several minutes and were now deep in a steep-sided valley rimmed by oak, hornbeam and ash. *Odd*. He hadn't seen any of the War Office escorts in a while, assigned as they had been to line his path. He was alone with the dead in this steep valley, when suddenly, a stag bounded across his path.

It froze at the sight of them, tail up in alert. It was a fine eight-pointer, with velvet hanging in shreds from each tine, and he marvelled at its wild beauty. The stag raised its head and bellowed into the trees, before springing away. But as it landed, its forelegs buckled, and it crashed to the ground, head swinging, hind legs thrashing.

"No no no no!" cried Sebastien. He leapt from Ash's back and rushed to the stag's side, dropping to his knees. "Not this time. Please, no."

He raised his hands and held them over the deer's heaving flank. But soon, the head lolled, and the thrashing stilled.

"Please, don't."

He had brought Ivy back from the dead. He had given life to Crown Prince Rudolf. Surely, he had this ability.

He closed his eyes and called on Ghostlight, felt the familiar cold rush down his limbs and into his palms.

Life, he thought. *I trade Death for Life.*

And he laid his hands on the stag's flank. Slowly, the dead turned their skulls to watch.

I am the Crown Prince of Death and I command Death to retreat.

Green eyes full of life. Mouth sideways in a quirky smile. Freckles dusted across her nose.

Life.

Ice crackled from his hands, turning the tan pelt white with frost. In a heartbeat, the sides, legs, neck and head were frozen, desiccated under his touch. Before he could remove his hands, the carcass dissolved into the frosty grass.

He dropped in hands in his lap, lost.

"I'm sorry," he said to the stag.

Sophie was a liar, and he a fool to have believed her.

"I'm sorry," he said to Ivy Savage, whom he would never see again.

The Crown Prince of Fools.

"I'm sorry!" he shouted to the steep-sided valley. It echoed and echoed until it faded into nothing.

Ash snorted and he looked up. Along the rim of this steep-sided valley, cannons pointed down at them from above.

Chapter 9

Of Madness, Monsters, and Mayhem on the Road

'I have love in me the likes of which you can scarcely imagine and rage the likes of which you would not believe."

– Mary Shelley, Frankenstein: the Modern Prometheus

He remembered the name of the valley was Devil's Kneading Trough, that there was in fact no city close by, and he vowed he would never trust anyone ever again.

The cannons boomed from above and in a flash of instinct, he called the Deadwall to shield him from their blast. The earth exploded with impact, and through the ice, he saw the bone army shatter into a thousand gruesome pieces all around him. The icy walls splintered and cracked under the cannon fire but held firm, and he closed his eyes again, surrendering to Ghostlight and her eerie ways.

All along the steep rim, the dead began to rise, pushing up through the earth with skeletal hands. They grabbed soldiers and scrabbled over cannons, creating sinkholes in their wake. The army scattered and the cannons tipped, some plunging into the pits, others sliding down the very steep banks of the Kneading Trough. He surrendered to Arclight and orbs sprang up, swallowing cannons and soldiers alike. He didn't know where they went. He didn't care. The War Office had created him, so long ago. It was time their bill came due.

Suddenly, the world roared, and he was slammed into the earth as the Deadwall shattered all around him, sending ice shards like shrapnel all across the grass. He couldn't hear. He couldn't feel, and he vaguely remembered the airship that had been following. He had forgotten about it, and knew that, just like the *Blood and Iron* fleet, it had likely dropped a bomb directly above him. He was grateful to Ghostlight, then, and the coffin of ice that had shielded him from the force of its impact.

He pushed to his feet. The ground was blistered by fire, and he staggered across the uneven terrain. But he heard the whistle of a second bomb and this time, called an orb for himself. He lunged through as the world erupted behind him.

***

"It started with the brothers," said Sidonie. "The brothers de Lacey."

Sidonie was translating since her mother was almost deaf. She also spoke a form of *Ch'ti*, a northern French dialect that was as difficult as it was distinct.

Sylvette Nédélec was indeed old. She looked like a withered apple wrapped in shawls and wool, and she sat on a stool by the kitchen table, drinking black coffee and smoking a very thin cigar. Christien liked her immediately, though he'd never admit it.

"Renaud and Rupert?" he said. "Those brothers?"

"Non," said Sidonie. *"Maslin et Marcel.* Many years before your father was born. Generations, I believe."

"It's always brothers," grunted Christien. "Bloody brothers."

"Twins," said Sidonie. "According to the story."

"Oh god," said Christien. "Even worse."

Valerie looked down at him and he could have sworn the steel had softened somewhat.

Sylvette spoke again.

"The de Laceys were a well-heeled family," Sidonie translated. "With two sons, Marcel *et* Maslin. Maslin lived in a fine house in Paris and Marcel ran this estate here in Caen. There was no love lost between the brothers, but when Maslin's son got in trouble with the law, Maslin was given a choice – a life in prison for his son or a life of exile for him and his family."

Sylvette leaned in to her daughter and spoke rapidly. Her voice was as thin as parchment.

"It was rumoured that Marcel was behind the offer," said Sidonie, "As he wanted both estates for himself."

"What did the son do that warranted such a penalty?" asked Valerie.

"He broke a man out of prison," said Geraud.

"Smashing," said Christien. "And which fate did they choose?"

"Exile," said Geraud.

"Well, that's a very sad story," said Christien. "But many families are cutthroat when it comes to inheritance. How does that affect our family now?"

Sidonie asked the question, answered a beat behind Sylvette.

"Because during all this, Maslin went blind. He and his two children fled France and moved to a small cottage in Germany, but it was very difficult for them. They lived in extreme poverty, and bad luck followed them even there. The little cottage burned down, and they swore it was set deliberately by…"

Sidonie leaned toward her mother, asked a question and Sylvette grew animated.

"Oui, hein," she said. *"Un monstre!"*

Sidonie sat back.

"The fire was supposedly set by a monster."

"A monster," said Christien. His heart sank.

"We did say myths, yes?" Sidonie smiled. "Naturally, no one believed them. After the fire, Maslin grew ill and they say he went mad, so the family returned to Paris to ask for help. Once again, Marcel refused them, and Maslin called *him* a monster. When Maslin died, his children publicly cursed Marcel and his family to a never-ending cycle of madness and monsters."

Sylvette grunted and puffed on her cigar for emphasis.

"Madness and monsters," said Christien. "That sums us up pretty neatly."

"That does not explain the lockets," said Valerie.

"No," said Geraud. "But it does explain the de Laceys."

The old woman turned in her seat and reached for Christien's hand. He frowned but let her take it, surprised at how papery and light her skin was. He could see the veins and the tendons, the age spots and the bones.

She leaned toward him, spoke a phrase that rolled out of her aged mouth along with the smoke.

"She asks, which one are you?" said Sidonie. "Madman or monster?"

He said nothing, and they sat for a long while in silence, to the bubbling of the soup and the ticking of the grandfather clock, Sylvette's raspy breath and the pulse of blood in his ears. From the rattle of the silverware in the drawer to the trembling of china cups on an old wooden shelf. Outside, a horse whinnied. And then another. And another.

Geraud crossed the stone floor to the door and peered out.

"Mon dieu," he breathed.

Christien joined him and his breath caught in his throat.

Over the rooftops of the stables and above the canopy of the bare trees, he could see three Sentinels thundering down the road toward them.

***

He was in a forest, with old spruce and pines covered in snow.

He slapped a hand across his brow.

"Not again," he growled. "I don't want this. I just want to go home."

But something was different, and he realized he was alone. Ash hadn't come with him, and he wondered if the horse was in one piece or many. He wasn't sure that would make a difference. The horse had survived being cleft in two by the *Gardien* in Calais. He wasn't a living thing, after all. Not living, not dead, just one of the many things in between.

This place was familiar now, like a recurring dream, and he dreaded each step as he crunched through the snow. Clearly, something was bringing him back. Arclight was bringing him back to this cottage with the low, thatched roof and rough timbers for a frame. The thin windows and no shutters, the family sitting by the fire. The old man, the young man and the two women, one fair and one dark. As idyllic as it was, he realized that the lack of free will had turned it a nightmare, for he was as stuck as a moth under glass, just waiting for the pin.

It was mercy then, that he saw the spirits and ducked as a spade sliced through the air for his head. He wheeled in the snow, sliding back as the figure rushed him again. The spade split the space between them with such force that had it struck, a normal man would be cleft in two.

He swung again and the Mad Lord sprang back, but his heel caught on a stump and for a moment, he flailed. In that moment, the spade struck his skull with the flat side and the clang of metal echoed across the wood.

Sebastien stumbled and hit the snowy ground on hands and knees. Lights popped behind his eyes, and he shook his head, surprised he was still conscious. The spade came down again.

"Accipere hoc ligonem," he barked.

Arclight flashed and the spade was swallowed in light. His attacker howled and staggered back, but Sebastien was fast. He sprang and lunged, grabbing the man's wrist and sending the cold deep, deep into the flesh. But the flesh didn't freeze, and the man didn't scream. He slammed his fist into the Mad Lord's belly and Sebastien doubled over, dropping to one knee in the snow.

"I told you!" the man snarled. "I will kill you! My mind is bent to injury and death!"

Lies, lockets, War Office, bombs. His life had been shaped by death since his birth, and it was continuing to be shaped by it. Death at every dreadful twist and turn. It was impossible now to stop the rage that flooded through his mind and raced to his limbs. With a roar, he lunged forward, taking the larger man's legs out from under him and together, they crashed into the woodpile. Both lockets began to spin, and Sebastien staggered apart and pulled his pistol, ethereal light spilling from his eyes and flashing across the wood. He stood over the man, the three barrels aimed square in the middle of the forehead. But at the sight of the face, a chill swept up his spine and he was forced to hesitate.

"What in God's name are you?" he breathed.

Not a monster, but not quite a man.

"I would ask the same of you!" the man cried out, shielding his eyes from the flashing of the lockets. "Please, if you shoot, the family will be afraid! Do not, I beg you! Their lives are difficult as is!"

Sebastien stepped back, and back again. He threw a glance to the cottage, where there was a crack at the door. A face peered out.

He closed his eyes, willed the lockets to quiet their dance. When he opened them, the 'not-quite-a-man' was gone.

He looked back.

"Hello?" called a voice from the door. "Who is there?"

He cursed under his breath, summoned an orb, and disappeared.

***

He couldn't remember the last time he'd been on horseback. He knew less about horses than he did about almost anything else in the world, despite Rupert's efforts at teaching. But he had to admit, Sebastien was right. French Warmbloods were now his favourite breed and he vowed to take a greater interest in the registry if any of them managed to survive the impending apocalypse.

The End of the World, and horses. How like Sebastien his life had become.

They'd barely made it out of the stable courtyard as the Sentinels rumbled in, and the horses fairly flew down the snow and dirt road faster than the mechanical men could follow. They maintained a gallop until they reached the ten-mile marker, then they slowed to a trot to let the horses, and themselves, catch their breath.

"We can make Bayeux tonight," said Christien. "But we'll need to find an inn. It's too cold to spend the night in the open air."

"So, we find an inn, after all," said Valerie and she smirked. "You see? I always get my way."

"I'll be far too sore for anything, tonight, *cherie*," he said. "Besides, we need to get a message to your airship. Perhaps they could meet us in Cherbourg-en-Cotentin. It'll be faster than a ferry or heading back to Calais."

She turned her head, and he admired her profile. She was a brilliant rider. Perfect seat, perfect poise. But of course, it made sense. Her mother, Empress Elizabeth, had practically grown up on horseback. It was only natural she'd impress that skill upon her youngest, most favoured daughter.

"Will this town…" she began.

"Bayeux."

"Bayeux. Will Bayeux have a teslagraph office?"

"I have no idea."

"Do you have a teslagraph in your arm? A fingerpress?"

He surprised himself by laughing.

"Well," she pouted. "You said you find new things every day."

"Quite true," he said.

"So, you will not share my bed still?"

"Valerie…"

"No?"

"No. I will not."

And she reached down to her ankle, pushed the layers of long skirt aside, and slid a pistol from her boot.

"Steady your horse," she said, and, raising the pistol to the sky, she fired.

The horses startled as a flare shot upwards. Up, up, up it went, before bursting into a rain of golden stars.

"What the devil?" he gasped.

"A daughter of the Gilded Emperor is never far from his golden arm."

Within minutes, the underbelly of an airship sailed into view.

***

London Times News
Dreadnaught Sighted over Coventry

Invention or invasion? A metal-clad airship has been reported over the skies of Coventry, under a solid black canvas.

"It was the strangest dreadnaught I ever seen," says part-time miller Ted Billings. "It looked like a bloody whale swimming through the clouds."

Billings is not the only witness to this unidentified flying object, with almost seventeen sightings reported since this morning across the lower borroughs, in a fairly direct path northwest towards Lancashire.

"It's likely the product of a backyard aeronaut," says Freddie Wrexham of the Royal Airships Society. "The World Fair is in Paris this year and amateur inventors are looking to make their mark."

The War Office has declined to comment. The London Times will continue to investigate.

***

While Franny had owned a steamcar for several years, it had only been named in the last two months. *Veritas*, she called it. Latin for Truth. Ivy was certain there was more to the name, but time had been short, and Franny had been giddy. At least that, of all things, hadn't changed.

It was noon before they left Wimpolldon, and the sky stayed heavy for the entire drive. The road was cobbled from Over Milling to Lancaster, and from Lancaster to Wharcombe, but on the final leg from the bayside town to Lonsdale Abbey, it was dirt. With spring only newly arrived, the road was mud with ruts freezing overnight, and the steamcar chugged and bounced roughly on its way up to the wrought iron gate. In the distance, they could see the Abbey itself, a huge Gothic mansion with weathered red brick and limestone over doors and windows. Three large stacks puffed smoke and steam into the gray sky.

"Well, that's a fright," said Fanny.

"It's quite remarkable inside," Ivy said as she hopped out of the back. "I've never seen a hospital quite like it. Or any building, for that matter."

"Is it, in fact, an Abbey?" asked Fanny.

"Or a sanitorium?" asked Franny.

"Yes," said Ivy.

Ivy stepped up to the hex-key code set, trying not to remember the time she'd cracked it while Sebastien lay dying at her feet.

"Seven sevens," she muttered to herself, punching the code into the panel with seven distinct clicks. "Laury, you are not so hard to decipher once you have the code."

The black iron gate shuddered to life. The articulating gears groaned overhead and wheels inside the lintel began to spin. Suddenly, an alarm blasted, and Ivy staggered back into Helmsly-Wimpoll arms. The three of them clung to each other as slowly, menacingly, the gates began to swing.

A shadow passed over them, silhouetted in the indigo sky.

"Oh, look!" gasped Franny. "A flying man!"

"Welcome home, Lord de Lacey," came a mechanical voice from the gate. *"By orders of Crown Prince Edward and the Imperial War Office of Steam, you are placed under arrest. Please surrender yourself peacefully and allow yourself to be escorted to the infirmary for detention."*

Behind the gate stood three figures – a young woman with an axe, a wild-looking man with sword and shovel, and between them, Agnes Tidy in nursing cap and long skirts, holding a blunderbuss in her arms.

Chapter 10

Of Truth, Daughters, and Time

"A mind of moderate capacity which closely pursues one study must infallibly arrive at great proficiency in that study."

- Mary Shelley, Frankenstein: The Modern Prometheus

Arvin Frankow's office was unchanged since her last visit, but then again, it wasn't surprising. As much as Ivy felt like it had been years, it had only been a matter of months since she'd been here to fetch her mother. It was now as it had been then; tall, mullioned windows, roaring fire, copper wires and eclectic bookshelves. There were several capsules untouched in the pneumatic pipes, and a cup of cold tea, also untouched, upon his desk.

There was also an axe buried into the wood of the door and Ivy couldn't help but smile to herself. Constancy, thy name was Lizzie Borden.

Ivy sat next to Fanny in a tattered armchairs while Franny contentedly explored the room. She had forgotten to remove her steamcar goggles, and while it made her an eerie sight, she seemed to fit right in. She peered out the windows. She scoped out the gears. She examined the book spines. She handled the lenses and tubing and glass. Where Fanny was a taut bolt of wires, Franny was a clockwork fly on every wall, seeking, learning, thinking, adapting. For all her quirks, she was, Ivy realized, the most unfettered woman she'd ever known.

"Oy, if it isn't the greedy girl," came a voice and they looked up to see Lizzie Borden standing in the door, one palm on the handle of her axe.

"Hallo, Lizzie," said Ivy. "Where is Dr. Frankow?"

She shrugged and cast her eyes over the sisters, before pulling the axe from the wood with a mighty heave.

"That's a dandy axe," said Franny.

"I like your goggles," said Lizzie.

"Me too," said Franny.

Tap, clank, hiss. Tap, clank, hiss.

"Uh oh," said Lizzie. "I've got to go."

And she spun on her heel and disappeared down the madly painted corridor.

Tap, clank, hiss. Tap, clank, hiss.

The sound, as familiar now as the chimes of a grandfather clock. Fanny sat bolt upright, glancing from Ivy to the door and back again. Franny was frozen, eyes bulging in her steamgoggles, an aluminium letter opener in her hand.

Tap, clank, hiss. Tap, clank, hiss.

The door swung open, and Arvin Frankow walked in.

Indeed, he also had not changed, and she rose to her feet, stifling the strange urge to hug him. He smiled at her, his own eyes bulging behind his great rimmed spectacles, and he turned to the sisters.

"I am Dr. Arvin Frankow," he said. "Who are you?"

Fanny rose to her feet, curtsied very slightly.

"Fanny Helmsly-Wimpoll, soon to be Helmsly-Wimpoll-Liddell. Ahem."

She and held out her gloved hand and Frankow took it, gave it a little shake.

"Congratulations, Miss Helmsly-Wimpoll, soon to be Helmsly-Wimpoll-Liddell."

"And this is my sister, Franny Helmsly-Wimpoll of Wimpolldon."

Frankow released her and turned. Franny held out her hand, but in her hand, the letter opener. Frankow reached out and shook it at the tip.

"Enchanted, truly."

"I love it here," said Franny.

"As do I." He turned again. "And Miss Savage. It is always a pleasure."

"Thank you, sir," she said. "I assume you know why we're here."

"I know why *you're* here," he said, and he took his seat behind the desk. "But you have surprised me once again with your companions, and that is a difficult thing to do."

"You must come away with us," said Ivy. "Now."

"And why must I come away with you, Miss Savage?"

"Because he's coming for you, Dr. Frankow."

"Who is?"

"Please, sir. Don't trifle. You know what I mean."

Frankow leaned back in his chair.

"Does he want to kill me, Miss Savage?"

For some reason, her chest grew tight, and her eyes stung with impending tears.

"Yes," she said. "Yes, sir. He wants to kill you."

"And bring about the end of the world," said Fanny.

"Oh, my," said Frankow. "Once again, I am surprised."

"Please sir," she said again. "Come with us. We can get you far away."

"To Lasingstoke?"

"Further. Some place he'll never think to look."

"If he still sees with the eyes of a cat, he won't need to look. He'll know."

"Doesn't that bother you?" she asked, leaning forward now, and clasping her fingers tightly in her lap. "That he intends to kill you?"

"If anyone had a right to kill me, it would be Sebastien."

She lowered her eyes. He was right, of course. Sebastien had been through hell at the hands of Frankow and his father. To hell, and back, repeatedly.

"We have to stop him," she said. "I have to believe we can stop this without any more bloodshed or death."

"Does he have the locket still?"

"Two," said Franny.

"Two?" The man made a series of faces, made even more remarkable by the multiple lenses on his spectacles. "Ghostlight *and* Arclight?"

Ivy nodded.

"That is problematic. Not the third, though?"

"No," said Ivy. "He doesn't know where it is."

"But he's coming here to find it."

"I…" She frowned. "I suppose, yes."

"Before or after he kills me?"

"Is this so hard to take seriously, sir?"

"Oh, I assure you, I am taking this very seriously. But I also know Sebastien. He is perhaps the most stubborn man I have ever met. If he has it in his mind to kill me, I'm quite certain he will succeed."

"But if he brings about the end of the world, as he has claimed," said Fanny. "Then he also intends to kill me."

"And me," said Franny.

"And all of us," said Ivy. "And he hasn't thought that through. The lockets are clouding his judgement, overriding his good sense."

"They are addicting," said Frankow. "He is addicted to their voices."

"He is, sir. He is chained to them like to opium. And I must help him."

"Why, Miss Savage?"

She cursed him because he knew. He knew and she knew, and he was simply being himself in drawing the truth out of her. There was no point in fighting.

"I must help him because I love him."

There. She'd said it. She didn't bother to resist the tears. It was a relief to let them go.

"I love him, and I know this is not him. It's not what he wants. It's not how our story should end."

Fanny took her hand.

"And I will fight for his story to end rightly," she went on. "I want the chance to make it right, to let him live free from these demons that plague him. I don't know if I can, but I'll be damned if I'm not going to try."

He cocked his head, and his lenses whirred making his eyes bigger and bigger still.

"Are you so certain this what he wants, Miss Savage? Or is it simply what *you* want?"

"He said," she swallowed the lump in her throat. "He said, in me, he saw life. Me, this silly, stubborn girl in his mother's red dress that was far too big, and much too bold. He said he saw life. And we danced across the ballroom of the Hofburg until Arclight came to call. But he was happy. For one brief moment, he was happy. He was free. And I want to give that back to him, whatever it takes."

Frankow studied her for a long moment. She couldn't read him. She never could. She didn't know anything that he was thinking. He was, and always had been, a puzzle with several pieces missing.

"The study of life and death is a dangerous game," he said finally. "One fraught with success and failure, victory and loss. I have played that game all my life, and I have lost more than I have won. People have died, and I could not save them. People have lived, whom I should not have saved."

"Sophie," said Ivy.

"Sophie Friederike Dorothea Maria Josepha von Habsburg-Lorraine, yes," said Frankow. "Yes."

"Gadzooks," said Fanny.

"Ooooh," breathed Franny, eyes wide, smiling like a cat.

"It is an unnatural study, all-consuming and all-encompassing," Frankow went on. "So, I too, am an addict, Miss Savage, to science. To the hope that, one day, there will be no more death or dying, or pain or suffering. But Sebastien has paid that price, over and over. I understand his quest to the end of all things. The voices deafen him. He merely seeks to silence them. He is desperately searching for peace."

She nodded. It was true. How a fox in a trap would chew its own leg off to be free, Sebastien would bring the world crashing down to find relief from the curses set upon him by that world.

"How will he end the world, Miss Savage?" Frankow asked. "I do not know if that is something Ghostlight could do on her own, and I am unfamiliar with Arclight. Was she responsible for Crown Prince Rudolf's death?"

She sighed.

"In a way, sir," she said. "But Arclight is different than Ghostlight. She makes holes in time and space. I'm convinced it's the only way Sebastien has been able to travel so far so quickly. Well, that and the Pale Horse…"

"Pale horse?"

"Yes. From Revelation," she said. "That one."

Frankow raised his brows as he processed the information, laced his fingers together across the desk.

"Is it true he travels with a bone army?"

"Also true, sir," she said. "It's frankly terrifying."

"And last question before I decide, I promise," he said. "Do you think Sebastien can sense the lockets? What I mean is, did he go to Vienna to get Arclight, or did she bring him to Vienna to get here?"

"I…" She frowned now, looked at her hands. "I think they'll use anyone as stepping stones. Ghostlight used Crown Prince Edward to ferry her from London to Vienna, and he's – forgive me for saying so – a bit obtuse. Sebastien is particularly in tune with their voices. I don't know if he can track them or find them on his own, but then again, I don't see with the eyes of a cat."

"Hm," said Frankow.

Fanny and Franny exchanged glances, but they all sat in silence for a long moment, until there was a rap at the door. A man in a tweed cap peered in.

"Beggin' yer pardon, sir," said the man. "But there's a Sentinel on the road."

Ivy's heart froze.

"Ah, the Wharcombe Sentinel," said Frankow. "I was wondering when they'd send him. Thank you, Carl."

Carl closed the door behind him.

"Please sir," said Ivy. "We have to leave soon. Anywhere, just not here."

"Wimpolldon?" suggested Fanny.

"It's a start," said Ivy.

"Very well. I agree," he said. "I will give you the chance to save my boy and I will place myself in your hands to do so. Is Seventh still standing?"

"Seventh? Well, yes, it is. To be honest, I'm not sure why. I should have thought Rupert would have had the place razed."

"Rupert St. John," sniffed Fanny.

"The Scourge," sniffed Franny.

They rose to their feet.

"Where is Mumford?" asked Ivy.

"Mumford?" said Frankow. "Why do you ask?"

"You said the voices deafen him, yes? Well, Mumford gives him quiet. Mumford soothes his restless soul."

"Yes," he said. "Mumford does, indeed."

"Perhaps Mumford can help him again in that regard? Maybe he can help break through the voices of the lockets."

"That is a sound presumption," he said.

The lenses whirred the other way, and his eyes grew smaller and smaller as he thought.

"Unfortunately, Mumford is at Lasingstoke. I sent him there with Carl when you and Sebastien returned from London in November."

"Lasingstoke is besieged by Sentinels," said Fanny. "We can't get in."

"Veritas," said Franny. She had been staring out the window for most of the conversation, and she spun around, now with a magnifying glass in her hand. *"Veritas Temporis filia."*

"Truth is the daughter of Time," said Frankow.

"Indeed, she is. She truly is!"

She clasped her hands under her chin and smiled like the sun.

"I think I have a plan."

***

The Gilded airship did not have to wait long to dock at the tower of Big Ben. It was an Imperial vessel carrying a royal guest during a time of political turmoil. Those ships carrying returning citizens were forced to circle while strings were pulled, and politics was played. Still, both strings and politics were efficient, and the Archduchess and her companion were deposited at the very top of Big Ben before the airship glided off into the night.

It was surprisingly busy on the streets of London for so late in the evening. Word of the Pale Rider and his legion of the dead was on every tongue, and in every broadsheet and paper. The Toxic Fog was thick, but few wore masks, evidence that they were more distressed by headlines than health, and Christien was glad when the hansom cab had two sets available on the seat.

The cab took them to Pall Mall, between the Reform Club and the Athaneaum, and it struck him how much had changed since he'd been here last. Then, he'd been eager and innocent, and more than a little desperate to discover the source of his family's trauma. Now, he was an entirely different man, weary and broken, not at all inclined to put any of it back together. Still, he knew so much more of his history, and couldn't be certain whether it had helped or hindered his journey.

The brass plaque beside the door read *The Ghost Club - London, est. 1862*. So many fine names. So many elite members. Science and spirituality met in the Ghost Club of London, as did research and religion. He wondered when the morality of it all had been lost.

With a deep breath, he glanced at Valerie. The woman was a trooper. In fact, she seemed as eager as him to find answers to the spider's web of questions. She caught his gaze and nodded swiftly, so he turned, headed up the steps and pushed open the door.

Wood-panelled walls and gold-framed portraits, elegant furnishings, and books. It smelled of pipe smoke and brandy and old, old money. At the foot of a spiral stair, there was a large banker's desk, and at the desk, and automaton.

"Hello, CHARLES," said Christien.

The automaton's red eye scanned him up and down.

"Welcome back, Lord de Lacey," it said. "It is pleasant to see you again."

"Is the club meeting?"

"Upstairs, in the Amber Lounge, sir." The automaton's red eye scanned Valerie up and down. "Please forgive me, but this is a Gentlemen's Club. Women are not allowed."

"She is not a woman," he lied. "She is an automaton, like yourself, but fashioned to look as lifelike as is possible."

The red eye scanned up and down, up and down.

"I am the latest model from the Gilded Empire's finest craftsmen," Valerie said, making her voice as thin and mechanical as CHARLES'. "VALERIE."

"VALERIE?" asked CHARLES.

Valerie cocked her head, robotically.

"Very Alive-Looking Experimental Representative for Intelligence and Etiquette."

Barely a heartbeat missed. Christien bit back a smile. By God, she was good.

"That is why I'm here," Christien said. "To show her off to the Club. She's all the rage in Vienna."

"All the rage," said Valerie, robotically.

The red eye flashed and flashed again.

"I am unsure of this protocol," CHARLES said.

"Don't worry," said Christien. "I've got this. Come along, VALERIE."

And he trotted up the stairs, Valerie following, robotically, behind him.

*****

The night was cold, but the fog had not turned to frost yet, and for that, Ivy was grateful. It would soon, she knew, once Sebastien was in the shire.

She tugged Victoria's fur coat around her shoulders, also grateful for its warmth and weight. It made her feel sheltered and protected, shielded from far more than cold or fog. She'd need all the resources she could muster if tonight had any hope of succeeding at all.

She swept her eyes across the pebbled drive, where two steamcars sputtered, hissing steam into the night. *Veritas,* and the *Lonsdale Lune,* which Ivy had to admit that it was as clever a play on words as she'd ever heard. Fanny sat in the seat of the *Veritas,* bundled in a woollen blanket borrowed from the Abbey's storeroom. Franny sat in the dickey, goggles set, and scarf wrapped snug round her chin. She was smiling like a madwoman, which Ivy thought was fitting since her plan was entirely mad. Something about machines taking on other machines, and she was reminded of her friend, H.G. Wells and his claim that machines would somehow begin the end of the very world.

Machines or Mad Lord. It seemed the world was doomed, regardless.

Carl finished checking the gauges and dials on the *Lonsdale Lune* and climbed onto the dickey. For a four-wheeled steamcar, it was larger than Franny's, but without the extra set of tires, it presented a suspiciously unstable appearance. This would tip in a heartbeat, Ivy reckoned, when meeting the first sharp corner or herd of cows on the road.

Lizzie marched up to the Lune, axe in hand, and glanced up at Franny at the dick.

"Nice car," she said. "Do you like pigeons?"

"I do," said Franny. "Do you like lasagna?"

"I don't know what that is."

And Lizzie climbed into the *Lune* next to Grigori Rasputin, pushing him with her axe and complaining constantly in her sharp American accent.

Ivy studied the *Lune*'s passengers and swallowed. This was a reckless, dangerous plan, but truth be told, she had nothing better. Wisely, Mr. Home was intending to accompany them from the air. Once again, Ivy marvelled at how this had become normal for her, but her world had grown larger since she'd first set foot in Lonsdale. Everyone had a story to tell, a yarn to spin, a talent to share, and the world was far too fantastical to let it end on account of some lockets.

"Tea," said Agnes Tidy as she handed Fanny a flask. Her great winged cap made it seem like she'd soon be joining Mr. Home and changing earth for skies at the next gust of wind. "For the road. It's a chill night tonight."

"Brilliant woman," said Fanny. "The Czech is lucky to have you."

They could have been sisters, thought Ivy. Both organized and particular, skilled and confident. She hoped they'd become friends at the end of it all, if she herself didn't make it out.

That left one and Ivy turned. There was no tap, clank, hiss this time as Arvin Frankow approached from the Abbey. He was sporting his traveling wheels, and they reminded her now of the TANC Sentinel on the bridge at Strasbourg. He too was bundled in an oversized woollen overcoat, and she recognized it from the night he drove the undertaker's carriage, fetching Sebastien's body from London. It seemed so long ago. A lifetime.

And more than one death.

He was carrying a black hat in his hands.

"It seemed to me that you were missing something," he said.

It was a bowler. Her throat grew tight.

"And while you have considerably more hair than me, I think our heads might be, ironically, the same size."

"Brains?" she squeaked.

"That must be it," he said. He passed it to her, and she happily patted it on her head. Home.

"Much better," he said. "Shall we go?"

She could tell he was scared. Scared of leaving Lonsdale, of facing Sebastien, or of facing his own impending judgement, but the lenses made his eyes larger than normal, and she could see the cracks.

"Let's go," she said, and she turned to the steamcars. "Into the fray, my friends? For the fate of the world?"

"For the fate of the world," cried Fanny.

"Huzzah!" cried Franny.

"For the pigeons!" cried Lizzie.

"If we are the cavalry," said Frankow. "Then I fear the world is doomed."

With a grin, she followed him to the car.

Chapter 11

Of Clubs, Kisses, and Politics Bollocks

"It was the secrets of heaven and earth that I desired to learn; and whether it was the outward substance of things or the inner spirit of nature and the mysterious soul of man that occupied me, still my inquiries were directed to the metaphysical, or in its highest sense, the physical secrets of the world."

– Mary Shelley, Frankenstein: The Modern Prometheus

The heavy scent of cigars led them as surely as the voices, to a set of double doors near the end of a long hallway. With a glance at Valerie, Christien pushed them open and stepped through. The Ghost Club looked up, shocked at the pair of unexpected intruders. They were a group of well-tailored gentlemen, some sitting around a large wooden table, others standing, holding tumblers full of ice and bourbon.

"de Lacey?" asked one.

"A woman?" asked another.

"Archduchess Marie Valerie Mathilde Amalie von Habsburg-Lorraine of Austria, daughter of His Royal Highness Franz Josef, Emperor of the Gilded Empire, to be exact," she said. "But yes, a woman."

The men were at a loss. Some bowed, some looked away, but one, a slim man with a marvellous white beard, rose slowly to his feet. He took a long drag of his cigar, not even sparing a glance for the archduchess before him, rather fixing his small, stony eyes on Christien.

"Leave us," he said, and the Club's men slipped out of the room through many secret doors.

"Christien de Lacey," he said. "I'm surprised to see you here."

"Where else should I be in an apocalypse, Dr. Crookes?" asked Christien.

"Is it an apocalypse, boy?"

"If we don't stop my brother, it will be."

"Does he have the locket?"

"He has two."

"Damnations," Crookes said, and he studied his cigar.

"Is Dr. Williams in the Club tonight?"

Crookes shook his head but didn't look up.

"In Wales. Retired. Amassing an extensive library, or so I'm told. Which lockets does your brother have, exactly?"

"Ghostlight and Arclight."

He did look up now, and Christien could see the fierce intelligence behind those stony eyes.

"And he is searching for Lostlight?"

"Yes. Once he has it, he will end the world."

"Can he do it, boy?"

"I have given up guessing what Bastien can or cannot do."

"Is it true he travels with an undead army?"

Christien shrugged.

"Army is not the word. Caravan, perhaps? Horde?"

Crookes grunted and finally turned his sharp eyes on Valerie.

"Your Highness, we've had many conflicting reports from the papers these last weeks," he said. "Is it true Lord de Lacey killed your brother?"

"*Nein,*" she said. "He resurrected him. He is a hero to the Gilded Empire."

"Will wonders never cease," he muttered.

"Sir," said Christien. "I need to know what the Club knows about these lockets. *Everything* it knows. And now."

"Why, you're almost as belligerent as your brother, wot?" came a voice from behind and they turned to see the great bear-like figure of Edward, Prince of Wales and Earl of Chester and heir to the Empire of Steam. "Valerie, m'dear, splendid to see you, as always. It's only been a few days, hasn't it? From funerals to fugitives! Will wonders never cease? Ah HA! Ah HA!"

"Your Highness," said Christien. "I thought we left you in Paris?"

"Finished m'business," he said. "And needed to get home to protect my realm."

"If you truly do value your realm, you can't keep me in the dark anymore," said Christien. "Surely, you know more about these lockets than you've let on."

"You may be right, there, m'boy," said the Crown Prince. "I know a tad more about many things."

And he slid his shiny eyes to Valerie.

"But you, dear girl, you also know far more about this 'Arclight' than you've let on, don't you? Come, let's have us a parlay, and reveal all of our secrets together, wot? Just like family."

In his arms, was a tattered leather-bound book.

"A big, battling, buggered-up family…"

He pushed into the room and closed the door behind.

***

He hated them both.

He hated Ghostlight for tipping the balance of his finely-fraught life. He'd been able to manage, all things considered. He'd been able to cope until she glittered like a star across his night sky. Then came Arclight, warping reality and bringing him back to the same place, the same time, over and over and over and over. He didn't know what the lockets wanted, if in fact a locket could 'want', and it was maddening to think he might be caught forever in this loop of time. That said, the man was not quite a man, and for some reason, that was as intriguing as it was distressing. Perhaps there was a lesson to be learned. Perhaps just another death yet to be earned.

He stood on a bank by a river that was swiftly freezing, and the ice glittered as it moved. He didn't know which river – Medway, perhaps? Avon? Surely not Thames. But then again, he never knew where Arclight was going to bring him, or even when. What sort of alchemy could harness time and place the way this locket did? If Ghostlight channeled because of antimony, what on earth did Arclight use?

Or maybe, it wasn't 'on earth' at all.

There were no lights from nearby homes, farms or stables, so he turned and trudged over to the stand of ash at the river's edge. He sat, knowing the perfection of the landscape would be short-lived, once the dead began to sprout. They ruined everything as they pushed out of the ground, and he was sure it would take years to repair the roads and fields destroyed by their passing.

Odd, how they hadn't come yet.

He wrapped his arms around his knees, tried to focus on the cool night air. He could feel his chest expand as he breathed in, and as a test, he held it. For a long time. Longer than was possible as a living, breathing, fully alive human. He let it out, knowing that he didn't need it but wondering what it meant.

It frosted the air on his lips.

He pressed his throat with numb fingers, hoping to feel a pulse. Nothing, but then again, he'd never been much of a medic. With horses and dogs, he knew what to do. He could tend almost any injury, bind almost any strain. People were a different story, one he'd never cared to read.

Stories. Ivy was good with stories. He wondered where she was, if she was comfortable, if she was afraid. She was such a plucky thing and he regretted pulling her into his life of madness and monsters. She was as stubborn as a spaniel, and just as tough.

She had kissed him once.

No, three times, he remembered: once at Lonsdale and the second time on the edge of an icy river much like this. Yes, the Danube. He had pulled her from the water and kissed her. It had been foolish and impulsive, and he had regretted it instantly, but to his surprise, she had kissed him back. In fact, she'd kept on kissing, and she pushed him backwards into the snow and he remembered wanting to be swept away in her arms and hair and kisses forever.

He stopped himself. No point in remembering. He had felt warm then. Alive. But then came Melk and the relics and Vienna and another kiss in the Hofburg chapel. It was a good kiss, the best of his miserable life, but then a bullet from Sophie's pistol, and everything had changed.

No, he had changed. The thought of another locket had changed him, and he had willing given in to it. When he'd had Ghostlight, he felt complete. He'd simply wanted that feeling again, as destructive as it was. Why did he chase them so?

It was quiet for the first time in weeks, and again, he looked around. Still, no dead. Had the airship's bombs truly taken them all out while he'd been transported to Germany and the strange little cottage, and the not-quite-a-man?

He rested his chin on his knees, trying to recall the man's face. Long and grey, mismatched eyes. Lines of stitches across cheeks, chin, nose and brows, as if he'd been put together in a third-rate factory. *My mind is bent to injury and death,* the man had said, in an accent that Sebastien couldn't place. Not German, not French, perhaps a blend of the two, but guttural and raw. And the spirits – always seven. But then again, seven had always been his own particular number. Perhaps there was nothing more to it than that.

He sighed and closed his eyes. He could still see, courtesy of the lockets, but it provided a moment of calm. Without the dead, maybe it was possible to find his way home in peace, live quietly in a place that wouldn't endanger Rupert, Cookie and the others at the estate. Maybe a small north cottage in the Hebrides or the Orkneys. Somewhere he was unknown and unbothered and free. He could cut firewood, catch fish, drink Scotch, just be.

Would Ivy come with him? Would he dare ask?

He sat for a while longer, enjoying the sounds of the night. The crackling of the ice on the river, the scrape of bare branches, the distant cry of a fox on the hunt. He remembered all the nights he spent with Gus as his only companion. Quiet nights after violent deaths, doing the Crown's work with a pistol in his hand. He had one more bullet, had only threatened the not-quite-a-man with the tri-barrelled piece, but he wasn't sure he'd need it again, not with Ghostlight and Arclight along for the ride. Unless Sentinels were in his immediate future, of course.

Which was entirely possible.

He opened his eyes and looked around, surprised Ash hadn't found him by now. At the very thought of the pale horse, the river began to crack, and a glimmering shape emerged from the ice. The horse looked like a Kelpie, trailing water like smoke as it made it on to the shore. The horse stood before him, didn't shake like most horses, and once again, Sebastien recalled that Ash wasn't actually a horse. Just a creature that lived in between.

Immediately, the dead began to rise, pushing through the frozen ground with bony hands and arms and skulls, and the Mad Lord's eyes widened as the realization sank in.

He brought Ash with his thoughts. He brought Ash but Ash brought the dead.

Ash brought the dead, not him.

This changed things considerably.

He rose to his feet and stepped between the risen corpses.

"Not my fault," he said quietly to himself. "Not my fault."

There was a sound and he glanced across the river. The lockets allowed him to see beyond trees and branches and scrub brush and banks. In the grasses, there was a sniper with a rifle aimed directly at his chest.

***

"Algernon deWinter was the name of the metallurgist," said Crookes. "He was commissioned by Romain de Lacey, grandfather of Marcel and Maslin de Lacey. Romain was deep into the study of astrology and astronomy, and was fascinated by all facets of alchemy, including the metaphysical uses of antimony."

"That's a hell of a lot of *A's*," muttered Christien.

"*Tut*," said Bertie. "You should be taking this seriously, m'boy."

"And you should've been more honest," he said. "We're dealing with the end of the world, here, Bertie."

"Bertie? You call your future sovereign Bertie?"

"Your titles won't spare you when it all ends, sir," said Christien. "And I'll not watch it all go down because of some goddamned rules of Monarchist etiquette."

Bertie's eyes gleamed behind his spectacles.

"By God, you've got nerve," he said. "I like it."

"May we continue?" grumbled Crookes.

"Please do, Bookie. Please do. Ahem."

"As far as we know, there were supposed to be five lockets," the physicist said. "One for each principal branch of metaphysics."

"But didn't the bugger die before the last two could be fashioned?" asked the Crown Prince.

"Radiation poisoning, no doubt," said Crookes. "Atoms are notorious unstable."

"Indeed, indeed," said Bertie.

"What is an atom?" asked Valerie.

"New science," said Christien.

"Fifty years of study, boy," said Crookes. "I'd hardly call that new."

"Atomical physics is a small and very specialized field," said Christien. "You can hardly expect the general public to know about it."

"And that," said Crookes. "Is the problem with our society. Not enough exposure to the natural, let alone supernatural, fields. It's all commerce and industry and politics bollocks."

"Steady on there, Bookie," said Bertie. "There ain't no commerce or industry or science without the politics bollocks."

"I shan't be swayed," said Crookes.

Christien sighed.

"But the lockets," he said. "What do they *do?*"

"Well now, that's the problem," said Bertie, and he opened the book. It was obviously a very old journal, with formulas, sketches and side notes filling the margins. The cover seemed seared in places and the pages themselves were yellowed, torn and laced together with thread-bare ribbons.

Christien leaned forward. Large blocks of scribbles were so blackened by ink as to be illegible.

"What happened here?"

"Redacted," said Bertie. "This is the only notebook of deWinter's to survive to this century and as you can see, it's been censored."

"By whom?"

"God only knows, boy. God only knows."

"So, what we do know is only based on what we have seen," said Crookes. "Which is in itself a completely acceptable method of deduction. Ghostlight appears to use the antimony to open gateways to the spirit world. Identity, consciousness, transformation, death."

"My father had Ghostlight," said Christien. "Williams said he used it to hunt ghosts before it drove him mad."

"Again, was it radiation poisoning?" suggested Crookes. "These elements are still theoretical, their properties unknown."

"And Arclight?" asked Christien. "The things I've seen it do, opening holes in mid-air, turning flesh into bone, swallowing bombs whole and releasing them elsewhere…"

"Time and place, dear boy," said Crookes. "Arclight appears to open portals in time and place, like a conduit between realms."

"But that's not possible."

"And yet, you've seen it."

He grunted. It was true. No wonder he preferred the more concrete fields of biology, anatomy, and mechanics.

"The lab boys are calling them white holes," Crookes went on. "And the study of them is all the rage in Newtonian physics departments all over the world. I believe entire laboratories in Switzerland and Austria are currently working on unravelling and understanding their properties."

"Their *theoretical* properties," said Bertie.

"Oh, absolutely," said Crookes. "Highly theoretical."

"Studying white holes in Austria," said Christien. "Is that how Arclight got to Rudolf?"

"Absolutely not," said Valerie, and all eyes turned to her. She had been standing at the end of the table, arms folded across her chest, eyes shining like daggers, edgy and sharp. She was her father's daughter, all the way.

"Go on, girl," said Bertie. "We're all ears."

"I only know what my mother has told me," she said. "That *Archelicht* was given to Charles XVI of France as a wedding gift. Charles then gave it to his new wife, Marie Antoinette, daughter of Gilded Emperor, Francis I and Maria Theresa, who was the Empress of All the World."

"Spoken like a true Gilded Girl," said Bertie.

She raised a brow, knowing it to be true.

"From what I understand," she went on. "They never knew how to harness it. Not Antionette, not Charles, none of the royal courtiers or scribes. All they knew was that it spun everything into gold, much like your Ghostlight. It kept the French coffers full until the revolution."

"Explains, much, wot?" said Bertie.

"Ghostlight does spin everything to gold," said Christien. "Hollbrook House is full of chests turned to gold because of her. Lasingstoke, too."

"Cellars filled with Norman gold was the rumour," said Crookes.

"Not entirely inaccurate," said Christien. "Considering the lockets were from Normandy."

"Going to have to raise your taxes, eh, m'boy?" Bertie grinned. "Cellars full of gold, indeed."

Christien rolled his eyes, wishing the Crown Prince would disappear into a white hole himself.

"Did your mother say who gave the locket to Charles?" asked Crookes.

Valerie hesitated, let her eyes fall on the surgeon.

"Marcel de Lacey," she said. "Baron of Caen, in an attempt to ingratiate himself to the king."

Christien's shoulders sagged.

"You never said anything," he muttered. "Back in Caen. You knew but said nothing."

"Old habits are hard to break," she said.

"Secrets your stock in trade, wot?" said Bertie, his eyes gleaming beneath bushy brows. "That's a Swan for you."

"I am not keeping secrets now," she said.

"Until it benefits you to do so," said Christien, and an awkward silence descended on the room.

"Emotions and unnecessary complications," said Crookes after a long moment. "You see why we don't allow women?"

"Not helpful, sir," said Christien.

"But true." Crookes looked to Valerie. "Please continue, child."

"You may call me Your Most Royal Highness," she said.

Crookes grunted but said nothing.

"According to my mother," she began. "Because of the political unrest in Fra—"

"Ah HA!" said Bertie. "See? Politics."

Crookes grunted again and Valerie went on.

"Because of the unrest, the court knew their time was short, so before her death, Antionette sent *Archelicht* back to Austria. She hoped that her family would find a way to turn back time and save her life."

No one spoke. The weight was implied.

"Naturally, that did not happen, and *Archelicht* stayed in the Hofburg treasury ever since."

"Until Rudolf," said Christien.

"Until Rudolf," said Valerie.

"He took the damned thing to Mayerling," said Bertie. "And now, look where that's got us."

"Mary Vetsera wanted it," said Valerie. "She was a Black Swan, so she was undoubtedly working for someone."

"I wonder whom," said Crookes.

For his part, Bertie looked at the book in his hands and said nothing.

"So, Lostlight," said Christien. "What does that one do?"

"Damned if we know," said Crookes. "We know nothing about it because it has never been seen or recorded in recent history. To be honest, we all thought only Ghostlight survived because of your father."

Christien thought a long moment, wishing for a cigarette but knowing there was enough smoke in the room to account for ten.

"One last question, Your Highness," he said.

"Anything, boy."

"Ivy told me you spoke about a pact between the Empires of *Steam*, *Gild* and *Iron*. That each of you would have a locket and keep the balance of power firmly within your grasp. Is that true? Was that the plan? Three lockets for three empires?"

Crookes glared at him, and Edward cleared his throat.

"Empty words, dear boy, based on wishes and possibilities. Besides, even though he's my nephew, Wilhelm is a brute and needs to be preoccupied."

"You knew the whereabouts of the sister locket?" Crookes asked. "And never thought to inform the Club?"

"The Crown knows many things, Bookie," said Bertie. "And has no obligation to inform anyone of anything, not even the Club. In fact…"

He looked at Christien.

"Your brother is himself property of the Crown."

"Well, he works for the War Office," said Christien.

"He *belongs* to the War Office, body and soul," said the Crown Prince. "And has since he was an infant, when your father made him a ward of the Crown. In return, we turned a blind eye to his paranormal activities with Frankow. So yes, we have a keen interest in the Mad Lord's escapades with the lockets. They are *all* assets of the Empire of Steam, Sebastien *and* the lockets, and right now, he is putting that Empire in a very precarious position, internationally."

Christien lowered his eyes. He knew it was true. Sebastien would always be shuttled off for secret meetings with the queen, would often skip sessions in the House of Lords only to be seen at the War Office that same day. He had never wanted to know how his brother served the Crown. He had desperately tried to forget that side of his life.

"So," said Crookes. "May we assume that Lostlight has, in fact, survived, and more than that, Sebastien de Lacey is actively seeking her?"

"Yes," said Christien. "We may assume that."

"So. Any ideas where she may be, m'boy?" asked Edward, dropping a mechanical hand upon Christien's shoulder.

"Any ideas at all?"

And he tightened his grip.

Christien felt a wave of cold sweep up from his belly. He could feel Valerie's eyes on him, knowing that he was in possession of a critical photochrome. But he knew that if he shared that photochrome, there would not be an inch of Lasingstoke left unscathed in the search for her. While he felt no particular fondness for the family's English estate, he did care for Rupert far too much to let that happen.

"None whatsoever," he said flatly. "I've never seen it in either Lasingstoke or Hollbrook. Perhaps Egypt? My father kept a property there and I've heard it has plenty of gold rooms."

"Egypt, wot?" said Bertie. "That'd be a damned good place to hide a gem like her! Splendid, m'boy! I'll contact the embassy straight away!"

Christien rose to his feet.

"If you'll excuse us, sir," he said. "I'm afraid this whole escapade is catching up with me and I need some rest. I'll be at Hollbrook House in Kensington if you need me."

"Jolly good," said Bertie. "We'll sort this mess out, don't you worry. And Valerie, it's been a pleasure, as always."

Her curtsy was as crafted as her identity, and together, they turned for the doors.

"To Hollbrook?" she asked under her breath.

"God no," he answered. "We're going to Lasingstoke."

***

"Follow them," said Bertie.

Chapter 12

Of Snipers, Sleuths, and Shots in the Dark

"The different accidents of life are not so changeable as the feelings of human nature."

    – Mary Shelley, Frankenstein: The Modern Prometheus

There was an army rifle aimed directly at his chest.

He swept his eyes across the banks of the river. Many rifles actually, in the hands of snipers laid flat in the bushes. Odd, how he hadn't heard them approach, but then again, the War Office had entire departments that worked in secret. It made sense that their divisions did too.

He pushed through the crowd of swaying dead to stand at the river's edge, counting five soldiers hidden in the trees. He'd taken many bullets in his short lifetime, most of them in the last week, and he wondered if they'd have any effect on a creature such as he. He was a man caught between worlds, much like the not-quite-a-man of the German forest.

My mind is bent to injury and death, the man had said.

Was his?

If he were dead, truly dead, would that effectively halt the end of the world? Would it end the end?

Ash snorted, tossed his sticky head.

It was time to choose. It was time to end this, once and for all.

No.

Once and for Ivy.

Slowly, he spread wide his arms, daring them to shoot.

Willing them to shoot.

The wind picked up and the lockets began to hum.

He shook his head, blinked away the burn behind his eyes.

The riflemen adjusted positions; their fingers pressed to the triggers.

Arclight snarled, stabbing him with sound.

"Silence!" he barked. "It is my choice!"

But light burst in his skull and he clutched his head as waves of pain rocked from the sockets and he knew orbs had been created. The crack of gunshots echoed across the river, followed by screams, but he felt nothing in his body, and he forced himself to look up. A wave of orbs swept through the trees, snatching the first rifleman and slurping him away in a flash of colourful light. The others swung their weapons as orbs spun closer and the night flashed again and again as the riflemen fired hopelessly into them. Trees were snapped in half, rocks split, and shrubs shredded as the white holes sucked all things into their ominous depths as they travelled through the wood. The last rifleman bolted, tossing his weapon and making a break along the banks of the river, and Sebastien watched in horror as an orb spun into life in front of him. The man skidded along the icy ground, twisting his torso to change directions even as he slid, but the orb pulled him mercilessly into its well. The man grabbed at twigs and saplings and grass, but it was useless, and he was drawn, feet first and screaming, into the hole.

The white hole closed, and the orb disappeared, leaving a twitching hand in the frosty grass.

Sebastien released a long, shuddering breath, causing ice to float to the ground like snow. It was only a matter of time before more troops came, along with airships and cannons. This had not been anything he had wished for, nothing he had summoned, and yet, the lockets had created orbs on their own, independent of him. As if they controlled themselves and used him only as a vessel to bring them together for their own purpose.

That changed things entirely.

"I don't want this," he growled as he surveyed the far bank. He could see pieces of soldiers left behind by the orbs. Two hands, a foot, an arm, part of a face. It reminded him of the not-quite-a-man from the cottage in Germany.

Slowly, Ash pushed through the dead, nudged him with a long pale nose.

"I don't want any of this," he said. "I don't want this crown."

Arclight stabbed him with pain yet again, and he waited, hand over his forehead until the waves had gone.

Yes, this changed everything.

He needed to find peace and quiet, a place where he could think, go deep inside himself to find the way. He'd become disoriented over the last weeks, dispirited. Lost. He needed a place he could be found.

He grabbed a handful of sticky mane and swung up on the horse's back. Sat for a moment as he tried to remember.

"A church," he said to Ash. "The church at Seventh. That's where we go."

He dug his heels into the pale mount, and they leapt northward, leaving the dead behind in their wake.

***

Ivy peered over the grey stone wall, Fanny and Franny on either side of her. It hadn't taken long to drive the dark roads from Lonsdale to Lasingstoke, and now, they were parked a half-mile before the gate where two Sentinels stood, guarding the entrance. In the darkness, she could see the flash of red eyes both near and far, and oddly enough, it was the best showcase for the layout of the seven houses of Lasingstoke Hall. First, Second and Third were situated in the middle of the property, while miles apart, Fourth, Fifth, Sixth and the nefarious, hidden Seventh flanked the diagonals. She could see faint flickers of red at those corners and she knew the Sentinels were there, watching and waiting and ready to strike.

"How many are there?" she breathed.

"Six, I believe," said Franny.

Suddenly, a beam of red flashed along the wall between the Sentinel at Fourth and the one at Fifth. Ivy yelped and Fanny shrieked. Franny lost her balance and fell back onto the road with a thump.

"What the deuce?" gasped Fanny, as she peered over once again. To the sound of whirring gears, Frankow rose slowly on his mechanical legs to the height of the wall.

"It is ingenious," he said. "Watch."

Another beam flashed but this time, in the distance between Seventh and Fifth. And then again, but between Fifth and Fourth, and again between Sixth and Seventh. Again and again, the flashing beams continued, but in different patterns and at different intervals.

"They are electrifying the perimeter," said Frankow. "Preventing anyone or any *thing* from going in or out."

"It's completely random," said Franny, her goggles making her eyes look as large as Frankow's. "There's no way to predict where or when a beam will come."

"That's worse than we expected," said Ivy. "How are we going to combat that?"

"The mad girl's plan is sound," said Frankow, after a moment. "You are small and I…"

His legs whirred and he rose in the air higher, and higher. And higher.

"…have other resources…"

"Golly," said Ivy.

"Right," said Fanny. "Shall we begin?"

Ivy swallowed and dropped back to the road. They all followed suit, and Frankow whirred down to normal height. Huddled together at the base of the wall, Lizzie Borden, Mr. Home, Grigori Rasputin and Carl Feigenbaum were waiting.

"Listen. I've seen these things kill," Ivy said. "They will show no mercy if they believe you're a threat. So please, my dear friends…"

She swept her eyes across the handful of peculiar, eager faces, tried to stop the tightening of her throat.

"Please be careful. If I were to lose any one of you, it truly would be the end of the world."

Lizzie grinned and tapped her axe hilt into her hand. Mr. Home raised his hands and began to rise. Grigori laughed and pulled a shovel from behind his back.

"Where's the sword?" asked Ivy.

"He fancied the shovel," said Frankow.

"Right," said Ivy. "What's the signal?"

Carl Feigenbaum dropped a satchel at their feet.

"Fireworks," he muttered. "From Guy Fawkes and Agnes Tidy."

"*Veritas Temporis filia!*" said Franny, and she patted the hood of her car.

Soon, the roar of two steamcar engines filled the night.

***

They did, in fact, go to Hollbrook House first, to the sheer delight of Pomfrey who had determined that he'd never see his master again. But it was a mere whistle stop, to stock up on some cold meats and warm bread, and a change of clothes for the ride. It was the steamcar Christien was after, the one he'd unknowingly bought last spring. It had proven itself useful on more than one occasion, and now, provided the quickest, most direct way to the north country.

Pomfrey led them up the stairs, chatting the entire time, and they showed Valerie to the Blue Room.

"With Miss Ivy's unexpected comings and goings," Pomfrey said, "And most of them involving a goodly amount of mud and blood, I've found it prudent to keep this room stocked with an equally goodly selection of women's apparel. I do find it most enjoyable shopping for women's apparel. Why – the colours, the fabric, the prints, the styles! Most enjoyable indeed."

"Miss Savage is considerably smaller than I," said Valerie.

"I bought a variety of sizes," said Pomfrey. "In fact, I tried most of them on myself. You and I are close to the same build."

"Indeed, we are," she said, and she smiled at Christien. "Almost identical."

She slipped inside the Blue Room, her eyes shining, and closed the door behind her.

They continued down the hall and stopped outside his room.

"The steamcar is charged and ready to roll, as they say, sir," said Pomfrey. "And I'll pull together a basket for the road. Lasingstoke is a good chug by steamcar, so biscuits, apples, two pork pies, and a sealed pot of tea should suffice. I will slip in a brandy flask as well, for the night is chill and dark, and the brandy is neither."

"Thank you, Pomfrey," said Christien and he turned. "Is the PHAX machine still working?"

"The Photochrome Hydraulic Ambient Xeroradiograph?" asked Pomfrey. "Why yes, sir. It's in the study."

He slid a paper from his waistcoat. It was the photochrome of Jane with the locket round her neck.

"Send this to Rupert St. John at Lasingstoke," he said. "Tell him to show Ivy. It's got to be there somewhere."

"I will, sir," said Pomfrey. "I will, indeed."

And the man turned on his heel and disappeared back down the stair.

Christien waited for a long moment, simply staring at his bedroom door. He hadn't been here for months, but it seemed like a lifetime. This place was no longer familiar, and he wondered if it would ever feel like home again. Truth be told, he wasn't sure it ever had.

Slowly, he pushed open the door and a wave of sadness hit him. He'd loved this room, once upon a time. The green wallpaper, the large, mullioned windows, the rich Persian rug. Dark wood shelves were neatly arranged with books and clocks and dials and many other small gadgets that had tickled his fancy over the years. There was a wire cage by the window, and he remembered that he'd once had a bird. It was a sparrow that he'd saved from a cat. He'd brought it back to health and enjoyed its chirping company, only to find it dead one morning with a broken neck.

It was only then that he realized he'd likely been the one that killed it.

He sank to the bed, sat with his arms draped over his knees, overcome. It was useless to hope, pointless to try. He'd never be anything but a madman's lesser son, a failed surgeon, a spurned lover two—no, three times over. He had money and he had looks, but his heart had been torn out when he was a child the moment his father had torn out his mother's. Any spark of happiness crushed by horror; any hope of significance stolen by a cruel twist of fate. Or maybe was it a knife?

His eyes slid over to the medical bag beside the door. He'd been a physician once, a surgeon in training, and the instruments within that bag his stock in trade. Now, it was full of ghosts. Devices that were meant to help save lives, took them; those meant to solve crimes, committed them. Even this noblest of professions had been ripped from him because he wasn't strong enough to fight the demons that came to call, neither those of flesh, nor those of spirit.

He wiped a tear that had spilled down his cheek. Life mocked him at every turn. Why did he still fight for it so?

There was a quiet rap at the door. Valerie peered in.

"Leibling?" she asked.

He said nothing. He felt nothing, not even when she sat on the bed next to him.

"Madness and monsters," he said finally. "It's true, what Sylvette said. That's my life. Madness and monsters."

"You are neither mad nor a monster," she said.

He looked up at her.

"You don't know what I've done, Valerie," he said.

"You don't know what *I've* done, dear Remy," she said.

"It's not the same."

"Why not? Because I am a woman?"

He shook his head.

"Are you the same person now as you were then?" she asked. "The same person as when you did these monstrous things?"

"I'm not sure who that person was, to be honest."

"You see? The person I know is a good man and a great physician who is currently trying to save the world. That does not sound like a monster to me."

"I'm not a physician anymore," he said. "Not with this hand."

"Are you completely serious?" She stared at him with those piercing eyes. "You put the heart and bowels back into a dead man, and he now lives."

"Bastien brought him back—"

"But without the organs in correctly, he would have died once more, and Rudolf is very much still alive. Perhaps it is not as bad as you say.

Perhaps the precision of your clockwork hand made that possible?"

He frowned as her words sank in.

"It may have begun as a curse," she said. "But you are a remarkable man, so now it's a miracle."

She was so very beautiful, and part of him wanted to believe.

"Not a madman?" he asked quietly.

"Not a madman."

"Nor a monster?"

"Definitely not," she said. "Miracle."

She wiped a tear from his cheek and smiled.

"Oh look," she said. "We are currently sharing the same bed."

She smelled of brandied peaches.

"Must be the end of the world," he murmured.

She leaned in to kiss him and this time, he did not pull away.

Suddenly, the sound of pistol shot shattered the air and Hollbrook House was plunged into darkness.

Chapter 13

Of White Ladies, Black Airships, and the Lonsdale Lune

"What can stop the determined heart and resolved will of man?"

- Mary Shelley, Frankenstein: The Modern Prometheus

"Wait," said Valerie, and she grabbed his wrist as he bolted to his feet.

"Valerie, we can't—"

"Wait, Remy."

She rose to her feet and moved swiftly to the window, silently unhooking the latch and leaning out. While the room was dark, moonlight streamed in through the mullioned glass, and he felt a blast of cold air. She glanced down to the mews below, then up to the sky.

"Look," she said, and he stepped over to peer up. A dark shape blocked out the stars.

"What is that?" he asked. "Is that the *Stahl Mädchen?*"

"It's a dreadnought, yes, but not the *Mädchen,*" she said. "She would never leave Austria."

"You shot us down over Alsace-Lorraine."

She glared at him but did not answer, instead reached down to pull the flare pistol from her boot. She took a deep breath and fired it into the sky above Hollbrook House.

The whistle and crack shattered the night.

"There," she said. "Whoever that is, now knows help is coming."

"I have to get down," he said. "Pomfrey—"

His voice caught in his throat. Pomfrey. Odd, hovering, meticulous Pomfrey. The man had been with him for years, had cared for him when he had no other family who would.

Valerie crossed the floor and pushed the flare pistol into his hand.

"There is one shot left," she said. "It will kill, so be careful with it."

"Stay behind me," he said. "You may be a Swan, but they have iron."

She pulled a small woman's flint from her other boot and grinned.

"Let's go find your Pomfrey."

God, he could fall a thousand times over.

In darkness, they opened the door.

***

This was a sacred place, this old priory, and it now lay in ruins on a road outside Wolverhampton. Most of it was gone, remnant rocks buried half deep in the winter grass, but the cold stones spoke to him. The arches called his name.

It had an old cemetery as well, and he knew it would only be a matter of time before the dead rose at his presence, so he'd left Ash in the trees overlooking the priory. Now, he sat under a stone arch on a square slab, breathing it all in as if home.

The last time he'd been in a church, he'd killed an Archduchess, maimed a German Emperor, raised a Crown Prince, and made a dread bargain in the name of love. This time, he only needed to learn to control two lockets. That should be a relatively simple task.

It was twilight and the moon struggled through rolling dark clouds. He closed his eyes and thought of his little chapel back at Seventh. All Souls Christchapel was its official name, but he only ever called it the chapel. He breathed deeply, not needing to but knowing somehow it was important to the clearing of the mind. Breathe in, breathe out. Silence the singing of Ghostlight and the whispers of her sister. Silence them, overwhelm them, bring them under his control. Feel the earth tremble at his feet, feel the moon cold on his face. Silence the sisters along with his breath. His was the Crown, his the rule. They had no choice but to obey.

Still, they sang and whispered, and he grunted in frustration. He could also hear another voice far, far away, and he knew it was Lostlight calling him home. Oddly enough, she was speaking in Latin.

It was useless.

He rose to his feet and stepped out into the embedded stones. Headstones, capstones, fieldstones, hearth. Cold stones covered in winter. Still, creeping over them all was English ivy, red-tinged from the frost. He looked up to study the arch.

"Alba feminarum," he read aloud. "The White Women? Ah, the *White Ladies Priory.* Yes, that makes sense."

He turned to head back to Ash, but several white forms greeted him.

Women, dressed in white. These were not risen dead, not revenants like his current companions. No, these were spirits of old, the kind he'd see before he'd gone to Vienna and changed the world.

"I can't help you," he said. "I'm not that man anymore."

They said nothing, merely hovered.

"Alba feminarum," he said. *"Abito."*

They blew away like early morning mist.

He frowned.

"Alba feminarum," he said again. *"Ostendite vos."*

They rippled back into shape.

Did Lostlight speak Latin?

He gazed over to the trees. Ash's pale coat gleamed in the moonlight. The horse was surrounded by revenants, the bone army standing, waiting, immobile until he gave the word.

"Populus mortuorum," he began. *"Revertere ad terram."*

Within a heartbeat, the dead crumbled. Ash remained, sticky mane waving in the breeze.

He turned back to the spirits.

"Thank you, sisters," he said. *"Gratias sororibus."*

They smiled and disappeared.

He released a vain breath, and headed back to the horse.

***

Mr. Home began to rise.

He had been standing at the foot of one of the two Sentinels. They hadn't noticed him, for it was dark and he was quiet, but at the roar of the

Lune, he raised his arms and began to rise. Higher and higher he went in the night sky. Up to the mechaman's hip joints, around the massive metal arms, past the shoulders to the iron face. It was only a matter of moments before the great helm noticed, turning ever so slightly as the beam of red shrunk to a pinpoint in the inhuman eye.

"*Desist*," boomed the voice.

With a sound like the grinding of gears, the head of the second Sentinel looked down at its feet. A tinny clang echoed again and again and again, the sound of an axe on an iron knee.

"*Desist*," boomed the second Sentinel.

An engine roared, growing louder and louder as a pair of steamcars barrelled toward them.

The red eyes began to glow.

***

The main stairs of Hollbrook House were far too exposed to risk going down, even with the house black as pitch. Instead, Christien led Valerie down the dark hall to the servants' passage, a back stairway that connected the three levels of Hollbrook, from scullery on the main floor to Pomfrey's quarters on the third. It was narrow and cold and, given that there were no windows to bring in the moonlight, utterly black. They moved slowly to dull the creaking steps, listening for any sound of struggle. Finally, they made it to the scullery entrance on the ground floor, and the moon shone faintly through a small, leaded-glass window. Christien pressed his ear against the door for a long moment, before pulling away and shaking his head. He raised the flare pistol and slowly, pushed open the door.

The room was cold, despite the hearth's crackling fire, and the door to the outside banged on its hinges. He could smell coal and fish, bread and oil. But there was another smell, one he was intimately familiar with, and his heart thudded in his chest.

"Oh, sir," came a small voice. "I'm so glad it's you. It *is* you, isn't it?"

He flung off Valerie's warning hand and rushed to the hearth. The fire cast a warm glow across Pomfrey, who lay in a pool of glistening red.

"They're gone, sir," he said. "But I'm sad to say, they've quite taken the photochrome."

His voice was thin and shredded, like tissue in water.

"Where are you shot, Pomfrey?" Christien asked, working the buttons on the man's waistcoat and tugging at the starched collar.

"I'm not certain," he said. "I'm afraid I don't feel anything at all."

"Remy," said Valerie, looming over them both. "We need to go."

"Get my medical bag," he said. "It's back up the stair in my room."

"Remy—"

"Now!" he snapped.

She whirled and disappeared back up the passageway.

"I tried to stop them," Pomfrey said. "I brandished the poker quite menacingly. It would have been sufficient, had they not a pistol. I do so hate pistols."

Christien peeled back the man's shirt. It was sticking to the skin around his belly.

"Pomfrey, I'm going to try to turn you. I need to see if the bullet went through or not. Do you understand? I need to turn you."

"I do, sir. I shall attempt to let you."

He took Pomfrey's hand with his mechanical one and rolled the man toward him, eliciting a rattle of breath and a fresh spray of blood.

He laid him back down.

"It's gone through, Pomfrey," he said. "So that's a good thing. But I think it's nicked the ventral aorta, so we have to patch you up right quick. But…"

Once again, his words caught in his throat.

"But I'm not sure I can," he said. "With my clockwork hand, I don't know if I have the control. I could kill you."

"The aorta is important, yes?"

"Yes."

"Nicking it is also bad, yes?"

He nodded. His throat was tight beyond reason. He had no words for this dear, dear man.

"So, whether you don't try to help me, or you *do* try to help me and fail, I die, yes?"

His eyes were stinging now.

"So, if you don't mind," said Pomfrey. "I would prefer you try. Sir. Yes, I prefer you try."

And he smiled a weak smile. Christien took his hand again and squeezed it.

Valerie dropped the bag at his knees.

***

The *Lune* crashed into the metal leg of the first Sentinel, causing it to

167

lurch. From the hood of the car, Grigori was flung forward, slamming into the welded shin of the mecha-man. He didn't fall, however, and he began to climb, clinging to the vents, ports, and bolts along the construct's thigh. Up, up, up the hip, belly, side and spine until soon, he was straddling the shoulder, a mad cowboy on an iron bronco. He raised the spade and began smashing the mechanical helm until sparks flew into the night.

Lizzie Borden rushed from the shadows of the wall, swinging her axe into its metal knee once again with a clang. The Sentinel raised a hand as if to swat a fly, but Mr. Home floated ethereally in front of its face. The great hand swung toward him now, but Home ducked away, navigating the night breeze like an owl and pulled a pistol from his coat. It was a vintage piece, clearly meant to shoot flares, but he fired, point blank, into the eye of the Sentinel. Sparks burst from the socket, as the explosion rocked the metal head, waves of light and power crackling inside it. It took a step, but its knee was compromised, and it shuddered under the weight. Franny Helmsly-Wimpoll laughed madly as she drove her steamcar, *Veritas,* into the leg. It teetered above them all, while the *Lune* backed up, readying herself for another run.

Slowly, from the gate, the second Sentinel whirred on its torso, the sound like grinding gears and thunder. Its eye glowed red in the darkness.

Fanny raced between the great iron feet, slipping firecrackers in the joints.

"Take that, you faceless monstrosities!" she cried.

And quickly, she began to light the wicks.

＊＊＊

Ivy was grateful that Frankow had shrunk to normal size as they slunk along the wall between Fourth and Fifth House. It was unnerving seeing him tower over her like that, as if he were a man perched on the top of a tall ladder, teetering in the breeze. His wheels allowed him to keep up with her, which was impressive given the dark and uneven terrain. They also enabled him to navigate over roots, rocks, and ruts with equal ease, much like the TANC wheels of the Strasbourg Sentinel.

She shuddered, remembering how much she hated those things.

Finally, she came to a halt, leaned against the stone wall to catch her breath. It was cold and damp, but not frozen, and they were making good time. Frankow stood quietly, not winded at all, and she cursed the marvels of his clockwork legs.

"Lasingstoke is a mile square," she said. "And the Hall not centred. This should be the shortest route when we get over the wall—"

She stopped herself.

"If we get over the wall."

"We will get over the wall."

She released a breath, nodded once.

"But then, we have to run across the fields and pastures to get there. First is closest, and I don't even know if Rupert is there, or in Second."

"Someone will be there," said Frankow. "I understand there is a cook and several servants. Is there a wife now?"

"Sort of?" she said. "Mary Jane, or Marie Jeanette, the new lady of the house. And Davis! Oh, I can't wait to see Davis again!"

"He is fully recovered, yes?"

"Yes," she said. "Laury saved his life."

The great spectacles whirred and clicked.

"You call him Laury now?"

"I…I do. He asked me to. Is, is that wrong?"

"If he has asked, then it is not wrong."

She nodded again.

"Right. Sentinels can blast rockets across fields, so even if we make it over the wall—"

"*When* we make it over the wall."

"When we make it over the wall, we'll have to, I don't know, weave and dodge if they start shooting."

"I understand. I am not so adept at the weaving and the dodging, but with the wheels, I am fast."

Along the top of the wall, a beam blasted from west to east, Fourth corner to Fifth, and she shrank back at its heat. Frankow rolled forward, lenses huge.

"That's not electricity, Miss Savage," he said quietly.

Her heart sank. This was madness.

Suddenly, a shrill whistle echoed through the night, followed by a boom. Red beams flashed and stars popped across the skies at the main gate.

"Fireworks!" said Ivy. "Is that the signal?"

"Undoubtedly," said Frankow. "This has Mrs. Tidy all over it."

She took a deep breath.

"Here we go."

And she pulled herself up onto the wall as Frankow began to rise.

Chapter 14

Of Men that Work and Machines that Don't

"How mutable are our feelings, and how strange is that clinging love we have of life even in the excess of misery."

– Mary Shelley, Frankenstein: The Modern Prometheus

"What the devil?"

Rupert leaned against the window glass. Red, white and blue lights crested over the main gate like fireworks.

"What is it, luv?" asked Mary Jane from the fire.

"Looks like bloody Guy Fawkes Day," he grumbled. "Is this how the world ends, then? In a show of bloody fireworks?"

"I luv fireworks," she said. "I want fireworks when the baby's born."

Rupert grunted. In the distance, red beams flashed along the walls, and he knew the Sentinels were moving again.

"Damn those Sentinels," he muttered. "And damn the War Office for all of this."

"I didn't think the Sentinels could bloody move," said Mary Jane. "I thought they was just for show. To send a message to the criminal types, y'know? I never thought they'd actually move from their spots. Rusty-ass tin machines, they are. Ugly, overgrown automabobs."

Over his shoulder, he looked at her. She was so beautiful, her strawberry curls spilling from the streetwise bun, content as a barn cat brought in from the cold. One hand rested on her belly. She was barely showing, and he wondered if it had begun to flutter inside her. Again, he marvelled at his fate. How he, a resolute bachelor, could have ended up with this wild young force of nature was blessing upon blessing, and he was not a religious man.

"It will end soon, won't it?" she asked. "They can't think he's coming 'ere…"

He said nothing, and Mary Jane looked at him.

"He's not coming 'ere, right?" She narrowed her eyes. "Ruby, tell me he's not."

"This is Laury we're talking about, my love," said Rupert. "I have no clue what he will or will not do."

She let out a deep breath, that sounded like a growl.

"Well, he ain't the Mad Lord for naught."

"C'est vrai, ma chere," he said quietly. *"C'est vrai."*

And they fell into a kind of silence, he watching the flashing lights, she watching the fire, until the sound of footsteps echoed in the hall. Soon, a figure rushed in, a sheet of paper in his hand.

"Sir," said Davis. "I think you might want a look at this."

And he held up the paper. It looked like a cheap photochrome.

"From the PHAX machine, sir!"

"I didn't think *that* worked, either," Mary Jane muttered. "House full of bloody machines, but none of 'em work…"

Rupert crossed the floor, snatched the paper from Davis' hand.

He was certain his mechanical heart skipped a beat.

This time, Mary Jane rose to her feet and moved to his side, slipped an arm around his waist.

"Who's that, then?" she asked, head on his shoulder. "And why's she wearing that bloody locket?"

***

Ivy flattened herself along the top of the wall, eyes tightly closed and praying that a beam wouldn't fry her before she could swing over the side. But there were fireworks at the main gate, so she knew she had time before the Fifth House Sentinel noticed her on the wall. She swung her very fine boots over the stone cap and let herself drop to the grass on the other side. In one piece, sound, undamaged.

Alive.

She rolled to her backside, watched as Frankow began to step cleanly over the wall, his long mechanical legs revealing the hydraulic pistons that allowed him remarkable mobility. He raised one metal foot, and she held her breath. One beam could slice him in half, and that would be a horrible way for any man to go. Then again, he was a self-confessed science addict. He might welcome the novel, and technologically superior, demise.

There was no beam, and she watched his wheeled foot touch the ground. He didn't wait for it to stabilize, however, and swung his other leg over the wall as soon as the first one hit. The wheels slipped and he teetered, but quickly, began to shrink the pistons that were his legs. Soon, he was his normal height, and he glanced over at her, eyes wide. She was surprised to see a smile stretch across his face.

"That was exhilarating, Miss Savage," he gasped. "Shall we run?"

"Yes," she said. "Run."

She rolled to her feet and together, they bolted off across the winter fields.

***

It was surreal, working by the light of the hearth and the single candle that Valerie had found. Pomfrey slipped in and out of consciousness as Christien worked, cleaning the wound with medicinal alcohol and securing both tissue and vessels with forceps. Sweat ran down his forehead and dripped from his hair, but his clockwork hand worked with unnatural precision. Wire, stitch, twist, press.

 It was impressive, it was exact, but it wasn't enough.

He sat back.

"What is it?" asked Valerie.

"I have no silver nitrate," he said. "To cauterize the bleeding, I need silver. I have no cautery. I have nothing."

"There's nothing in your bag?"

"I worked on corpses, Valerie."

His shoulders sagged.

"He's going to die."

Lights flashed rhythmically through the kitchen window, accompanied by the now-familiar *whup-whup-whup* of an airship engine outside Hollbrook House. She knelt beside him.

"I am sorry, Remy."

He looked down as she laid her hand on his mechanical arm. It had worked perfectly. In fact, he was shocked at how well it responded to his thoughts. Skills he had honed over years in the profession became art, became poetry. Wire, stitch, twist, press. He was more machine than man, he told himself. Not madman, not monster, not even miracle. Simply machine.

"The Gilded airship is here."

The last time he had used his medical bag, he had murdered a woman, left her in pieces in another woman's bed. The last time he'd wielded a blade, this hand had devastated. It mattered little that he remembered nothing, that he'd been the unwitting host to a murderous spirit. Five women were dead, more if his brother were to be believed. Didn't matter. His surgeon's hand wielded death, not life. He'd been foolish to hope otherwise.

"We need to go, Remy." Her voice, like a distant drum.

He studied his wired fingers, now slick with blood. They weren't surgeon's fingers.

"Remy…"

But neither were they the Ripper's.

In truth, this wasn't the same hand. *That* hand had been caught, torn off, and crushed beneath the engine wheel at St. Katharine's Dock. The guilty hand sentenced, punished, executed, excised. Gone, like the dock herself into the icy waters of the Thames. But this hand was new, clean, and scientific. Unblemished by death and spirits. It was blameless, faultless, free.

The War Office gave you a bloody garrison in that arm.

He thought 'pen.' His index finger disappeared, to be replaced by a fountain pen.

"I'm sorry you can't save him," a voice was saying. "But we have to get to Lasingstoke."

He thought 'cigarette.' His middle finger disappeared, replaced by a cigarette.

Pistols and lockpicks and cautery iron nonsense.

"Good lord," he breathed.

He thought 'cautery iron.' His index finger disappeared. A short, slim wand appeared in its place, a spark crackling along its wire tip.

"Oh," said Valerie.

Not madman. Not monster. Not even miracle, if he was honest.

"Goddamn machine," he grinned, and bent back to his work.

***

The Sentinel lurched again as the *Lune* rammed into it a second time, but this time, Fanny watched Carl's head smack against the window glass. He slumped forward, dazed and unmoving, behind the wheel.

Lizzie rushed between the iron feet and with a mighty swing of the axe, the knee buckled and gave way. The squeal of metal and grinding of gears echoed through the night, and the mecha-man began to tilt.

From the giant's shoulder, Grigori leapt into the air and twisted like an acrobat, plunging the spade into the metal chest and slicing it through as he slid down. The Sentinel's entire body sizzled as it tipped, off balance and splitting, and the Russian launched into the air, leaving the spade embedded like a spear. Mr. Home caught him mid-air as the Sentinel crashed down, exploding into a thousand fiery pieces when it hit the ground. But a slab of iron slammed into the chassis of the *Lune*, crushing the engine and crumpling the dickey. Coal spilled from the tank and steam hissed into the night.

Home had Grigori by the arms, but the weight pulled them awkwardly downward. The second Sentinel thundered toward them, every footfall a boom, shaking the ground like an earthquake. Home dropped the Russian to the hissing, smoking grass, before launching back up with flare pistol toward the second Sentinel. Its mechanical hand swung, striking the man with a sickening crunch, and sent him rocketing skyward.

"No!" cried Lizzie, and she rushed the Sentinel even as it marched, but the great steel leg swept onward, knocking her to the ground and sending the axe flying. Fanny was at the *Lune*, swinging the door open and grabbing Carl by the arms. His leg was entangled in twisted chassis, and sparks sizzled at her feet as they landed in the coal. With a burst of light and heat, the flames began to spread.

"Берегись, сумасшедшая женщина!" Grigori shouted from the grass.

"I'm so sorry, good man!" Fanny shouted and she yanked Carl free of the twisted *Lune*, both of them tumbling backwards into the grass. Blood sprayed from his shin. Fireworks shrieked and the ground thundered as the second Sentinel towered over them. Fanny managed to drag him just out of range as an iron boot thumped down on the hood of the *Lune*, crushing the steamcar like a beetle.

There was silence for a moment, as it turned its head, single eye focusing on them and growing red.

"Don't look," she said, tucking Carl's head into her chest.

The boot swung up, up, up over their heads, blocking the moonlight and the stars and the wispy clouds of night.

She closed her eyes.

***

Dearest Ivy,

I can't say I think about death often. I'm far to engaged with life for that. What, with Mama and Papa and Franny and my Ninny and of course, you, how could I dally with such a discouraging notion. But Granny's health is in constant question, and I must admit the thought has crossed my mind. I think I shouldn't want to die, but if every single person that I know and love is gone, then I will do so, and happily. I suppose all this is to say that if we are unsuccessful and you are unable to prevent the end of the world, do not feel guilty on account of it. We've had tremendously good fun in our short time, and I wouldn't trade it off for... well, for the world.

Besides, I'm quite sure they have tea in heaven.

Yours until the end, and beyond,

Fanny Helmsly-Wimpoll

***

Pomfrey's colour was returning, the blue cast of his lips turning a more natural pink as Christien packed the wound with dressing from the bag. He sprayed the dressing with carbolic acid and wrapped the man's waist tightly with strips of gauze and linen. He pulled a syringe from the medical bag, filled it with liquid from a glass vial, held the hypodermic up to the hearth light to gauge a dose. A drop glistened at the tip of the needle.

"What is this?" asked Pomfrey.

"*Pyocyanate*," he grunted. "*Blood and Iron* surgeons are having marvellous luck with it, but I have no idea where it goes."

"Whatever do you mean, sir?"

"Artery? Heart? Muscle? No idea."

"Wherever you put it, I'm sure it will be better in me than in the bottle."

And Pomfrey smiled weakly.

Gods, he loved this man.

With a deep breath, Christien plunged the syringe into Pomfrey's bandaged belly, emptied its contents in one go.

After a long moment, the houseman relaxed.

"Thank you, sir," he said, his voice frail as a dry leaf. "But it may be a while before I am able to properly scrub the floors. Blood does stain so."

"I'll give you a day, then, maybe two," Christien said, patting the man's hand. "But I'll want it spotless before the week's out."

"Spotless it shall be, sir," said Pomfrey. "Spotless it shall be."

And he closed his eyes, the smile waning on his thin face. He was asleep within moments.

Christien rose to his feet.

"He needs to get to a hospital. St. Bart's, maybe, or the Royal."

He grabbed a bar of carbolic soap from the bag and crossing the floor to the butler's sink.

"Can you call a neighbour?" Valerie asked.

"I need you to take him," he said. "In the airship."

Turned on the water, began to scrub.

"I need to take him," she said slowly.

"Yes."

He felt the water cold on his skin and the soap slick between his fingers, watched with weary eyes as the blood swirled down the rusty drain. He dried the arm of flesh with a linen cloth, slowly, methodically, feeling intimately the sensation of fabric against his skin. Next, he sprayed the mechanical hand with carbolic acid, polished them with the same linen cloth. The tendons clicked and gleamed in the firelight.

They were a bloody miracle.

She stepped closer.

"Me," she said. "Not us."

Deliberately, he turned.

"Not us," he said. "I must go to Lasingstoke. Me, Valerie. Not us. But I do need you. I need you to help me."

Her flawless face betrayed no expression.

"This man is important to me so I'm asking you to help him. By doing that, you help me. I know that it's not in the thick of things where you like to be, but if you care for me at all, *truly* care for me as you say you do, you will do this one thing. For him. For me. Please."

There was a sound, and Gilded soldiers appeared at the kitchen door. One man spoke rapidly to her in high German, and she nodded.

"The dreadnought is gone," she said. "It was not the *Stahl Mädchen,* nor is it any one of ours. They didn't recognize the design, and there was no ensign on the canvas but there was a name on the transom."

"What was it?"

"*Vanguard.* They say it was heading north."

She turned to look at him.

"I do not know where your St. Bart's is," she began. "But I can take him to the Royal. I will tell them that he is an aide to the *Gilded Empire* and must be received as such."

His eyes stung once more.

"Then, once I am convinced that he will be duly cared for, I will come to you at Lasingstoke." She set her jaw. "Provided the world has not ended by then."

He nodded swiftly.

She commanded, and the soldiers rushed to attend Pomfrey by the hearth, sliding table linens beneath him to help with the lift. Together, they carried him out of the kitchen and into the night.

She took a long breath, clearly marshalling her resources, but her eyes were swimming.

"I am not allowed to choose," she said.

"I know," he said. He stepped toward her, took her hand. "I know."

She laced her fingers and raised their hands between them, and he marvelled at the sensations. Palm to palm, skin to skin, nerves and flesh and tendon and bone. So simple, so raw, so human. But then, she reached for his mechanical hand and raised it between them. She kissed the tips of his clockwork fingers, intertwined them with hers.

"Not monster," she said softly.

His head was swimming.

"Not machine."

God, his heart.

"Just a man who is loved by a woman."

And she kissed him.

He wished it could have ended, right then, just like that. The world would open up and swallow them both, take Hollbrook, Kensington-Knightsbridge, take all of London for that matter. There could be no better end, no more fitting finale, and he lingered, dreading the rush of cold air between them. Deep calls to deep, like to like. They were the same. Children of privilege, drowning in loss. No, not drowning anymore. Treading, perhaps. Fighting against the buffeting currents, desperately searching for a raft. One day, they'd find a shore but today was not that day.

He pulled away. But this time, there was no cold.

"Goodbye, Christien Jeremie St. John de Lacey," Valerie said, stepping away. "Go find your little writer and save the world. Save your brother, too, if you can. He is not so different from you."

Then, she turned and was gone. The lights flashed through the windows, the house rumbled with the propellors and the engine, *whup-whup-whupping* into silence.

He wiped the tears from his cheek, and turned to the door, the mews and the steamcar that would take him home.

***

From the remaining corners of Lasingstoke, the Sentinels looked up, red eyes flashing in the black night.

"Desist," they said, three voices echoing as one across the fields. *"You are under House Arrest by Order of the War Office. Desist."*

And as one, they turned on their axes, swung their great feet, and began the mile-long trek to the main gate.

***

"Damnations," Christien muttered, and he knelt down for a closer look. The steamcar's tire was flat and, in the moonlight of Hollbrook House's back lane mews, he could see that it had been punctured by a very thick blade. Not a coincidence, and he knew that the same villains who'd put a bullet in Pomfrey had put a shiv in the wheel.

He straightened, rubbed the soot from his face with a sleeve.

It was then that he heard the engine.

It wasn't the sound of an ordinary steamcar. Not at all the chug-chug-chug or rattle and bang of a typical four-wheeler. It wasn't even the purr of a six-wheeler, which boasted a finer engine and cleaner steam. No, this was something utterly different, a growl, a snarl, a roar, and it was getting louder.

He automatically shrugged his shoulder, calling the rifle stock into his clockwork hand as an obscenely long steamcar rolled up, blocking the entrance to the mews. The moonlight caressed its sleek shape—the curved chassis, the polished hood, mirrored windshield, and arched tailfins. Oh yes, and its eight wheels.

And suddenly, all manner of coincidences clicked into place.

The door swung open, pushed by the tip of a cane.

"Get in, boy," said Edward, Crown Prince of Steam. "We have a world to save."

Chapter 15

Of Metal Legs, an Assembled Man, and a Variety of Men on Horseback

"And when that time shall come, when a rational knowledge of what the great change—the mortal putting on immortality—actually is, shall be substituted for the dreadful fear of death which so often frightens man from his propriety and which enslaves his mind with a worse than Egyptian bondage, what imagination can picture the vast increase that will flow to the happiness, the wisdom, and the purity of man!"

– Daniel Dunglas Home, Incidents in My Life

***

Ivy heard it at first, the strange whistle coming from the skies, and she skidded to a halt in case it was a rocket. Suddenly, a shape thudded into the grass ahead of her, sliding for several yards before slowing to a halt. Together, they peered through the moonlight and her stomach lurched as she realized what it was.

"My god, that's a man," said Frankow.

They rushed to his side.

"Mr. Home?" he asked. "Daniel?"

Frankow folded slowly, mechanically, to his knees.

"Daniel? It's me, Arvin."

Even in the darkness, Ivy could see the man was utterly broken. His jaw was askew, joints bent at wrong angles, and blood seeped from mouth, ears and nose. But as he looked up at the skies, eyes burst, seeing nothing, he smiled. Most of his teeth were gone, but still, he smiled.

"I was so high, Arvin," he gasped, each breath a struggle. "So very high…"

"Daniel," said Frankow. "Can you describe it, Daniel? I need to hear it. I need you to tell me. Stay awake, Daniel, and tell me what you saw."

"Arvin. I saw, I saw …"

Every word a victory.

"…God."

The smile froze and, for a brief moment, there was silence.

Ivy had no words. She had known him only a few months during the time her mother had been at Lonsdale. Daniel Dunglas Home had been a gentle, happy, inquisitive soul and clearly, as brave as a bear. A devout spiritualist, she hoped he could now discover new spirits, new realms, new life. Quietly, she pulled the fur coat from her shoulders and draped it over the man's broken body.

Frankow pushed to his feet.

"Bertie will pay for this," he growled. "I swear by all that is holy. And by all that is not."

"I'm so sorry," she said. "It's not fair."

"No," he said. "Daniel was a good man and a good friend."

She studied him, this strange, curious, brilliant man. It was hard to imagine him having friends or any sort of life before Lonsdale. Then again, she knew he loved Sebastien like a son and that hadn't been hard to reconcile.

A metallic screech echoed in the distance, and she swung around.

"Damnations," said Ivy.

Even from the middle of the field, she could see a Sentinel thundering outside the stone wall from Fifth corner to Fourth. Even so far away, its head swivelled, and its red eye locked upon them.

"At least there's nothing coming from Sixth," she said, and she turned.

"Damn and blast…" she growled.

There was a Sentinel coming from Sixth.

"Remember that weaving and dodging?"

"What is the phrase?" said Frankow. "Wheels up."

Suddenly, the earth exploded as a rocket hit the field between them.

***

It seemed like only yesterday that a person of royal blood had invited him into their carriage. That being Valerie and this being a steamcar made no difference. The aristocracy played with lives as if people were toy soldiers to be moved across a game board, then discarded when the stakes were raised, or the rules changed. He hated this game now. He hated the players even more.

They were well out of London, and he kept his face expressionless as the eight-wheeled streamcar roared down the dark road heading north. In fact, he was exhausted. The roar of the engine was strangely soothing, and he had to fight to keep his eyes open. Surely this was the longest night of his life. With Bastien in the country, perhaps day would never break.

"Sorry about your steamcar, wot?" said Edward. "To be sure, the Crown will pay for a new tire. A fine new tire, in a set of fine tires. Ah haaa."

This time, there was no forced laugh, merely a release of breath like the grumble of a weary dog.

"Will the Crown also pay for a new man servant?" asked Christien. "I don't know if mine will survive a brush with the Empire's own."

"Collateral damage, boy," said Edward. "And they were not the Empire's own."

"No?" said Christien. "That ironclad dreadnought? The *Vanguard*? Not yours?"

"Of course not, m'boy," he said. "Surely not. We're the good ones."

"That's ironic. Then, whose?"

"Willie's perhaps? Or even Franzie. Your brother has shown the world what those lockets can do. All the empires want them now."

"They took the photochrome," said Christien. "No one knew about the photochrome."

"Everyone knew about the photochrome, boy," said Edward. "Valerie found it in Caen, yes? And you flew to London on a Gilded airship. Was she with you every moment of the way?"

He kept his face masked. He'd been good at that, so long ago.

"Why, a copy is likely circulating in all the science journals and hack broadsheets in the country by now."

"As far as going to Hollbrook House, I only told you."

"And Valerie, and Bookie. Your logic is faulty, Remy m'boy. No place and no *one* is secure."

Christien sat back and gazed out the window. They were heading north at an incredible speed, by the looks of the trees that whipped by on the side of the road. He probably had a compass in his arm somewhere, if he'd had a mind to look. He had all manner of gadgets in there, along with the cautery iron that had saved Pomfrey's life.

"Why, I wouldn't wonder if she had a direct line to her dear old papa, wot? Or to the very Black Swans themselves…"

Pistols and lockpicks and cautery iron nonsense.

He kept his eyes straight, face a tight porcelain mask.

"You never know the lengths some governments will go to when the stakes are so damned high," Bertie continued.

In fact, it had been Bertie and the surgeons of St. James who had arranged for the clockwork arm. Had been the War Office who had installed Jekyll next door as his neighbour in Kensington to keep eyes on the lockets and the last of the de Laceys.

*He **belongs** to the War Office, body and soul,* Bertie had said, back at the Club. What if it was not just Bastien? What if he did too?

"Just can't trust the Frenchies, wot? Ol' Boney spoke about a *rapprochement,* a resurrection of old alliances with the Russians to present a front against *Steam, Gild* and *Sun.* Why, I can absolutely believe that they have a man or two on the inside…"

The same way he'd simply 'thought' and the cautery tool had popped out, he turned his mind to other devices. Listening devices. Tracking devices. Tiny implants that allowed the MoD to know his every step. A dictograph or phonautograph.

"…or maybe their man is indeed a woman…"

…phonautogram…

Click.

He glanced down. Perched on the end of his clockwork thumb was a tiny metallic device, the size and shape of a ladybird beetle.

"You say all the empires want the lockets," he began slowly, eyes fixed on the tiny device. "Why? Without Sebastien, they will not work. What could an Empire possibly do with them?"

"You said it yourself, Remy," said Edward. "Gold. Entire rooms of gold. You think an Empire of this size runs on taxes?"

He grunted. Politics *was* the name of the game in this modern world. He closed his fist over the phonautogram, tucking it into his palm.

"They also bring chaos and death," he said.

"Chaos and death are merely tools of an empire, Remy," Edward said, and he leaned back in his great wide red velvet seat. "We might still be running Kabul and Kandahar had we enough chaos and death on our side."

"The world is ending, and you speak of politics."

"Is the world ending, boy?" And he thumped his cane. "Is it really?"

Christien frowned, looked over at the great bear of a man.

"Of course, it is," he said. "The ice, the dead, the rotting food and dying livestock…"

"Your Ivy was right. Damnations, that girl is right more often than I can fathom."

"I'm not following," he said.

"In the *Carolina*, remember? She made a point about the rivers thawing once your brother passes. It's all true. The food stops rotting, the dead stop rising, the livestock stop dying. All this plague and pestilence lifts once the Mad Lord leaves whatever region he's in. So, is he apocalypse or merely abomination? Perhaps we will never know."

"But he has two of the three lockets," Christien said. "Are all the empires of the world going to war to prevent him from finding the last one, or to take them for themselves?"

Edward gazed out the window, saying nothing.

"And are you hoping I will lead you to him, or to the last locket?"

And he held up his hand, the phonautogram flashing in the darkness. Edward looked at it, then him.

"It's just politics, m'boy, as I said to Bookie. Simply politics and bollocks. Nothing personal."

Christien reached over and took Bertie's walking stick, dropping the device to the steamcar's wooden floor and crushing it under the steel tip. Satisfied, he passed the stick back.

"You can't kill him," said Christien. "Surely, you know that. Surely you remember the *Walküre Eins?* All those *Blood and Iron* warships? Arclight dispatches threats with an orb of space, or time, or whatever the hell Crookes called it. No, Your Highness. Bastien can't be stopped. Not by conventional means."

"We might not need 'conventional' means…"

Edward reached under the steamcar's velvet seat, pulled out a package wrapped in tissue. He slid it across the seat with his mechanical hand.

"I might not have been entirely truthful back at the Club."

Christien peeled the paper away to reveal an ancient text. It was exactly like the one in the Ghost Club and he knew instantly that it was a copy of deWinter's notes. He didn't need to flip through the pages to know there would be no great swaths of ink.

"Why give it to me?" he asked warily.

"You see, I've been speaking with Mummie, m'boy," he said, great moustachioed mouth smiling, but eyes as sharp as flint. "And we have a proposition for you…"

***

Fanny opened her eyes at the horn of a steamcar, tearing up the road and ramming the Sentinel a second time. It was the *Veritas* and when she hit, the Sentinel teetered dangerously to one side. She held her breath as the iron foot slammed down just inches from where she huddled over Carl and chunks of earth and coal flew up all around. Hands fell upon her shoulders and suddenly she was pulled to her feet.

"To the wall!" cried Lizzie, and together, they dragged Carl out of the way of the Sentinel and its iron fires.

With the satchel and the last of the fireworks over one shoulder, Grigori leapt onto the second iron giant and began to scale it like a monkey. He quickly wedged the satchel into the articulating hip joint, before dropping to the ground, ducking as a massive hand slapped the spot where he had been.

Fanny looked wildly around for her sister, spied the steamcar backing up for one last run. The front was entirely crumpled, tires flat, and Franny had blood smeared across her cheek. Over the roar of the fires, the plucky little steamcar growled like an angry dog and the Sentinel's head turned slowly toward her now.

It swung an arm, and the rocket bay begin to glow red.

"Franny, dearest, no!" called Fanny. "Get out of the car!"

Grigori held up the flare pistol.

"For Daniel," he said, and he made the sign of the cross. He aimed the pistol at the mechanical hip and fired.

There was a split second when the sky was silent. As if through leaded glass, Fanny watched the flare shot track toward the Sentinel. She saw it hit. She saw the satchel catch and ignite. She saw the steamcar leap forward, her sister wild at the stick as it smashed into the iron pillar. The leg buckled it like a tree felled by a lethal axe. At the same moment, the satchel exploded, and with a blast of heat and light, Fanny was flung violently backwards. Bolts and screws sprayed in all directions. The Sentinel groaned as sheets of hip metal began to slide one way, while the massive torso slid the other.

As if underwater, Fanny looked up. Her ears were ringing. Her head was pounding. The fire and fireworks caused the air to shimmer and bend. The world was red and hot and black and loud as finally, with a deafening roar, the Sentinel smashed into the soggy earth, sending stones, coils and sparks to the sky.

***

"я хотел бы умереть." - Grigori Rasputin

***

She pushed herself to her knees, glanced around for Frankow. He was unmoving on the ground, and she crawled toward him, praying he hadn't joined his friend Daniel in the sky. His geared lenses were gone, and she spied one clockwork leg in the winter grass nearby. She grabbed it and dragged it over to him, frantically searched for a pulse. She felt a wave of relief sweep down from her shoulders when she found one.

"Dr. Frankow," she said. "Dr. Frankow, are you hurt?"

He opened his eyes. They seemed so small after the lenses.

"I am still here?"

"Yes," she breathed. "I'm afraid you are."

He pushed up on his elbows and patted his chest as if searching for something beneath the bulky overcoat. He sighed a breath of relief.

"Still here, yes."

He looked down at his leg.

"Oh," he said.

"I have it here," she said. "But I don't know how to put it on."

"Of course, you don't," he said, and he gazed over the field at the distant wall. The Sentinels had left, continuing their mechanical march toward the main gate from opposing sides of the estate, but there was smoke between the trees where the rocket had passed. The doctor turned to look at the Hall itself, its Georgian windows glowing with distant firelight inside.

"Go, Miss Savage," he said. "It may take a moment to affix this leg. Longer if the wheels have come loose."

"I can't leave you," she said.

"Those things don't want me," he said. "In fact, I don't think they even want you, but you have a job to do. Weave and dodge to the best of your abilities but get to the Hall. I may need to remove the wheels and simply walk, so it may take time. I will catch up once I am able, and dear Cookie will feed me tea."

"Are you sure?" she asked.

"Well maybe coffee," he said. "But yes. I am sure. Go."

She pushed to her feet and wiped her hands on her breeches.

"Weave and dodge," she breathed. "Dodge and weave."

And she bolted off across the field toward the house.

***

They were in a forest, with old spruce and pines covered in snow. He could see lights in the distance, and he prayed it would be different this time. It was not a church, not the little chapel by Seventh where he marshalled his thoughts and channelled the dead. Perhaps this was a church of a very different sort. Perhaps he needed to learn a different way to pray.

He closed his eyes and slid from Ash's back, feeling the weight press down on his shoulders. He leaned into the pale horse, laid his forehead on its damp neck. Ash was always damp, clammy, sticky. Christien would have a term for it. He was a medical man, a surgeon. No finer mind in all of England, he was sure of it.

Shame about the arm. However, with the lockets now serving as his eyes, he supposed they were both clockwork men.

Clearly, Arclight wanted him here and he needed to know why. His head still ached from where the shadow man had struck him. It was the second time the metal in his skull had saved his life. Perhaps, like his brother, he should be more grateful for the science and skill that had forever changed them.

He sighed and turned.

Perhaps you could teach an old dog new tricks.

Time for a new tactic.

He took a deep breath, left Ash and trudged through the snow on the forest floor toward the light.

It was the same as ever, a cottage with low, thatched roof and rough timbers for a frame. The same cottage with thin windows and no shutters, and the same family sitting by the fire. The old man, the young man and the two women, one fair and one dark. This time, he didn't curse the locket.

He blessed it.

He stepped back and turned. The seven spirits, and the not-quite-a-man, were waiting for him once again. He held up his hands.

"Wait," he said. "No fighting. Please. I need to talk to you."

"Why do you keep coming back here?" asked the man.

"I wish I knew," Sebastien said. "I believe Arclight brings me here for answers."

"Who is Arclight?"

"This one," he said, touching his eye. "I think. It's the one that hurts when I defy it."

"If I endeavour to answer your questions, will you leave us be?"

"I can only try," said Sebastien. "The lockets have a will unlike any other."

"Away, then, so the family won't hear us."

The figure turned and stepped quietly over the snow. Sebastien followed, amazed at the length of the man's stride. Clearly, he was almost eight feet tall. Impossible, yet he was here.

The man and his spirits stopped at the hovel at the side of the house.

"Ask your questions, child of the sun," said the man. "I will do my best to answer."

The Mad Lord took a deep breath, not needing it. Force of habit. Function of life.

"Where are we?" he asked.

"Germany, somewhere," said the man.

"And when?"

"When?"

"Do you know the current year, sir?"

"That, I cannot say. I am new to this existence."

"Me too," said Sebastien, and he placed a hand on his left temple. "Arclight keeps bringing me here, and I'm not sure why."

"Then, you should leave."

"I have. Repeatedly."

They stood in silence for a long while, the cottage's warm light flickering like a distant hope.

"Are you a murderer, sir?" asked Sebastien.

"Murder?" said the man. "A protector, rather. I have adopted this family to protect and serve."

"There are seven dead spirits hovering around you," said Sebastien. "It is a puzzle, but given my current affliction, not particularly surprising."

"I am an aberration," said the figure. "Created by the living from the dead."

"Interesting," said Sebastien. "I'm the same."

"Are you also a construct, then?" asked the figure. "Your face is pleasant, but your eyes have an unnatural look."

"They're lockets," he said. "Ghostlight and Arclight. I'm not sure how they got there, but because of them, I will bring about the end of the world."

"Please, don't," said the figure. "The family would suffer more in such an instance."

"I've no choice."

"You're a living man," said the figure. "Therefore, you always have choice."

"I'm not sure I'm living."

"Neither am I."

"Not living, or not sure?"

"Yes." The tall man turned to look toward the cottage and the light flickering within. "One day, I shall make their acquaintance. Until then, I protect, and I serve."

"Perhaps I should speak to them," said Sebastien. "I might find answers."

"Considering you aim to bring about the end of the world, you do not seem to be one currently wrestling with questions," said the man. "Do you really hate life so much as to wish to end it for all?"

"I don't hate anything, actually," said Sebastien. "It's simply my destiny."

"That seems a very definite path, and not one I can support." The man looked back. "Although it may only be an accumulation of anguish, life is dear to me, and I will defend it."

"I used to think that way," said Sebastien. "Death dissuaded me of the notion."

"To examine the causes of life, we must first have recourse to death."

"True enough," said Sebastien.

They stood for a long moment, staring across the snowy yard at the scene behind the leaded window. Contentment in such a meagre property, joy in each other's company. Perhaps the man was right, Sebastien thought. It was always possible that he himself was wrong.

"Sebastien de Lacey," he said, and he stretched out his hand.

The other man stared for a moment before offering his own. Sebastien was not surprised to see stiches running along a grey wrist with blue fingers. When their palms touched, Ghostlight whirred, and Sebastien saw the deaths of all seven, here, in one man. He was not the cause, however. He was the effect. A man assembled by the parts of seven others.

"de Lacey," said the figure. "That is your name?"

"Yes, my name."

"That is why you are here, then." And the man gestured at the cottage. "They are de Laceys. Pappa, Felix, Agatha and Safie. The finest, most noble living beings I have ever encountered."

"An old family cottage, I suppose, but…in Germany?" Sebastien looked up. "Are you certain we are in Germany?"

"I am not certain of anything, sir."

"And you cannot fathom the year?"

"I would agree that not knowing the year we are currently living in should be an anomaly. However, you yourself don't seem to know it, so I'm not alone in that regard."

Sebastien smiled. It felt strange upon his cheek.

"What's your name, sir?"

The man hesitated, gazed off into the trees for a long moment.

"Call me Adam," he said finally. "Perhaps the first Prometheus."

"Am I here because of them, or am I here because of you?'

"I cannot say. *I* am here because of my creator."

"Your creator?"

"He wished to bring life to the dead, so he made me from the dead. But I am too hideous to live, so he rejected me."

"You are a creation, then?"

"I believe so."

"I'm also a creation," said Sebastien. "And now, apparently, the Crown Prince of Death."

"Is this a crown you desire?"

"Not at all."

"Then don't wear it," said the man. "I'm an amalgam of seven men. I have no choice in my bearing. A crown should be an easy enough garment to remove."

"I haven't a clue how."

"How did you put it on?"

He frowned. How had he put on the figurative Crown of Death?

Sophie. Sophie had given him the locket. Arclight. He had died then. He remembered his last breath as a man in the caverns beneath Vienna, opening his eyes to a new, terrifying and bleak existence.

But Sophie von Habsburg was dead. He had shattered her into a thousand pieces in the Hofburg chapel. Had she set things in motion, events that he had unwittingly continued without question? If so, could he, wittingly, now stop it?

"A woman gave it to me," he said finally.

"Then perhaps a woman can take it back?"

Ivy?

How it all came back to Ivy.

"You've given me much to think about, Adam," Sebastien said.

"Go with God, de Lacey. Do not dismiss your life so easily. Once lost, it is not easily won. Now, please leave and do not come back."

Sebastien turned to walk into the forest. He took two steps but swung back.

Adam was gone.

"I'm not sure which is more curious," he muttered as he took one last look at the cottage. "An assembled man or de Laceys in Germany."

When he got back to the trees, Ash was waiting for him.

He took a deep breath and closed his eyes.

"Home," he said to the night sky and the lockets. "Take me home."

***

She only had eyes for Lasingstoke Hall, and the warm glowing windows of the distant First House. Rupert and Cookie, fires and tea. She could make it before her legs gave out. She could make it before the frost coated the winter grass. She had to make it before Sebastien stopped the clock and opened a hole that swallowed the world.

She heard the sound of hoofbeats thundering across the grass, and in the moonlight, she could make out a man on horseback. She slowed, remembering all the nights Sebastien had followed his horse home across the fields. She remembered the time she'd followed him; he pale and cold and covered in blood; she in her nightdress and Wellington boots, when he'd given her the saddle and left Gus in her care. If she'd known then what she knew now, would things had been different? Could she have chosen differently, knowing her involvement would lead to this?

She squinted, certain now that there were *two* men on horseback, and they were galloping toward her.

"Ivy! Ivy!"

It was Davis and the dam that was holding her tears almost burst at the sound of his voice. He reined in his mount and leapt to the ground, catching her in his arms as if he'd never let her go. The dam crumbled then, and she clung to him, sobbing as if she had never sobbed in her life. The terror, the trauma, the horror, the death, all swept over her in a sudden flood, and she wept in his arms until her breaths came in ragged gasps.

"I'm sorry, Davis," she panted into his shoulder. "Oh God, I'm so sorry for everything."

"Buckle up, skirt," said the second man. "Enough simpering for today."

Davis released her and she turned to face Rupert St. John, the Scourge of Lasingstoke. She opened her mouth, but once again, no words came out. Her chin quivered and the tears threatened anew.

He reached out and pulled her to him, and she sank into his embrace, wishing now she could just sleep for ever and ever and ever.

She feebly gestured to the field.

"Frankow," she said. "I couldn't fix his leg, and, and Mr. Home is dead, and…"

She gestured to the distant gate where the last arcs of fireworks crackled and sparked.

"And Fanny and Franny and Lizzie and Mr. Raspberry and Carl…"

"Is all of bloody Lonsdale here, then?" asked Rupert.

"I think so, yes," she sniffed.

"Those Sentinels are converging on the gate," he said. "But they'll be calling in reinforcements from all over the county. Soon we'll be surrounded by machines, and I'm not convinced we'll be safe."

He looked down at her.

"Skirt, I got a message from Remy."

She took a deep, shuddering breath, wiped her cheeks and her eyes.

"We'd best get on it, then," she said.

He grunted, turned, and swung up onto his horse, reached a hand to swing her up behind. She wrapped her arms around his waist, grateful for the warmth of human bodies.

It occurred to her that Sebastien was most often cold.

"Davis, go fetch that bastard, Frankow, and bring him back to the Hall," Rupert said. "Then, you are free to use any, and all, of your inventions to dispatch as many Sentinels as you can. With my blessing."

Davis grinned up at Ivy.

"I been busy," he said.

Rupert hauled on the rein and the horse whirled, kicking up grass as it sped toward the Hall.

***

"Franny!" Fanny cried, and she pushed herself to her feet. "Franny!"

The sound of mad laughter rose over the roar of the flames.

"Hahahaha! *Veritas Temporis filia!*"

And the steamcar sputtered and chugged into view, with Franny at the stick.

"Oh darling!" cried Fanny and she rushed to the car, pulled her sister from the dickey with surprising force.

"We did it," said Franny. Her face was blackened, her scarf singed, but her smile had not disappeared. "I knew we could."

"But look," said Lizzie, and she gestured with her axe over the wall. "More."

Moonlight glinted off metal and red beams cut across the dark fields.

"How many?" asked Franny.

Grigori scrambled up the wall.

"три," he said.

"Three," said Lizzie.

"More coming," muttered Carl from the base of the wall. "Likely a Place Setting."

"A Place Setting?" Franny grinned from ear to ear.

"What's a Place Setting, dearest?" asked Fanny.

"Twelve."

"Oh dear," And for the first time in hours, Franny's face fell. "Well, I'm sure we can manage a few more…"

Suddenly, a strange wind picked up. The flames hissed and sputtered and finally died, choked by a creeping blanket of frost.

Grigori stepped forward.

Fanny was certain that her heart stopped beating, for, through the billowing smoke and fog and steam, there was a man on horseback.

"*наследный принц,*" Grigori said.

"Your Lordship," said Carl.

"Wonderful to see you again, Carl," said the Mad Lord of

Lasingstoke.

Chapter 16

Of Lost Loves, Lost Lives, and Lostlight

"Life, although it may only be an accumulation of anguish, is dear to me, and I will defend it."

– Mary Shelley, Frankenstein: The Modern Prometheus

"Well, that ain't Frankow," said Davis, and he laid the fur coat back over the dead man's face. He stood, put his hands on his hips, and cast his eyes across the dark fields. There were stone walls and styles, stands of trees and piles of dead branches, but no sign of Lonsdale's doctor anywhere.

"Dr. Frankow!" he called. "Oy, Frankow! Where are ya?"

There was no response, save the fading fireworks from the Sentinels that sputtered at the main gate. *Why the main gate*, he asked himself? Not like a Mad Lord riding an undead horse leading a legion of skeletons was going to be stopped because of a few ironmen at a gate.

"Cor," he breathed. He could already see the illustrations for that

205

one.

"Frankow!" he cried, one last time, but he stopped as his breath frosted in front of his face. He looked down. Ice was creeping across the field like fingers, and he wrapped his arms around his chest. The last time he'd seen ice like this had been at Seventh, where he'd almost been torn apart by dead women. Or so he'd been told. He still remembered nothing, which Lottie called a blessing.

No, ice like this only meant one thing.

He swung up on his horse and wheeled toward the Hall.

***

She'd never been so happy to see the straight limestone walls and ivy-covered borders of Lasingstoke Hall as she was now. Never been so thrilled to walk the long halls, cross the well-trod rugs, glimpse the old, gold paintings. A healthy fire roared in the study. The dogs had whined and kissed and bumbled. Castlewaite shook her hand most vigorously and Lottie had welcomed her with a great warm hug. Cookie even cracked a smile as she plied her with tea, toast and jam. She was ravenously hungry but there was no time for rest, and her mind was racing as Rupert shoved the PHAX paper under her nose.

"The War Office is jamming the Teslagraph signals," he grumbled through his cigarette. "But no one uses PHAXs anymore. Why we still have one is beyond me."

"So, this is from Christien?" Ivy asked over her tea. "Did he find it at Caen or Hollbrook?"

"Caen," he said.

"Jane, yes?" said Ivy, and she glanced up at Rupert. "Before the wedding?"

"Yes," he said. "Before."

"Come, child," said Cookie, taking her daughter by the hand. "We'll best leave them be."

"You don't have to—" Ivy started but Cookie waved her hand.

"Call us if you've the need. But some things are best kept private."

"Thank you, Cookie," said Rupert.

"Come, dogs," said Cookie. "Bones in the kitchen for ye tonight."

She and Lottie slipped from the room, followed by the dogs.

Rupert moved to the hearth, blowing a stream of smoke through tight lips, and Ivy looked up at him. The Scourge of Lasingstoke. He'd lost his heart so long ago, cobbled it together with the care of Jane's two orphaned sons.

"Do you remember her ever wearing it?" she asked softly.

"Never," he said. "But then again, unless it's a wedding ring, tell me what man notices a piece of jewellery?"

Ivy looked back at the chrome.

Renaud Jacobe St. John de Lacey. Twin to Rupert, but so easy to tell them apart. There was something in the eye, a sharpness, a drive, and she wondered why Jane could have chosen him when a man like Rupert was hers for the asking.

"Hard enough to remember birthdays and anniversaries and the lot," Rupert muttered more to himself than her. "We simply don't pay attention to the seemingly little things. And when they're gone, we realize perhaps they weren't little at all."

She ran a finger over the image of the locket. It looked innocuous enough, but then again, so did Ghostlight and Arclight, when separate and on their own. She remembered when Christien first gave her Ghostlight, how it danced and spun and called the light. There was something otherworldly about them. *Extraterrestrial*, her friend Wells had said. *Supranatural*. It made sense, really. Spiritualism was all the rage in London. Even John Williams hadn't escaped.

"We need to see more photochromes," she said. "If we can pinpoint the last time she wore the locket from an image in a chrome, that might help us narrow down its location."

"Mm," he said.

She looked down at the chrome in her hands.

"I know it's not allowed, but…"

"You want permission to open the master room."

"I think I must."

"Does he really have two?"

"Ghostlight and Arclight, yes," she said. "They're in his eyes."

"Oh, God…"

"I'm afraid I put them there," she said. "I thought he was dead. Well, he was, actually. So was Crown Prince Rudolf."

He studied the cigarette between his fingers.

"Just tell me he wasn't the one who shot Rudolf. I don't care what the hell else happened in Vienna, just tell me he didn't murder a Crown Prince of Europe to get a bloody piece of jewellery."

"No sir," she said. "He didn't. Of that, he is innocent. Involved, yes, but innocent."

"And Rudolf is now alive, yes? Or is that sensationalist nonsense?"

"Very much alive, sir," she said. "On account of Laury *and* Remy."

"Not you, though."

"No, sir. I had very little to do with it."

"So, what the bloody hell do you think you can do about it now, skirt?"

So many retorts tumbled through her mind, some strong, some weak, some esoteric, some rude. But if there was one thing she'd learned in the last few months, it was the power of an honest answer.

"I have no idea what I can and cannot do," she said. "But one thing I do know is that, for the first time, I'm not wearing a skirt."

He grunted again and tossed the cigarette into the fire. She could have sworn there was the hint of a grin.

"Right," he said. "This way."

And he strode past her towards the door.

***

Frost swept up the shattered Sentinels, splitting the metal and causing it to curl.

"Oh, well done on those Sentinels," said the Mad Lord. "Did you do that, Carl? Or was it Grigori?"

The Russian stepped toward him, before falling on his knees and clasping his hands beneath his chin.

"наследный принц," he said again. *"наследный принц."*

"All of us, m'lord," said Carl and he struggled to his feet. "But mostly her. It was her idea."

And he pointed to Franny, who smiled like the sun.

"Two machines to take out two machines."

"Clever," Sebastien said. "Hello, Lizzie. Where's your axe?"

Lizzie stood up straight, smoothed the mud off her thighs.

"The iron giant smacked it away. I need to find it."

And she ducked into the shadows to search.

A tall, thin woman stepped over the sizzling grass.

"Why are you doing this?"

"Do I know you?" he asked.

"I am Fanny Helmsely-Wimpoll, soon to be Liddell," she sniffed. "The best bosom friend to Ivy Savage, who adores you to no end and, to my eyes, for no earthly reason!"

"Ivy," he said, and his cheeks ached with a smile of his own. "Is she here at Lasingstoke?"

"IF she were, I'd not tell you!"

"She's here," said Franny.

"You have no right to do this," snapped Fanny. "You are like a spoiled child with lazy parents."

"I have no parents," he said.

"You have no right to end the world for so many others who are only beginning to live. It's not right and it's not fair and you are simply being selfish and cruel. Shame on you, you Mad Lord. Shame on you!"

"Have you lost someone?" he asked.

"We have all risked life and limb to fight what you have started," she said. "It's simply not right."

"наследный принц," said Grigori.

"Yes," he said to the Russian. "But Mr. Home?"

"в воздух," he said.

"Hm," said the Mad Lord and he looked up, his eyes spinning. "I see he's found peace. I am glad for him."

"You're glad he's dead?" asked Fanny. "You are a ghoul."

"Death is not the enemy," he said.

"Death is the end," said Fanny. "And for those of us who utterly delight in this thing we call Life, it is most certainly the enemy. It is a thief and a robber and a brute, like you."

"Once lost, it is not easily won," he muttered.

"She's gone to the Hall," said the woman in goggles. "Ivy has gone to the Hall with the Czech."

"Franny, no!" snapped Fanny.

"Frankow is here?" he asked.

"Oops, right. No," said Franny. "Not here. Somewhere else that is not here."

And the ground beneath their feet began to rumble.

"Veritas Temporis filia," And he let his gaze settle on her. Ghostlight wanted her, the odd blonde woman with the goggles and the scarf. "Truth is the daughter of Time, but with Arclight, I am the Lord of Time."

Franny's eyes grew wide.

"And at this moment, you do not speak the truth."

Both sisters shrieked as the earth burst with bones and corpses began to push their way from the depths. Lizzie grabbed her axe and began swinging, shattering as many as crawled from the soil. Grigori slammed the spade into the ground as they pushed forth, took off heads and cleft arms and splintered spines. Still, the grass heaved, and the bones rose.

"Prohibere," said the Mad Lord, and he raised his hand. The dead froze. *"Revertere."*

And with two words, the skeletons collapsed, shattered, turned to dust and settled on the snowy road. But the ground continued to rumble, and he looked up. Through the lockets, he could see Sentinels, one rolling from each corner of the estate. Their red eyes sliced through the darkness as they rumbled toward the gate.

"Can you handle those?" he asked.

"Not at all!" snapped the one named Fanny.

"Absolutely," said the one named Franny.

"Very good," he said. "I'll leave you to it, then."

And he turned to Franny.

"Be careful, friend of Ivy Savage," he said. "Truth may be the daughter of time, but not of authority. You may not see the light of day."

"What does that mean?" snapped Fanny and she swung between him and her sister. *What does that mean?"*

"I have one more lesson to learn," he said. "Therefore, one more stop to make."

He raised his hand, cast a circle with his fingers and a great round orb sizzled to life between them, large enough for him to urge his sticky horse through.

"Adieu, my friends," he said. "You will all be remembered for your bravery."

He paused, thought a moment, and looked up.

"If the world doesn't end tonight, that is."

The portal snapped shut behind him as two more Sentinels rounded the corner of the gate.

***

"There ye go, luv," said Cookie, and she slipped the padlock from the door. "Try not t'make a mess, please? Ah don't want my last breath t'be cleaning at the end of the world."

"Can you please check on Mary Jane?" Rupert asked. "Her symptoms were very bad today."

"She's almost at the end of the first trimester," said Cookie. "She'll have an appetite soon enough."

"Thank you, Cookie," he said quietly, and patted her hand. "I hate to say it, but I couldn't do this without you."

"Ah know it, sir. Ah do know."

And she disappeared down the corridor.

Ivy smiled at him, remembering their very first meeting. He'd been abrasive, rude and insulting, but now she knew that the Scourge of Lasingstoke had indeed a very soft heart. Ironic, considering that heart was now made of gears. He grunted as if reading her thoughts, so she turned and pushed the door open.

It was beautiful.

In fact, she was quite surprised. She wasn't sure what she'd been expecting, but it certainly hadn't been this. High ceilings, tall windows, ivory crewel paper on all the walls. While the rest of Lasingstoke was a study in either brooding masculinity or aristocratic elegance, this room was simple and utterly lovely, and Ivy knew that it was all Jane. Jane Penteny of Eccleston.

Unfortunately, there were few photochromes on the walls in here, unlike the corridor which was filled with them. There were a few on a chest of drawers, however, and another on an oaken bookshelf, and Ivy slowly crossed the room toward them. She paused, turned back to the door where Rupert was standing, arms folded across his chest, outside.

"Are you not coming in?" she asked.

"The last time I was in this room," he said, "I had to pick up the pieces of the woman I loved."

Ivy looked down.

"That included her two sons."

"I'm sorry, Rupert," she said.

"Two brothers torn apart by loving the same woman," he said. "One wins, one loses. One gloats, the other resents. The brokenness goes so very deep."

So many families. So much grief.

"I loved Jane, and she loved me, but she chose my brother, and we all paid the price. But the thing is…"

He shook his head, but she could see that he was somewhere else, some*when* else.

"I'll never know why."

His voice caught now, and she could see his eyes glistening.

"I don't think she was greedy, but my brother stood to inherit the estate. I was just the second son; a twin, yes, but second-born. What could I give her? I didn't fight for her because he could give her a far better life than I ever could. I let him win and because of it, she danced with kings and queens."

He looked at her now and she could have sworn there were tears.

"And I know women aren't prizes to be fought for and won," he said, releasing a breath. "But could I have stopped all this, if only I had fought? Just a little?"

Gads, how much more could her heart take.

"And I know I never say it – God forbid I encourage a stubborn young thing like you," he said. "But either of my boys would be lucky to have you."

Slowly, she raised her head.

"What's that?"

"You're bright, stubborn, independent, free. You may not have the most astounding common sense and you're as silly as a spring colt, but you're curious, clever and resourceful beyond measure." His smile was sad and lazy, like an old cat by a fire. "You make them happy."

Her eyes welled with tears now, her throat tightening at his words.

"They've had little contact these last ten, fifteen years. They've lived such vastly different and separate lives, but they're still brothers and I have to believe they care about each other, even in some small way. God knows they both care about you, so maybe they could fight, just a little."

"I don't want them to fight," she said finally. "Not over me. I love them both, but so very differently."

"So, what has changed?"

"Well, everything," she said. "The world, Sebastien, the lockets—"

"I mean, in you."

He leaned on the side of the door, arms still folded.

"Two weeks ago, before you barrelled onto an airship and decided to take on the world, you told me that you had no idea what you wanted," he said. "Has that changed?"

"It's changed," she said quietly. "I think I know what I want, and how I want it. But *I'm* the one who has to fight for it, not them, and it's terrifying."

She wrapped her arms round her chest now.

"I'm not any of those things you said. Bright, clever, independent, free. I'm not any of that, not really. That's Penny Dreadful, my character. *She's* bright, stubborn, independent, and free. I…I use her. I draw on her. I pretend to be her, but when I'm just being me?"

She lowered herself to the edge of the bed.

"I'm afraid all the time."

"Tripe. You're as bold as a terrier on a rat."

"I'm not. I'm terrified of everyone, and everything, and I have been since I can remember. My tad is a bobby, and his job is dangerous. We were always afraid one night, he wouldn't come home, so I got to know the other bobbies in his squadron, tried to tell myself it was fine, easy. See? Just a normal life with all the other tads. But I was so scared that he'd be killed on the job by some bludger. I was so scared for him, all the time."

She shook her head.

"My mum lost five babies, but I never let myself remember that Davis and I *also* lost five babies. I was still a child, but I lost five brothers and sisters before I was eight. Every other year, there was another little coffin. And then Tobias. He lived until he didn't. When was it Davis' turn? When was it mine?"

She swallowed, looked down at her hands.

"And when I began to lose my mum, I had to take care of both her *and* Davis. I was eleven, but I was his mum *and* hers. I had to clean the house and arrange the meals and shop for food and handle money because tad was working, and, and…"

Her chin quivered and she looked up.

"I was only eleven! I was so afraid I'd mess up, fetch the wrong food, or not enough and we'd go hungry. I'd forget to order the coal and we'd freeze, or I'd forget to watch Davis and I'd lose him, just like my mum lost Tobias…"

The tears spilled now, and she was helpless to stop them.

"I had to be so ordered, so *orderly*, to keep all our lives together. I had to work so very hard to be an adult, but I was just a little girl, so when I met Remy, it seemed like it would be so easy. It would all get taken care of by the slipping on of a ring. I could finally let go and let someone else carry it all for a while, just a little while. But then…"

She looked up at Rupert now, met his eyes, kept them.

"Then I was afraid that I'd lose him too. I wasn't smart enough, good enough, rich enough, pretty enough. I couldn't plan those elegant parties, learn to play whist, take up embroidery and fashion and art. But Penny could. She was all those things, and I could slip her on like a pair of very fine boots. It was jolly good fun for a while, but for the rest of my life? I simply couldn't and that's when we began to crack.

But then I met Sebastien, and everything changed. Upside down and sideways. He just wanted me to stop pretending and just be me, but I didn't know who that was, so I fought him too. He told me to reach higher and I tried. I fought so hard to be smart enough for them both, good enough for them both, but I wasn't. I never was. I was just a scared little girl in far too deep and dreading it but not knowing how to get out, or even if I wanted to."

Her voice broke, and she gasped for air, wiped her cheeks with her palms.

"I'm still scared, because now, if we don't fix this, everything dies, and it was all because of me. I could have told him no, we weren't going to

Vienna. No, we were staying here, up north, away from the madness, with his horses and his dogs. But I didn't because who am I to tell him this? I'm not his wife or his fiancée or even his 'special friend' like Mary Vetsera. I wanted to kiss him in the gorse bushes or crawl into his bed that night on the *Chevalier,* but I didn't because I was too afraid of what would change if I did. And now I'm scared of airships and scared of Sentinels and scared of dying and scared of losing him and just as scared of loving him because I don't even know what that means. I'm just so, so scared."

She closed her eyes and dropped her head. What a mess, she was. What a complete and utter calamity.

The bed sunk and she felt him sit beside her. He lifted her chin and dabbed her eyes with a handkerchief. Pressed it into her hand and stared at her a long moment.

"Look," he said. "I am in the room."

She tried to smile.

"Yes," she said through her tears. "Yes, you are."

"I dread this room with every beat of my heart, but I will stay until you are finished. I can't help you with your fears, but I won't leave if you won't."

"I won't leave." She took a deep breath, then another. "We have a job to do."

"Saving the world rubbish."

"That too."

He patted her hand and helped her to her feet. She held up the handkerchief.

"May I?"

"God, keep it. I don't want it back now."

She grinned weakly and turned back to the photochromes on the bookcase, feeling considerably lighter than she had in years. With another deep breath, she began to pick up the frames to study them more closely. There were smaller and more personal than those decorating the corridor walls. Those were family and friends, business associates and momentous occasions, but these were candid images of Jane and her dogs, images of Renaud and his horses. The boys together and separate, with parents and without. None of them showed Jane wearing Lostlight, however; none but one. It was a wedding chrome, and she narrowed her eyes.

"Rupert," she said aloud. He moved to her side, peered over her shoulder at the frame in her hand.

"Jane's wearing Lostlight, but Renaud is wearing Ghostlight. How was there no chaos?"

"No key?" said Rupert.

"Sebastien," she breathed. "He was the key. But how? I still don't understand."

"Neither do I, skir—" He caught himself. "Ivy."

She smiled again.

She laid the chrome back on the bookcase and moved on to the chest of drawers. There was an image of Jane pregnant, with Sebastien she assumed, and again, Lostlight glittered like a star around her neck. She picked up another gold frame. This one was the whole family–Jane, Renaud, young Sebastien, and baby Christien. It was so beautiful. The perfect family. But interestingly, Jane was not wearing the locket.

Ivy frowned. Sometime between her first baby and her second, Jane stopped wearing the locket. She was narrowing down a time, but how in the world did that help her narrow down a place?

She picked up the last photochrome in the room. This seemed to be a candid image of Jane holding baby Sebastien. Since it was monochromatic, she couldn't tell the colour of his ever-changing eyes, and she smiled seeing his face as an infant. There was clearly a resemblance, but before the effects of growth and time and life. And death.

"Was Jane a spiritualist," she asked. "Like Sisi or Renaud?"

"Mmyes," said Rupert. "More like Sisi than Renaud, or Williams, or Bertie, or any of this modern mob."

She looked back at the chrome. Mumford was in the picture as well, as freshly knit as the young lord, with both ears and no frays.

"I have to remember to get Mumford," she said distractedly.

"Why?" he answered, equally distracted.

She ran a thumb across the photochrome, pushed aside a faint layer of dust.

"To help calm Sebastien," she said. "Frankow said he's in Laury's room here."

"Mumford's not here," said Rupert. "Hasn't been here since that night."

"What? He's not here?"

Mumford is a toy, Miss Savage.

"Frankow said he was here."

There was no locket around Jane's neck.

A knitted dog made for him by his mother at his birth.

"As far as I know, Mumford's at Lonsdale."

Latin is the language Mumford speaks.

"Oh my God," she breathed.

"What is it?" asked Rupert. "Ivy?"

Footsteps echoed down the corridor, and Lottie burst into the room.

"He's on the grounds, sir," gasped the girl. "The Mad Lord is home!"

Chapter 17

Of Horses and Dogs, Both Living, Woollen and Dead

"... the companions of our childhood always possess a certain power over our minds which hardly any later friend can obtain."
        – Mary Shelley, Frankenstein: The Modern Prometheus

They were in a forest, with old spruce and pines covered in snow. There were no lights in the distance, and he frowned. This was not the way of things. Something was wrong.

He slid from Ash's back, wishing for the warmth of a real horse. A horse of muscle and bone, tendon and hair. He'd loved horses, once upon a time. Perhaps he would again if he could find his way again. Horses and dogs, fields and trees. The cold stone of Lasingstoke Hall, the ivy that climbed her walls. He smiled to himself. He had been happy at Lasingstoke Hall. Sometimes, he had been happy.

He was glad to almost be back.

He took a deep breath, left Ash and trudged through the snow on the forest floor.

There were no lights, no windows, no thatch. The cottage was a husk, blackened and charred and near burnt to the ground. The family was gone, and the door gone too. He turned in circles, looking for spirits, but none rose and none hovered, and he realized that for the first time in ages, it was quiet.

He was quiet.

"Adam?" he called, his voice echoing through the trees. "Adam, are you here?"

Nothing. There was no answer, not even the whisper of monsters in the night, and it occurred to him that he was grateful for the silence.

He turned back to look at the cottage. Snow had settled on the charred beams and in the cracks of splintered rafters. He stepped toward the open doorway, leaned against the lintel to peer in. The furniture was burned to embers, but he could see the remains of the hearth where the fire would dance. He remembered the faces of the family that gathered beside it – the old man and the younger, the two women one fair, one dark. Laughing, smiling, talking, living.

Living.

Ivy lived.

Rupert lived, as cantankerous as ever with his clockwork heart and the acerbic young woman who shared his life.

Christien lived, dented and cynical, yet not broken, not bowed.

Something caught his eye on the side of the cottage, and he moved to investigate. Near the hovel attached to the cottage, was another smaller building, a lean-to that had likely housed pigs. In the low doorway, the pages of a book lifted and fell in the night breeze. Carefully, he reached down to pick it up. It was as charred as the cottage, but he recognized it immediately.

Paradise Lost.

He'd read it once, years ago. He tried to turn the pages, but they crumbled into ash at his touch.

Better to reign in Hell, than to serve in Heaven.

Was it, though?

He looked around the clearing, once alive and fraught with conflict, now silent, dead, cold. Works of art turned to dust; a pocket world ended because of a monster. Or was the monster merely a man? A man who lived between life and death, like himself.

Ivy lived.

Ivy lived. Cookie lived, and Lottie and Davis and Castlewaite. He smiled at the thought of Castlewaite. Good man, great driver, crackerjack airship pilot.

Frankow also lived.

He turned and leaned against the hovel's sooty walls.

Frankow. His chest ached at the name.

They'd shared port by the fire on so many stormy nights, debated philosophies and religiosity and piety and sin. Talked of violence and criminality and weakness and love. Shared family memories and the tragedy the came with both. Frankow had been his friend, his mentor, his father. Was he also a monster? How did one reconcile that horror with love?

Do not dismiss your life so easily, Adam had said. *Once lost, it is not easily won.*

He laid what was left of the book back down, and stepped away to take one last look at the little cottage that was home for both de Laceys and monsters.

Perhaps no lessons learned, but things gleaned, a heart mended.

He would never come back here again.

When he got back to the trees, Ash was waiting for him.

***

"Where's Frankow?" Ivy asked as they crossed the cobbled courtyard towards the stables, six dogs at their heels. It was dawn, and the sun was low and struggling through creeping fog. "Did Davis find him?"

"No, Miss Ivy," said Lottie. "He said only a dead man in a fur coat, but that it weren't him."

"Where could he be?" she asked.

At her side, Rupert growled.

"I don't trust him," he said. "Never have. But I doubt he'd do anything to hurt Laury."

"Other than kill him over and over and over."

"That was before."

"My God, Rupert. Do you hear yourself?"

He looked down at her.

"Have you not learned who we are, girl? Have you not been paying attention?"

She released a breath and nodded swiftly. He was right, and to pretend otherwise was to deny the truth. The de Lacey family was as cursed as a family could be, addicted to their spirits, their science and their secrets as any in the Empire of Steam.

"I'm sorry," she said.

"Don't be." He turned to Lottie. "Where's Davis?"

"Gettin' some gadgets in the streamshop," she said. "He wants to take down a Sentinel or two."

Rupert grunted.

They continued across the courtyard toward the steamshop at the far corner along Third House. The great geared door was open, and she could hear the growl of an angry engine inside.

"Lasingstoke has another airship?" she asked.

"Not an airship," said St. John. "Your brother is a very clever young man."

"I know it, sir," she said.

"He's bloody brilliant," said Lottie and she smiled.

They paused at the machine shop's open door. The roar of machinery was deafening, sending echoes across the courtyard and smoke billowing into the menacing sky. Ice was settling into the cracks between the cobbles, crawling up the limestone walls.

"The Mad Lord," said Lottie.

"Now, girl," said St. John. "You go and release the horses into the fields."

"All of them, sir?"

"All save Rue and Blaise. Get Castlewaite to saddle them up. We may need them soon enough."

"Aye, sir." Lottie curtsied and sped off toward the stable, her boots clacking on the cobbled stone.

Rupert turned.

"So, you're saying the locket has been here all along," he said.

"Well, not here," she said. "In Mumford, wherever he is."

"God, that makes sense," he said. "The locket was the only thing protecting her from Renaud, so she gave it to the one who needed more protection. She hid it in that damned knitted bear."

"Knitted dog. Mumford taught Laury to speak. Mumford speaks to him still."

"So it's the locket that's speaking, yes?"

"I can't think of any other explanation. It has to be Lostlight, hidden in Mumford all this time."

The growl from the machine shop was a howl now and Ivy glanced around the courtyard.

"Are you certain you have no other airship?"

"Only the one," St. John said. "What the hell is he doing in there?"

"It is rather loud," said Ivy.

Rupert grunted.

"Do you think Frankow knows the locket's inside the bear?"

"Dog," said Ivy again. "I think he may. Why else would he lie?"

"But *why* would he lie in the first place? Why not grab the bloody bear—"

"—dog."

"—dog, and just bring him here, to Lasingstoke?"

"Oh!"

She gasped and looked up, eyes wide.

"Oh! I know where Arvin Frankow's gone!"

Suddenly, the sky grew dark as an ironclad airship roared over the machine shop, the name *Vanguard* painted on her hull.

***

Seventh House was the same as before, but with wooden boards over the windows and chains across the doors. Black peaked roofs, gothic wrought iron, winter ivy, and stone. It was all stone, and it had been his favourite laboratory so many lifetimes ago.

Frankow had found his way through the dark wood easily, through the thick trees and twisted roots that kept most out. The graveyard was a familiar haunt too, its stones serving as pavers, the crosses like markers on a highway. The dawn sky was red, but losing its fight against the looming fog, and he thought it fitting for this morning to end all mornings. It would most certainly be his last. Frost worked its way along the forest floor, and he knew Sebastien was on the way.

"Hello, dear friend," he said to the house. "It has been a long time, yes? Fifteen years, maybe? Sixteen?"

There was no birdsong in this part of the wood. There never was at Seventh. No birds, no bees, but there was a sound, now rising on the morning breeze. It was low and lethal like the growl of a great cat.

"He is coming for me, so I must be ready. Will you let me in?"

The sound grew louder, deeper, higher like a hurricane wind as the walls began to move.

"You have no claim to me," he said. "My sins are against him, and him alone. You understand this, yes?"

Shutters rattled and stones heaved, and the chains smacked against the doors. Winds whipped around his legs, buffeted his overcoat and lifted his cap from his head. It was immediately snatched by the branches and carried high into the blood red sky.

"Temper, temper," he said. "Open your door."

The house howled now, mortar shaking loose as its very frame convulsed. Light beamed from cracks in the stone and, behind the boards, windows shattered, sending shards of glass blasting like shrapnel and he ducked away to avoid the cuts. From the wood of the door, a shape began to bulge, an oaken hand with skeletal fingers, reaching for him, pushing, pressing, clawing.

He slipped a hand inside his overcoat and pulled out a floppy shape of brown wool.

Immediately, the house grew quiet.

"I brought a friend."

After a long moment, the hand and the chains fell away. The door creaked open into the dark.

***

The orb sizzled shut behind him, and he took a deep breath. He didn't need to, but it felt good to breathe in the fields of Lasingstoke. It was dawn, but the sky had closed in, covering the angry sun, and an eerie fog was settling over the pastures. This was the closest thing to home for him, outside the Hall in an early morning mist. Most nights had been spent hunting down villains and murderers, most mornings spent rambling home. He knew each tree, each fence, each stone and meadow in this great estate, and it lifted his spirit to see it again. He'd been so afraid he never would.

The main gate was far behind him. Fortunately, the orb had deposited him in the middle of the estate on a bit of higher ground. He could see little, save the stands of trees cutting through the fog like rocks in a river. The grass was tipped with silver, and he knew it wasn't because of the winter. It was him, bringing the frost like he always did. Bringing the killing, killing frost.

Could the Latin help him with that the same way it did with the dead?

There was a rumble, and he turned toward the distant outline of the Hall, waiting as horses thundered through the mist. *Odd.* Someone had released them into the field far too early this morning, but he suspected there was as much chaos inside Lasingstoke as there was outside. A large black shadow hovered over the rooftops of the estate. It looked like an ironclad airship, he thought to himself, but the fog was thick, distorting the sight. Bertie's maybe? Or Franz Joseph's? The only one he'd ever seen had shot them down over Alsace-Lorraine. It had been one of the first times he'd ever summoned an orb. He wished it had been his last.

His attention was drawn back to the small herd of horses racing through the grass. They were magnificent, and he lightened as he watched them, bucking and kicking, full of life and vigor. With splendid conformation, they were perfectly balanced between carriage horse and sport, and his heart swelled with pride. French Warmbloods. The finest breed in the Empire. Perhaps the world, but then again, he was biased.

The herd finally slowed to graze in a patch of thick winter grass, but one horse was alert. A dappled grey stallion stood on stiff legs, head high, tasting the air. *Montclair's Ghyslain d'Auguste.* Gus. He let out a squeal and left the herd, cantering across the field toward him and the strange horse at his side.

The grass thudded with his hoofbeats, and through the lockets that served as his eyes, Sebastien could see the muscles and tendons that fueled the great beast. As if aware, the stallion slowed as he approached, snorting and tossing his head.

It was then that the Mad Lord remembered the stag.

"No, Gus," he said. "Go back."

The stallion tossed his head again, stomped the ground. He was wire-tight, ready to bolt.

"Gus, my lad," Sebastien repeated, his heart breaking. "My fine, fine lad. Go back."

He raised his arms, waved them high and low and wild. Gus grumbled, took several steps back as the frost crept toward him like an arrow.

"Go!"

Ash lunged forward, snapping his skeletal teeth, and Gus wheeled, thundering off toward the herd. They bolted after him and disappeared into the mist like vapour.

Sebastien stomped his boot and let out a roar.

"I hate this!" he cried. "And I hate you!"

The horse blinked slowly at him, not comprehending.

"You've destroyed what was left of my life," he said. "I don't want you anymore. Go away!"

Ash snorted, pawed the earth with his hoof.

"Go away! I hate you! Go!"

Ash tossed his sticky head.

"I! Exite! Odi te!"

Slowly, the horse turned and walked away. Each pale hoof sank into the earth, deeper and deeper and deeper, pushing through it as though he were wading into a river. Within moments, he was gone. There was no pit to mark his passing.

Sebastien flexed his fingers, curled them into fists. He was a stranger here. Here, in the fields of Lasingstoke that were his heart's blood, and he cursed these lockets that drove him madly onward. He had intended to go straight to Lonsdale, but the lockets had drawn him here.

The distant sound of hoofbeats again, and he cast his eyes eastward, where the sun was struggling to break the fog. Another horse cantered across the field toward the little church and Seventh House. The horse was followed by a pack of six dogs, and, had his heart been working, it would have surely stopped. It was the bay mare – *Rouen Delfina d'Arc en Ciel*, or Rue, with Ivy Savage on her back.

***

She threw a glance over her shoulder at the rooftops of Lasingstoke and the looming shadow that was the dreadnought. Rupert had urged her to go, promised he and Davis could handle whatever came their way, and so go she had, grateful that Rue was tacked and ready for a gallop across a very wide field. They had even taken two small fences in stride. She had never jumped on horseback before, but she'd just tucked herself low to the horse's neck and let the mare take them both over. Fortunately, Rue was a good jumper, for she made it feel like a skip over a creek. She'd lost a few of the six dogs over the fences, but they knew the holes in the walls better than she did, and they'd found her quickly enough afterwards. She almost always had the pack of six bounding at Rue's hooves.

Suddenly, the dogs began to bark and the air in front of her frosted her breath. She drew the mare up to a halt and cast her eyes around the fields. Low stone walls, winter green hills, stands of alder, oak and hawthorn. The fog hung low over them, creeping over all things as if painted with a white brush. But no, she could almost feel him on the frost, and she turned her face to the west, where a figure stood in the mist.

He looked almost human, standing there in the field without the pale horse or the bone army to accompany him. Almost human, with his blanket around his shoulders, his hair wild, face gaunt. It was always extremes with him, either happy and sunny like a field of wheat, or skin stretched thin over hungry bones. Her heart ached at the sight of him. It always had.

The dogs whined now as the lockets flashed. She had put them there, thinking it a fitting tribute, a funeral rite for a paranormal prince, but she had been wrong. They controlled him like a puppet now, playing the strings on his life of pain. They were here heading for Seventh, the most dreaded house in the Empire, to battle over the fate of the world.

To battle.

And suddenly, she realized that she was indeed going to have to fight him for it. She was no longer the little writer girl from Stepney. She was the woman holding the fate of the world in her hands. She had no idea how it would unfold, but either way, it would take everything and more to save it.

She turned her head and dug her heels into the bay mare's side, leaping across the frosty ground toward Seventh.

***

He watched Ivy slow the mare to stop dead in the middle of the field, and the dogs stopped with her. She turned her face his way, and he knew that she saw him. He knew every line in that face, every curve, every freckle. She was Life, warm and free and constantly moving forward. He'd always been a cold man, while she was as bright as an early summer sun.

Do not dismiss your life so easily.

Had he dismissed even the chance of Life? When did that happen? How?

The dogs saw him too, then, and he prayed they wouldn't come. He prayed they'd follow her, away from him and the killing cold. He'd shattered one dog once. He couldn't bear the thought of a second.

Ivy turned her head back and spurred the mare onward, northward, toward the dark trees and darker stone of Seventh. Seventh House. Why was she going to Seventh House? Anyone going to Seventh was a bad thing. There was never a good reason, and yet, he would follow.

Happily, the dogs went with her instead of toward him. Even Tag, who lingered a moment before slipping off into the fog.

Once lost, it is not easily won.

Ghostlight and Arclight had him, wretched sisters both. Had he lost to them already? Had he even fought, or had he given himself over to them willingly, eagerly even? Was it so much easier to hide in winter than try to love that bright summer sun?

Lostlight would have the answers. Lostlight would set him free.

And this time, he knew that somehow, someway, Lostlight was at Seventh.

Arclight beckoned. *Make me an orb,* she urged. *Let me take you.* How the lockets spoke now. He could hear them like voices inside his skull.

"No," he said out loud to the fields and the fog. "No more orbs. This time, I walk."

He forced his lungs to draw a breath, turned, and set his feet toward Seventh.

Everything came back to Seventh. Always.

Suddenly, a shape bounded out of the fog. It was Tag, the needy, happy springer spaniel. Before he could stop him, Tag leapt up onto his leg and pushed his nose into the Mad Lord's hand.

***

The ironclad hovered over the courtyard of Lasingstoke, its canvas obsidian, its propellers slicing the fog like daggers. Rupert stood beneath it, hands on hips, almost daring it to strike. He felt Davis step in beside him, then Lottie, then Castlewaite. All of Lasingstoke held their breath, waiting for the next move.

From the hull of the gondola, a black hatch began to slide.

***

The howl echoed across the fields.

"Tag! No!"

The little spaniel dropped to his feet, shaking his head from side to side as ice shot up from his muzzle, burning his whiskers and crackling his long ears.

"No!"

Whining, he staggered back until his hind legs buckled, and his black and white body crumbled to the ground. His ribs convulsed as the frost consumed his trembling frame, and his brown eyes bulged as the cold did its work. His tongue froze in his mouth, and his whining grew softer, thinner. Then it ceased.

"…tag…"

The little dog lay still in the winter grass.

Sebastien sank to his knees, clutching his fists to his chest, tears burning rivers down his cheeks. He reached out to touch the fur, white and black and now crackling with ice.

"Tag," he gasped. He had no breath, like his dog. His silly, sweet, needy, old, good dog.

He gathered the body into his arms, pressed his face into the ruff, but the dog dissolved under his fingers, fell away to nothing in the frosty grass.

The earth began to rumble.

"No."

Tag was a good dog. The best dog.

He raised his head to the sky.

"No!"

The dead were coming.

He'd killed his dog. *He* had. This thing that he was, this monster.

"No!"

His cry echoed across the fields as he flung his arms wide. Grass bulged, trees tilted, and all around him, the ground erupted as bones burst forth. Hands, arms, skulls, ribs. The bone army of the dead. His army. His people. His was the Crown of Death.

Revenants rose all around him, swaying on decayed feet. He sat between them all as in a field of dead wheat. It didn't matter what Adam had said, or how his story ended. He had no life. He had no heart. He had no will other than that of the lockets. There was no controlling them, no fighting what would happen. There was only Life, Death and the Things in Between.

He was the Thing in Between.

The Thing. The Creature. The Monster.

Slowly, he rose to his feet and moved through the dead, and they parted for him like the Red Sea. Forget the little chapel. He would go to Seventh, find Frankow, find Lostlight, and end this for once and for all.

He turned his face toward Seventh.

Chapter 18
Of Fighting on All Fronts

"If I cannot inspire love, I will cause fear!"
– Mary Shelley, Frankenstein: The Modern Prometheus

"Oh no," said Franny, and Fanny looked up. A third Sentinel was rounding the corner at Fourth House, its great strides covering the ground on its way to the gate. Fanny turned and stood on her tiptoes to peer over the wall. Red beams flashed as a fourth giant could be seen through the fog coming from Fifth. She turned her head to see the last two, on their way from Sixth and Seventh. She sagged against the wall. They were surrounded and exhausted and down two men, leaving herself, her sister, the woman with the axe, and the mad Russian.

"We can do it," said Franny and she offered a thin smile.

"I'm not convinced we can, dearest," said Fanny. "But we must surely try. For Ivy."

Franny nodded eagerly.

"For Ivy!"

"Come, my friends," said Fanny. "We have a matter of moments, and they may be our last. But I am honoured to have fought this battle with you, and I'm immensely proud at what we have accomplished."

"I can fight," said Carl Feigenbaum, and he pushed himself to his feet.

"My good man, you can barely stand," said Fanny.

"But I can fight."

"Very well," she said. "We know their weaknesses, but we also know our strengths. Let's figure out how we take them down, one by one by mechanical one."

A flock of pigeons rushed overhead, and Lizzie pointed.

"Look!" she shouted.

They all turned to see the flashing red beams of six more Sentinels thundering down the road from Over Milling.

***

She remembered the last time she'd been to Seventh. She'd come back from London after the Mad Lord had 'died' and had promptly stormed the House to get him to reveal himself. It had been one of the most horrifying things she'd ever experienced, with living chains and claws of oak, and she'd barely escaped with only a few scratches. It seemed like so long ago. A lifetime.

The horse refused to enter the deep wood. No surprise there, Ivy thought. Animals were sensitive that way. So, she dismounted at the edge of the trees and looped the rein over the horse's neck. No tying this time. She keenly remembered that night in Milnethorpe, and Sebastien's words about a quick getaway. She wasn't sure if there would be any sort of getaway, this time, quick or otherwise. In fact, she had no illusions at her prospects for 'getaway' at all, or for that matter, survival.

"Stay," she said to the mare. Rue grumbled but did not move.

She looked around at the small pack of eager dogs.

"Stay," she said. "I'll be back soon, I promise. Just stay."

Jo and Birdie sat. Fergis, Clancy and Dickie laid in the leaves. No lolling tongues, no wagging tails. They were stressed and confused. They were in a bad place without their master, and she felt her heart ache for them as well.

"Tag?" she asked and looked around. "Tagger? Tagger, come here, boy!"

There was no answering bark, no snuffle or wagging hind end, and her heart skipped a beat. The dog had been with her when she'd seen the Mad Lord. She prayed he hadn't gone to him. She feared what would happen if he did.

She swallowed and looked down at the Lasingstoke pack.

"Please, stay."

They lowered their heads.

She turned and studied the snowy path into the wood. There were footprints and she knew they were Frankow's. He'd clearly exchanged wheels for shoes at some point. She released a breath and followed the prints, under the bare branches and dark canopy, deeper and deeper into the wood until she stood at the clearing where everything died.

There were no chains. There were no claws. The house sat quiet in the early morning fog, all grey stone and black windows, but she knew better than to believe. It was full of death and despair, murder and madness, and now, with ice crackling up the path, it would soon become the fulcrum for the end of all things. How on earth could she stop it? How in heaven? How in hell?

She stepped toward the door. No hands, no claws, no shuddering beams of light piercing from the cracks in the frame. Even in the early morning, no birds sang. Seventh was silent and all the metaphors ran through her head. As night. As a tomb. As the grave. It was always silent here. Silence was Seventh House. Seventh House was the Silence.

She touched one of the blackened door handles, prepared to snatch her hand away, but there was nothing. She turned the handle and pushed the door. It creaked into blackness.

"Dr. Frankow?" she called softly. "Dr. Frankow? Are you here?"

Silence.

She took a deep breath and stepped inside.

***

The gondola's obsidian hatch began to slide open, revealing rows of black boots. Rupert leaned sideways to Davis.

"Go fetch your gadgets," he said. "And be quick about it. And Castlewaite, go with him."

"But sir," the coachman began, but St. John cut him off.

"Go."

Aye, sir," he said and together, man and boy ducked back into the machine shop.

"Lottie, please get inside," he said. "Tell your mum to be prepared for anything but do *not* put yourselves in danger. This is not your fight."

"Forgive me, sir," she said quietly. "But Ah believe this is all of our fight."

He felt a rush of pride and damn it all if those tears didn't sting anew.

"Just be careful," he said.

She turned and rushed out of the courtyard, just as the gondola hatch clanged onto the cobbles.

Rupert pulled a cigarette out of his vest pocket and lit it, took several long puffs as a balding man strode down the ramp. He wore a black uniform and reflective goggles and was followed by at least a dozen others holding hydraulic rifles. The man crossed the cobbles to stand directly in front of him, while the others fanned out behind. His goggles swept the courtyard, before turning to face the Scourge.

"Rupert St. John," said the man. "Of Lasingstoke Hall."

"Indeed," said Rupert. "Who are you and which empire do you serve?"

"Where is Sebastien de Lacey?"

"Last I heard he was in Vienna," said Rupert. "Your accent is Russian, but your uniform is not. So, I say again, who are you and which empire do you serve?"

The man held up his gloved hand, gestured for the troops to fan out into the yard. Then, he held out a sheet of paper.

"Can you tell me whereabouts of this?"

It was the photochrome of Jane with the locket.

"Of Jane de Lacey? Good lord, man, she's been dead for years."

The backhand was as swift as it was savage, and Rupert staggered under the blow. Two men stepped in behind him, grabbed his arms and shoved him forward once again.

"Then let me be perfectly clear," said the man. "Where is the locket?"

"Cor, this a dreadnought, then?"

"Non!" barked a uniform behind and they all turned to see Davis leaning into the gondola's dark hatchway, his face and hands covered in grease.

"I ain't never seen a dreadnought. She's a right beauty, she is!"

And he banged on the walls and the metal floor.

"But, so heavy! How she fly, then?"

A soldier rushed forward, shoved the boy out of the way.

"I was just lookin'," he grumbled as he disappeared into the shop. "We don't get to see ships like that up here…"

"That sounded like a French *non*," said Rupert. "A Russian-French alliance, perhaps? Is that what Vanguard means?"

The man turned back, held up the chrome.

"This."

"I have never seen that piece of jewellery in my life," said Rupert. "But you are more than welcome to look. There are only six hundred acres or so. Should be fairly easy. Then, once you find it, take your bloody Vanguardsmen home with you, to Russia or Prussia or Paris or wherever the hell you come from and leave us in peace."

The man stared a long moment, moved as if to turn away but then swung back, striking St. John a second time across the cheek, this time so savagely that he almost hit the ground. The two behind caught him, set him back on his feet once again. He worked his jaw back and forth, spitting blood into the frosty ground.

"We shall search every inch of your six hundred acres," said the man. "And you will remain standing here until we find what we are looking for."

"Happy to oblige," said the Scourge.

And the man and his followers fanned out, disappearing into the many doorways of First, Second and Third Houses of Lasingstoke Hall.

Rupert pulled a second cigarette out of his pocket, slid it between his teeth, and lit the match.

***

Ivy wasn't sure what she had expected, but it surely wasn't this.

The floors were walnut parquet, each plank stained a different shade, with intricate borders that mimicked rugs. The walls were very high and very dark, possibly blue or grey, their colour virtually hidden by the many paintings and tapestries that covered them. An ornately carved staircase flanked the right wall, and a blackened fireplace sat at the far end of the room. Threadbare chairs were stacked, and shelves buckled under the weight of damp books. There were doors leading to other rooms, but they were bolted shut, and from inside the house, it was impossible to see the windows, boarded as they were. The smell of dust was strong, but there was something else, something *other*, and she knew from her days in the morgue with Christien, that it was chemicals, iron, and blood.

Along the walls, tables sat laden with cracked tubes and glasses, vials and beakers. Wires ran along the walls, and gas lamps perched at various intervals, corroded and empty. An ice box sat, door ajar, and a multi-armed automaton lay on the floor, spiderwebs connecting its limbs more surely than bolts or wires. On one table, blades of different sorts formed a fence, standing like soldiers stabbed into the wood.

It seemed like an abandoned laboratory that may have also served as a home, and it was almost a natural leap to think that may have been the case. But this is where her brother had almost died, and she knew there was nothing natural about this place.

She wrapped her arms around her chest, noticing a series of circles painted on the tile floor. Circles and triangles, numbers and symbols, and she wondered if it was Sebastien's doing, or his father's. The little church on the property was similarly adorned, and she knew it was either blood or ink painted across the tiles. It took a long moment before it occurred to her that she had originally thought the floor was wood. *Odd.* It was clearly brown and black tile – dusty and crusted with mud. One of the gas lamps sputtered and she looked over at the wall. Wooden panels. Elegant but worn, in need of attention.

She frowned. She could have sworn the walls were painted grey.

She turned. There was no staircase.

Turned back. The walls were stone.

The floor was dirt.

A chill swept up her spine. Seventh was a mad house.

She saw a small, woollen mound in the shadows, and with a deep breath, she carefully crossed the floor. It was Mumford and she stooped to pick him up from the dirt. She brushed him off and held him out to look at him. Buttons for eyes, the mouth and nose hinted by an X of thread, simple stitches in black wool. Patches on the belly, one floppy ear frayed and barely there. She squeezed him in the middle to see if she could feel the round shape of a locket, but the stuffing was lumpy and old. She pinched along his floppy arms and legs, his pathetic wisp of a tail, his tattered ears with a moth-eaten hole. He looked worn and forlorn, and she smiled to herself. This was Sebastien's best friend in the world. It had been sweet when she'd thought it merely a child's toy, but if Lostlight were truly Mumford's heart and soul, he became a decidedly more sinister thing.

She ran her fingers along the knitted head. Beneath the layers of wool and batting, was a small, hard object and her heart thudded within her. It felt like a nest, and she wondered if it had become tangled in fibres as the rings had spun their magics over the years. Would that slow its function, dull its lure? What on earth was its particular power, if Ghostlight beckoned spirits and Arclight opened doors in time and place?

Something dripped on the dirt floor at her boots.

She stepped back, clutching Mumford to her chest. There was another drip, and then a sound, like the hiss of held breath. Slowly, dreadfully, she looked up.

Up, up, up, past the beams and exposed rafters, past the decaying coffers and plaster and medallions and chandeliers, there was something pinned to the ceiling. No, something was *gripped* to the ceiling with wooden claws.

It was Arvin Frankow.

***

In First, the sweeper hummed happily down the corridor that led to the study. It was the Georgian part of the estate, formal yet with a genteel shabbiness that belied the classical symmetry of the wing. It swept the long wool carpets and the polished wood of the floors with equal proficiency and innocently bumped the walls as it went. Now, it happily turned the corner into the study that belonged to Sebastien Laurent St. John Lord de Lacey, Baron of Lasingstoke.

And while it was never a tidy room to begin with, the two thugs dressed in black had turned it entirely upside down.

They had ripped broadsheets off the walls, pulled books from the cases, rifled through every drawer in the grand oak desk. The little sweeper bumped and chugged over the debris, vainly attempting to clean the layered carpets beneath. It whirred over to one of the thugs, bumped gently against his foot. The man ignored the little sweeper, pushed it with his boot when it got too close. It was then that a wire popped out of the top and zapped the ankle with a jolt of current. In fact, the current was live, persistent, and surprisingly strong for such a happy little device and the man was frozen for several long, agonizing silent moments until the sweeper changed course and whirred happily under the desk.

The man pitched forward on top of a cushioned footstool before crumpling to the floor.

The second man turned around.

"Nico?"

The sweeper emerged, chugging toward him over papers and boxes and books.

"Nico? *Vas ist?*"

He looked down as the little robot innocently bumped his boot.

He snarled and stomped it, but the wire was out, and the current was live. It raced through his limbs and constricted his muscles. He was paralyzed, foot on top of the little sweeper, and the humming grew louder and louder. The boot began to smoke, and the Vanguardsman began to convulse. His eyes bulged and his tongue pushed out between his teeth and his heartbeat was interrupted. He was dead on his feet within minutes.

Finally, he toppled over, releasing the little sweeper, and it turned, carrying on out of the study in search of other dirty carpets and even dirtier thugs.

***

He heard them first, the growls and whimpers and whines, and what was left of his heart sank to his boots. The path to Seventh was a familiar as his own study, if not more so, and he knew that Ivy had left the dogs here along with her horse.

He turned to the bone army.

"Abito," he said. *"Ad terram."*

And just like that, they fell away, bones turning to ash, flesh sinking like dust. He looked back over the field where he'd walked. Ruined, destroyed, burst and raw. The dead had made it so. Or was it him?

He turned back to the forest and began to walk in. The dogs grew louder, barking now as he approached. He would not let them die like Tag, he told himself. He would make sure they survived this day, unless of course, he ended it all with the capture of Lostlight.

He paused.

If he ended the world, he ended the dogs. All dogs. All horses. All life. Life. He took a breath, felt it fill his chest. It still felt unnatural, but then again, he was never a natural man.

He saw the horse first. The little bay mare named Rue, and she shifted nervously, tail swishing, hooves dancing. But she was not tied, and he remembered a night in Milnethorpe when he'd been shot. Something about a row house by a factory. It was a blur, a vapour, a breath of fog on a fading horizon.

Once lost…

He spied the dogs next. They rose to their feet, unsure whether to wag or whine, and he called on Ghostlight, reached in to her frozen depths. He summoned a Deadwall to surround his dogs, a fence of ice that rose from the ground, corralling them together and safely away from him. Fergus was a wolfhound and therefore, the tallest, and he watched with anxious brown eyes as the ice of the Deadwall grew up all around him. Sebastien's heart broke anew as many paws scratched at it from within but he knew it would keep them safe until he was gone.

Tag should have been there with them.

Tag should have been there.

The mare laid her ears back and squealed at him. He passed her by without a word, but he stayed well away, glad the curse didn't affect horses the way it affected sheep and stags and cattle. He walked past her, and the ice raced on ahead of him along the path to Seventh.

***

"Get out of me kitchen!" snapped Cookie as four men pushed their way through the scullery hall. They ignored her and began to empty sugar tins and spice jars onto the tile floor.

"Here!" she cried. "You leave those be! Good Lord! D'ye see any gold? There ain't no bloody lockets in this kitchen!"

"Mum!" Lottie said as she rushed in from the storeroom, but the men whirled, pulling their weapons on her. One man grabbed her by the arm and swung her into the cupboards, but Cookie snatched a cast iron frying pan and lunged forward, smacking it onto the man's head. He struck the centre table and went down. Another strode forward and pushed her against the large combustion stove, dagger at her throat.

"Wait!" cried Lottie. "I can help!"

The man turned to look at her.

"I know where they keep the lockets," she said.

"Lottie, no," hissed her mother.

"Everyone knows," she moaned. "And Ah won't let them knick you on account of a trinket."

She turned, took a deep breath.

"They're in the cellars," she said. "They say the cellars are full of Norman gold, but they ain't."

She twisted her apron into knots.

"It's the lockets."

The three men moved toward her. One glanced down at their fallen comrade, a small pool of blood forming under his head. He nudged the man with his boot.

"Dead," he said.

"He were trying t'hurt me daughter," growled Cookie.

The Vanguardsman turned to Lottie.

"Take us, and we won't kill you," he said.

She nodded swiftly.

"But we take your *maman* too," he said. "And we will kill her first if you lie."

"Ah ain't lyin'. There's boxes and boxes of gold, and it's all made by the lockets."

"You lead," said the man. "We follow with your *maman.*"

She did, through the narrow hallways of the serving wings of Lasingstoke, past the storeroom and the boot room, past the women's sitting room and the pantry, to a doorway at the top of a very narrow stair. She grabbed a candle holder on a stool beside the door and lit it with a long match. She looked back at her mother, took a deep breath, and began to wind down the stair.

It was clearly a very old part of the house, and the stone steps were worn smooth from centuries of use. Lower they went, and the stairway grew narrower and darker still. Lottie paused at the last step and used the candle to light a wall sconce. Light flickered, revealing a wide grotto with bricked arches and limestone nooks. Old wooden crates lined the walls, and the smell of damp clay filled the air.

"This door here," said Lottie, and she led them toward a low oaken door with black latches and a great geared lock.

"No tricks," said the man, and he flashed the dagger at the side of Cookie's throat. "Or your *maman* will die."

"No tricks," said Lottie. "It's really a marvel, once ye see it."

And she turned to the geared lock, punched in a series of numbers, and a blast of air puffed out from the bottom of the door.

Light beamed out from inside.

She hauled on the door.

"See?" she asked. "I told ye."

The room was glorious. Gold walls, gold floor, gold ceiling, gold chairs. Golden boxes holding gold bars. Golden urns filled with gold coins. Everything in the room was cast in gold, even the mirrors that reflected the candlelight had taken a gilded sheen.

"I've never been in the room, m'self," said Lottie, "So I don't know where they keep it. But that's what it does, and likely, that's why yer a-wantin' it, yeah?"

The Vanguardsman said nothing, but he released Cookie, walking past her like a man possessed to follow Lottie into the room. The other two did the same, eyes wide, entranced, as they studied the walls, the ceiling, the floors, and the crates. It was a vast, low room, most certainly not a natural one, and they moved into the space with more than a little avarice.

Swiftly, Lottie slipped out of the room and as one, she and Cookie slammed the door, spinning the gears, locking the three soldiers in the golden cellar.

It was then that they heard the explosion.

***

"Dr. Frankow?" she whispered, surprised her words came out at all.

She could barely see him in the shadows, but faint light glinted from his metal legs and his lenses. The wooden claws tightened, pulling him deeper into the ceiling as if trying to make him a part of it. Blood dripped three stories to the floor below.

The floor, which was wood. This time, the floor was wood.

Seventh House was madness.

"Let him go!" she shouted, and she thrust Mumford up at arm's length. "You let him go!"

A bitter wind picked up, and dust swirled across the floor.

"The Mad Lord is coming and Lostlight commands it!"

The wind became a howl, shrill highs and dissonant lows, a

cacophony of sound like a Bedlam choir. Now a filthy crewel wallpaper, the walls began to smoke as if fires smouldered behind the boards. The swirling dust twisted the smoke, along with ash and bits of glass, into shapes like ink seeping into a glass of water. Ivy's breath caught in her throat as the smoke became wraiths with shadow eyes and gaping mouths. They seeped out of the walls, crawled along the ceiling and snaked across the floor. Mumford shuddered in her grasp, as phantom fingers reached for him, trying to coax him from her, trying to swallow him in their shadowy embrace. She couldn't let that happen. She knew she'd end up caught like Frankow if she let Mumford go.

"Lostlight commands it! She says let him go!"

The smoke wraiths swirled around her, their eyes hollow, mouths distorted, and the cold from them chilled her to the bone. She clenched her own eyes and turned her face to the ceiling, clutching the knitted dog.

"Lostlight," she said. "Lostlight, can you hear me?"

Her palms began to grow warm, but she didn't dare open her eyes.

"Lostlight," she said. "If you're in there, listen to me. Help him. Please."

The warmth radiated up her arms, but the shadow wraiths circling her were cold, and her fingers had lost their feeling. How could she keep hold of Mumford if she couldn't feel him?

"Mumford?"

The warmth became heat now, and her body began to tremble. She could feel the hollow faces pressing against her, their breath smelling like decay, their wispy tendrils stinging like wasps. Their howls shook the walls, the floor, and the beams, and above her, she could hear rafters buckle and crack. Tears streamed down her cheeks, as she pulled Mumford back to her chest and sank to her knees.

"Please," she begged.

There was a rattle above her head, and she opened her eyes.

"…wait…"

She hadn't thought it through. She hadn't thought.

Frankow's body swung like a pendulum in the high ceiling as, one by one, the wooden claws snapped. Splinters and blood rained down as they released him, and with an unbearable cry, he fell.

Her scream joined his as he plummeted straight down, three stories from the highest raftered peak, arms and metal legs flailing, unable to break his fall.

And then, he stopped.

He stopped with a terrible jolt, inches about the stone floor.

Face down, arms out, legs taut, he hovered, his scream cut off in his throat. The howling winds died and there was silence, as if, suddenly, Seventh was holding its breath.

Ivy knew what that meant. She buried her face in brown wool and wept.

The doorway swung open, and ice swept in, crackling and angry and deadly and swift as the Mad Lord stepped across the threshold of the Seventh House, home.

Chapter 19

Of Everything, Everywhere, All at Once

"It is true, we shall be monsters, cut off from all the world; but on that account we shall be more attached to one another."
– Mary Shelley, Frankenstein: The Modern Prometheus

"Let go!" came a voice from the Second storehouse door. "That's not yours, you bludger! He has a bad heart and needs his stick! You let it go!"

Wrapped in a woollen shawl, Mary Jane marched across the courtyard, struggling with a Vanguardsman over a fine black walking stick.

"Don't you lock horns with this pregnant frow, I warn you. I'll clock you one, I will! Don't you lock horns with me!"

She shook the man off and stormed over to the Scourge, passed him the cane. With a deep breath, he leaned forward and bent over on it, taking some of the strain of standing.

"What the bloody hell is goin' on, Ruby?" she snapped. "And who are these boffers tumbling my house?"

"Russians, I believe," said St. John. "Or maybe French."

Her eyes grew wide as she saw the blood at the corner of his mouth, and the blue cast to his jaw where bruises were beginning to form.

"Who did this, then?" she asked. "That bald bludger?"

"Not to worry, *chérie,*" he said. "I'm quite fine."

She turned to the men behind him.

"You done this, didn't you?" she snarled. "You have no pride, bustin' the chops of an ol' codger like this. He has a clockwork heart, and it don't always tick right proper."

"Marie Jeanette," he said.

"Well, it's true, and my baby needs his pop, he does—oh!"

She gasped.

"oh…"

And she doubled up, a hand on her belly. St. John leaned forward.

"Marie?"

"Ohhh," she moaned.

One of the guards stepped around, offered her his arm and she reached for him with both hands.

"Ahhhh! Ohhh…"

Still bent, she grabbed his arms and pulled him in close, and with a swift, savage motion, brought her knee up into his groin. She cupped her fists and swung them up, cracking him in the chin and sending him reeling backwards. At the same moment, Rupert spun, swinging the cane into the second guard's skull and the third man sprang back as Rupert lunged a second time, knocking the strange rifle out of his arms.

The Vanguardsman yanked a dagger from his belt as Rupert swung again, but the man grabbed Rupert's wrist, blocking the strike. He lunged forward and swiftly, thrust the blade up and into the Scourge's heart.

The cane clattered across the cobbles and the men locked eyes.

"I believe she did say 'clockwork' heart," said St. John.

The Vanguardsman blinked in confusion and Mary Jane brought the cane down his head. He dropped to the ground like a stone, and she stood over him, striking him again and again and again, savagely and without hesitation, blood spraying with each blow of the cane. She whirled and smacked each of the other two several times for good measure, before she slowed, her breath coming in ragged gasps. She turned to look at him. Her eyes were wild, her curls free of the knot, and he thought she'd never looked so glorious.

"Ain't no one hurts my Ruby," she purred. "Else they deal with me."

She reached up to stroke the Scourge's bruised face. He caught her palm and kissed it.

"Old codger?"

"*My* ol' codger."

"*Ma chère,*" he said, grinning, and then he turned. "Davis!"

There was a roar from the machine shed, and a clunky, copper machine rolled out on thin coach wheels. Castlewaite was at the dickey with Davis in the rumble.

"What the bloody hell?"

"It's a steam carriage, sir," grinned Castlewaite. "Young Davis 'ere took one of me old carriages and made it sommat new!"

"And look!" cried Davis over the roar of the engine. "A hydraulic blaster, just like the Sentinels!"

And he held up a strange weapon that looked part hose, part blunderbuss, with glowing orange tubes running the length of the stock.

"Bully, boy," said the Scourge. "Have you reprogrammed VINCE?"

"Last night, aye, and the sweepers too! They're right deadly, now, I reckon."

"And the airship?"

"Done, sir!" And Davis handed him a device with a yellow switch. "I tossed it in before they even saw me at the ramp."

"Off you go then," said St. John. "Take out as many as you can but be careful. They won't spare a thought for you. We'll handle the Russians or Prussians, or whatever the bloody hell they are."

"Aye, sir!"

And the steam carriage roared out of the courtyard and down the road toward the main gate, puffing white steam from its stack as she went.

Mary Jane turned to pick up the strange rifle. She tested its weight, scope and trigger mechanism, then looked up at him.

"This'll do."

Yes, utterly glorious.

"Well," he said. "There are at least twelve others to dispatch before the end of the world."

She grinned.

"What's that, then?" she asked, nodding at the device in his hand.

"This?" he said. "A VTF. Variable Time Fuse."

"Ah," she said. "A detonator."

"Let's get some cover, shall we?"

And they crossed the bloody cobbles to duck into the machine shed before he flipped the switch. With the heat of a thousand suns, the airship exploded into a massive ball of flame and steel behind them.

***

Dear Ivy,

Am I afraid of death or dying, you ask?

Not in the least. It's just another grand adventure I yearn to take.

Yours,

Franny

***

"Charge!" cried Franny, and the *Veritas* lunged forward into the path of the Sentinel approaching from Fourth.

The steamcar swerved in and around the iron feet, dodging eye beams that blasted ruts in the frozen road. Standing on the rumble seat, Lizzie waited until the last moment before she leapt up and swung her axe into one of the legs. It held and she clung for dear life, her boots scrabbling but her grip sure. As the iron helm swivelled to follow the car with its red eye, the young American pulled a corn cob from her skirts and tossed it into the joint at the knee. She sprang free, hitting the grass hard and rolling to a stop. She slipped her fingers between her teeth and whistled. Within a matter of moments, a fluttering mass swept from the sky and a flock of pigeons swarmed the metal leg, diving in and out as they swooped for the cob. The mecha-man jerked to a halt, its knee joint jammed with the darting avian bodies, its own massive frame now dangerously off balance.

With a roar of steam, the *Veritas* rammed her chassis into the other foot and the Sentinel teetered precariously over the wall, where a mad Russian happened to be waiting. Grigori leapt on to the arm and turned in time to catch the firecracker that Carl tossed up from the ground. Like a monkey, he scaled the metal frame and shoved it into the neck joint below the great grinding helm. That helm swivelled, and the eye socket glowed red as Grigori sprang back to the wall. The rocket hand also began to glow, and the hum and squeal of metal echoed across the late morning fog. At the iron foot, Carl pulled a pistol and shot straight up, and the neck began to sizzle and spark. Within seconds, the fireworks erupted, and the Sentinel lurched backwards, toppling over like an ancient oak and sending rubble in all directions. But on top of the crumbling wall, Grigori was unable to leap away. When the iron torso crashed, the Russian went with him, disappearing beneath a mountain of gears and stone.

Fanny bolted to the wall and dropped to her knees, pulling at rocks and wires, copper tubing and steel. It was impossible, for the sheer amount of wreckage that sizzled on the wall.

"Look out!" shouted Carl. Red beams sliced up the ground as another Sentinel thundered toward them, its red beam searching for signs of life. For her part, Lizzie was unaware, and she combed through the debris for her axe, pitching springs and gears to the side as she dug.

"Fanny!" cried Franny. "Pigeon girl!"

Atop the rubble, both women glanced up, caught in the flashing eye beam from the Sentinel. Its rocket arm swung up, glowing red in the pipes, and Fanny felt her heart sink. One shot and they'd be finished. One blast and she'd be gone.

The great red glow of the rocket arm was all she could see, and she sank to her knees, knowing this was it. The Mad Lord had won, and the world had lost. Not at all how her story should end. She steeled her jaw and closed her eyes.

"For Steam," she whispered. "And for Ivy."

"Not my sister!" shouted a voice over the din.

The musical horn of the *Veritas* sounded and the steamcar's engine roared with life. It leapt into the path of the oncoming Sentinel, swerving and squealing its way through the field of fallen robots. The helm swivelled and the rocket arm readjusted, firing a deafening blast onto the road. The *Veritas* almost tipped on its rickety four wheels, but Franny gripped the stick and bore down, mad scarf flapping, goggles reflecting the glowing red lights.

The rocket fired a second time and the road erupted, flipping the tiny car into the air. Over and over and over it flipped until it hit the ground and slid to bump, upside-down, against a great iron foot. The rocket arm swung directly down, and the muzzle glowed with red.

"Franny!" cried Fanny, and she leapt from the rubble onto the road. She raced toward the *Veritas* when suddenly, an orange beam sliced through the metal torso from behind. She slid in the slick earth, hitting the ground and covering her head as sparks rained in every direction from the iron giant.

High above her, the great helm swivelled on its geared thorax to look behind toward the main gate. The orange beam had carved clean however, and as the torso turned, the plates began to slide, taking each half of the giant in two different directions. Both pieces peeled away, and the Sentinel toppled like split firewood onto opposite sides of the road. Fire burst from each section as they hit, and the winter grass caught anew.

Through the wavering fire light, Fanny could see a steam carriage on the road, with a gap-toothed old man at the stick and a young man holding a very large weapon in both hands.

"Hydraulic blast!" shouted the young man. "I'm Davis Savage! You must be Fanny!"

She nodded.

"I got another one back there. Look!"

And he turned, pointing back toward the gate, where the fifth Sentinel lay in pieces, glowing orange from the rent seams.

But before he could utter another word, a red beam sliced through the air, blasting the weapon out of the young man's hands and he was blown off the steam carriage, and onto the ground. He rolled into the grass, his face and chest blackened by the shot.

It was the last Sentinel, the one that had stomped all the way from the corner by Seventh House. It thundered up the road, eye beams flashing through the fog, rocket arm glowing like the devil.

With a snarl on his craggy face, Castlewaite stomped the accelerator and the carriage rushed forward, its thin tires kicking up mud from the ruts in the road. He hunched over the stick and drove the carriage directly into the Sentinel's path, leaping out of the dickey just as the great foot came down. The carriage crunched and buckled, but when the mecha-man lifted its foot, the carriage went with it, stuck to the bottom of its iron sole.

Like a wiry old monkey, Castlewaite climbed onto the foot with a hose and cables in his hand. He set to work strapping the remains of the carriage onto the boot, yanked a cord and leapt to the ground. Immediately, something inside the crushed carriage began to inflate.

"Good Lord," breathed Fanny from the road. "It's an airship canvas…"

With a rumble of steam and compressed gas, the canvas inflated. The Sentinel tipped awkwardly, first forward then back, and its arm swung wildly to correct its lost balance. Red beams flashed from the eye, desperate to puncture the filling canvas but it was a futile attempt, and the great iron body toppled forward, smashing its helm against the wall and sending stones flying. Still, the canvas inflated, carrying the carriage, and attached foot, up up up into the air, dragging the leg, waist, torso and helm with it. As the head finally left the ground, the red eye began to fire wildly, slicing wall and trees and the wreckage of other Sentinels on the road.

"Fanny!" cried Davis, blackened and burnt but alive and pushing up from the grass. "Here!"

He tossed the hydraulic blaster through the air, and she scrambled to catch it. It was weighty and awkward, but she lifted it to her shoulder, squinted, and squeezed the trigger. A thin orange blast shot from the wide muzzle, arcing through the air like a new-fangled electrical current. She felt heat and vibrations sweep up her arms, but she held it steady as the current struck the helm, seeking the eye as if drawn to it. The eye exploded, then, showering sparks onto the road, and silencing its lethal beam. With a fading grumble of gas and steam, it disappeared into the clouds.

Exhausted, she lowered the blaster.

"Well done!" cried the boy called Davis and she released a weary breath.

"Well done," she repeated. "Well done, indeed."

She scanned the rubble. Hissing grass and sizzling coal, sparking gears and sheets of twisted metal. The wall was in ruins and the debris of steamcars were everywhere.

"…oh, fanny…"

Her heart skipped a beat, and she glanced around for the *Veritas,* crushed and on its hood on the side of the road. She dropped the blaster and raced over, dropping to her knees at the sight of her sister, pinned beneath the steamcar that she loved.

"We did well, didn't we?" asked Franny.

There was blood at her nose and mouth, and the goggles were shattered, pieces of glass embedded around her blue eyes.

"Yes, dear heart," she said, voice cracking. "We did very well."

She grabbed Franny's arm and began to tug, but her sister was completely pinned by the Veritas's crushed chassis.

"It's fine," said Franny. "I'm fine. I'm just happy my plan worked."

"No," said Fanny. "I just have to lift this damnable steamcar…"

She pushed to her feet and wrapped her hands around what was left of the doorframe. She heaved and hauled, but the *Veritas* did not move.

Her chin trembled, but she adjusted her grip, and hauled on the frame anew.

"Let me help the goggle girl," said Lizzie, and she slipped her axe under the bar and pushed down, using it as a fulcrum. The *Veritas* shifted but it was not enough.

"Here," said the boy, Davis. His face was blackened, his neck and shoulder burnt. "I can help."

And he grabbed the frame alongside her.

"Me too," said the gap-toothed man, Castlewaite.

"And me," said Carl.

"One, two, three," said Fanny, and together, they heaved the frame so that Franny slumped out of the seat. Fanny grabbed her by the arms and slid her out from under the car and into her lap.

"Ah can fetch Dr. Ferris," said Castlewaite. "He's in Milling, always on call."

"In what vehicle?" asked Fanny. "They're all destroyed."

"It's fine," said Franny, and she smiled under her sister's tender hand. "I'm fine."

"You are fine, dearest," said Fanny, eyes stinging. "You are the finest in all of Lancashire."

"My legs are still there, yes?"

Fanny looked along her sister's battered body. Skirts tattered, stockings red with blood. There was no movement from Franny's body at all and her throat grew tight.

"Quite there," she said thinly. "Although Granny will fuss about the mud."

"I like mud," said Lizzie.

A distant explosion echoed across the fields and wearily, they all looked toward Lasingstoke, where a cloud of flames and smoke billowed into the sky above the Hall.

"Oh, gadzooks," said Fanny. "I simply don't have the heart."

"Oy," said Castlewaite. "And o'er yonder."

He gestured with his bristled chin to the road to Over Milling.

"Bloody hell," said Carl.

"Curses," said Fanny and her heart sank. "I forgot about them."

"We're right pinned," muttered Davis.

Not quite a half mile away, six new Sentinels now stood at the far corner of the wall that marked the estate. Their eye beams flashed but they made no sound. In fact, all was silent, save the growl of a steamcar approaching through the fog.

It growled and roared until it rolled to a stop in front of them all.

"Cor," said Davis.

"Oooh look, Fanny," breathed Franny. "It has eight wheels…"

An elegant door swung open, a walking stick hit the ground, and Crown Prince Edward stepped out of the car.

***

Anton Boudin was a serious man, strict and self-disciplined and very, very thorough, so this search of an old English manor for an even older French locket was a satisfying task. His men had been sent out to comb the houses and while he had some faith in their abilities, he knew it would ultimately be up to him to bring the locket back to his superiors. It would be a painstaking process and likely take far longer than they had hoped, but he had his methods, his understanding of human psychologies, and he knew that if anyone could find it, it would be him.

He looked around the master bedroom. His search had been quite detailed, and now, he stood at the mullioned window, holding a framed photochrome in his hand. A woman was wearing the locket – the same woman and the same locket from the original chrome he'd snatched from the old manservant in Kensington. That had been far too easy. This would be much harder.

Slowly, he slit open the back of the frame and slid the chrome from its nest. He took one last look at it. It was a wedding photo, both man and woman wearing lockets. The man looked to be the same as the one standing in the courtyard, so he tucked the chrome into his coat. He would need to question the man further. It would be an enjoyable process.

There was motion from the window, and he glanced out. Another woman was headed toward the airship and the lord of the manor. He watched, amused then alarmed, as the pair of them quickly dispatched his three associates, then flinched as the airship gondola suddenly burst into a brilliant, bloody firestorm. Alarm turned to horror as flames swept through the gondola and raced up the canvas rigging. He threw himself from the window as, within moments, the entire balloon erupted, shaking the very manor house to its foundations, shattering the window's glass and twisting the leaded canes inward.

Boudin rolled himself up from the floor and sprinted out the door.

***

Dust rained down from the ceiling and shook the stones of the walls. It had snuffed out the wall sconce and Lottie was grateful they had left the door at the top of the stairs open. They ducked and pressed themselves against the narrow walls as a second explosion rocked the very foundations of the Hall.

***

She took a deep breath and looked over her shoulder. He was a silhouette in the foggy doorway, great coat billowing in the unnatural winds. But the lockets flashed from his eyes. Ghostlight was gold, Arclight blue, and in her hands, Mumford's face beamed white between the woollen threads.

The ice swept across the floor, but now, there was no floor. It was black and hollow, a void that dropped to the centre of the earth and beyond. She lifted her head. There was no ceiling, no rafters, no beams. There was sky, stars, moons, galaxies. She looked around. There were no walls. There was vast, endless emptiness. Nothing. Gone. All being consumed by the ice that radiated at every step of the Mad Lord's feet.

"Sebastien," said Frankow. His voice was weak, strained, as his body hovered, held by Arclight's reality-bending power.

"Iudicatus es et inventus es minus habens."

Sebastien's voice was hollow and echoed as if across a great valley.

"Ano," said Frankow. *"Přijímám."*

"How many times?"

"It doesn't matter."

The wind began to pick up once more, and Ivy shivered as a chill swept up her spine. He was right next to her, and the terrifying Seventh House trembled in his shadow.

"How. Many. Times."

She didn't dare look at him, kept her eyes firmly fixed on Frankow, suspended ghoulishly above the floor that now rippled like an inky pool. She could see him close his lids, and her heart broke. *Odd.* She thought there hadn't been anything left to break.

"Thirteen," he said.

"How?"

"Sebast—"

"HOW?"

The wind roared and the psychiatrist was flung across the room, slamming into a wall that wasn't there. He hung, rigid and stretched, arms wide, legs twisted, teeth gritted against the pain.

"You were seven," he croaked, his voice thin and stretched. "Something about chasing swans into the pond. Your father pulled you out and brought you to me at Lonsdale. There was no harm. You were already dead."

Slowly, Ivy looked up at the man standing beside her. His fingers were blackened, his fair hair wild and tipped with ice, and she could see sweat droplets frozen on his brow. But the lockets flashed inside his eye sockets, and she knew he could see nothing through them.

Nothing, and yet, everything.

"It worked," Frankow said. "The electrical currents stimulated the antimony I injected into your veins, and you lived. That was the first time."

"Twelve more times?" Sebastien asked, "Twelve more times before that night?"

"If we do the math—"

"You killed me twelve times in three years!"

Tears spilled from Frankow's goggled eyes now, ran down his face.

"Answer me!"

"Yes," he said. "God forgive me, but yes."

"God will not forgive you," said Sebastien. "I will see to that."

The lockets were flashing in harmony now, like a heartbeat and Mumford trembled in response. She clutched him tighter, as if her arms could contain a hurricane or tidal wave. As if her arms could do anything at all.

"Was I afraid?"

"…my god…"

"Was I?"

Frankow struggled with his breath, with the tears pooling inside the goggles.

"Yes," he said. "Most times, I think you were."

She broke anew at the thought.

"Please, kill me now, and find your peace," said Frankow. "I deserve any death you give me, after all I have given you."

"One last question."

Frankow nodded. The Mad Lord's hands curled into fists, but Ivy saw the tiniest twitch of his jaw, the quiver in his chin.

"Anything."

"Why?"

"Why?" asked Frankow. "Why did we bring you back?"

"Why did you do it?"

"Death is the final doorway, the last, best, worst leg in the race of humanity. It's every physician's quest, to find a cure for death—"

"*TO ME?!*"

He drew in a shuddering breath, and then another.

"Why did you do it to *me?!*"

"I'm sorry…"

"Why me, Arvin? Why?"

"…my boy…"

"Was it because I was so very bad?"

"No…"

"I know I was bad. Father always said it, and Mother always wept."

"No, Sebastien! No! It wasn't because you were bad. It was because you could! You lived! You, with your bright spark and big heart, you lived! Your courage and boldness and absolute lack of fear! You lived! And you kept living, time and time again! You were so strong and so brave, and we couldn't believe that somehow you were the key to answering the biggest question of the ages! Young Master de Lacey! You were a miracle!"

Ivy's own tears were making a puddle at her knees.

"Your father had been hunting ghosts with that locket for so many years. In fact, it was what drew your mother to him. She was fascinated by the spirit world, by life, death and those in-between. At first, she was delighted that you had this power, her little boy, the light of her life, but it changed after the third time. She said no more, but your father was obligated to the Ghost Club. They funded my work at Lonsdale. All the good I was doing was paid for as long as I helped them in their 'special investigations' into life, death, and those in-between. Soon, your father began to hate you because your mother loved you so very much. It became a problem between them…"

She saw the furrows in the Mad Lord's brow, the tears that froze the moment they spilled from his lashes.

"I think he began to kill you so I wouldn't be able to bring you back. But I did. Every time. That's why I set up my laboratory here. This was *her* house, the special place he gave her to host teas and invite friends and have long afternoons with books and solitude and prayer. It was very pretty, once. So very pretty…"

Frankow struggled with breath. He was still bleeding from the claws in the ceiling.

"She gave it to me so I could help sooner, bring you back sooner. And each time you lived, I think he died a little. He needed Ghostlight by then, like the opium or the laudanum. He couldn't think without the locket, and it twisted him into very different shapes. He was not the man I knew. Not the man your mother married."

"A monster," said Sebastien.

"Yes," said Frankow. "A monster hunting monsters."

"Like me."

The silence was deafening.

Suddenly, Frankow's body crumpled to the floor. It splashed like inky water.

Ivy gasped.

But he pushed himself to his knees and slid the goggles up onto his forehead.

"I saved you, Sebastien," he said. "And Sophie, and many others whom I shouldn't have, because I couldn't save my own son. His name was Bohdan. He wasn't yet two years. He died of the Scarlet Fever. In my arms, no less. In my arms."

"Bohdan," said Sebastien.

"Yes, my boy. My first boy. He was a miracle. Like you. Like all little ones, to be truthful. My wife could not live without him, much like your mother, Miss Savage. She drowned herself in the Vltava soon after and I buried them both together in the same grave. It was not allowed. An abomination, the church said, but still, I knew it was what she would have wanted."

"All these years and you've never mentioned him."

"I'm sorry, my boy. The memories bring with them pain."

"If I end of the world," said Sebastien after a long moment. "Then the pain of that memory will go away."

"But so will the memory of Bohdan," said Frankow.

"And so will the hope," said Ivy, her first words since he'd made his entrance, and she was surprised she had a voice. She looked up at him. "So will the hope."

"Hope…" It froze on his lips, like the tears. "I know nothing of hope anymore."

"Yes, Laury. Hope." She struggled to her feet, still clutching the stuffed dog to her chest. "These are the things we still live for. Hope, life, love."

He looked at her and the lockets whirred.

"Horses and carriage rides," she said. "Sunsets and sunrises. Warm rain. Hot tea."

"Scotch," he said.

She smiled.

"Scotch," she said. "Raspberry tarts fresh from Cookie's oven."

"Eggs for dinner."

"Upside-down days."

"Friends?"

Her heart thudded, and she stepped toward him.

"And lovers."

"I wouldn't know," he said, and he stepped back. "I can't stop it, Ivy."

"In fact, only you can."

He stepped back again, cast his otherworldly eyes all around Seventh. The starry ceiling and the inky floor, the nebulous walls and the smoky wraiths, hovering around the edges like mist on a pond. Reaching, cloying, shrinking, billowing.

"I don't want to stop it."

"I think you do," she said. "I think you just want to stop the pain."

"I just killed my dog."

"Oh." Her heart. "Tag."

"I didn't mean to," he said, his voice tightening. "I loved him."

"And he loved you."

"He was a very good dog."

"And you have five other very good dogs who love you and need you just as much. More now, without Tag. Don't leave them, Laury. Don't do that to them."

She took a deep breath.

"Remember you once told me *Every day spent living is a good day.* You told me that. I believed you."

"But I'm not living."

"Then it's not a good day," she said. "So, change it."

He was trembling now.

"How do I change it? They control everything—"

"They don't."

"They do. I've tried. Since Calais I've tried."

"Well," she said. "Let's try something different."

And she reached out her hand.

"No," he said. "You'll shatter like the stag. You'll die like…"

His words failed.

"If you die…"

"Then you'll bring me back, like you did in Vienna."

"I tried with the stag. I tried with Tag. I—" He winced, shook his head, hand moving up to his left temple where Arclight throbbed with power. But Mumford pulsed within her grasp, and she noticed Arclight dim. Slowly, he found his breath.

And she knew.

"I tried," he said quietly.

Mumford healed.

"I wish—"

Lostlight healed, and if she did, perhaps there was a way after all.

"Don't wish," she said. "Just do."

She offered her hand again, and trembling, his hand moved toward it. Their fingertips brushed and she made a fist, feeling the shock.

"You see?"

"No," she said. "It's just cold."

She took a deep breath and took his hand in hers.

The cold shot from her palm up to her elbow, then her shoulders, then her throat. She clenched her eyes, gritted her teeth but held on as he tried to pull away. Cold, cold, brutal, bitter cold. She was going to shatter into a thousand pieces, just like the dog, the dog, Mumford the dog. Mumford was glowing like a star. Like the sun. Mumford was Lostlight, and Mumford was warm. She leaned into him, called him, and pulled the Mad Lord closer. Sent the warmth from the woollen into his body through her own. The knitted dog made for him by his mother. *Jane, help me*, she thought, and she pulled him closer. Reached up with Mumford to caress his frozen cheek and he closed his eyes at the touch. *Jane, help me*. Tears spilled from his lashes, but they did not freeze. *Jane, help me*.

They did not freeze.

Lostlight, come home.

You are life, Miss Savage.

And she pushed up on her very fine boots and kissed him.

Long and deep, deliberate and sweet, she kissed him, and with that touch, she sent warmth and love and hope and life into his weary bones, chasing the frost with light, banishing the ice and the cold and the despair. His hands slid into her hair, cradling her head, discovering her back. *You are life, Miss Savage.* And suddenly, she knew it, beyond all shadow, beyond all doubt. Of all the powers in the metaphysical, parapsychical universe, Lostlight was life.

Not ghosts, not death, not time and place. Life.

Lostlight was life.

She looked up at him. His eyes were still closed, as if trying to keep the taste of her on his tongue. She laid a hand on his chest, validated to feel a heartbeat beneath her palm. He stepped away now, turned his back, and covered his face with his hands. Lights flashed and Seventh reflected them, mirroring Sebastien within her very batten and board. The galaxies above parted and lightning cracked across the ceiling/sky. The foundations rumbled beneath her boots and molten lava curdled in the very depths of the cellar. The walls breathed in and out, in and out, like stone lungs filled with cinders and the wraiths hovered between them all, caught between life and death and the Mad Lord of Lasingstoke.

He turned back to her and held out his hands. In his palms were the lockets, Ghostlight and Arclight, sparkling but still. She studied his face, the gaunt cheeks and sallow skin, his eyes bloodshot and cracked, but no clockwork in sight.

Her own tears spilled.

"Brown," she said with a sob. "Your eyes are brown."

She could have knocked him over with a feather.

"Why do you have Mumford?" he asked in a voice as thin as leaf in autumn.

She looked down at the knitted dog.

"It's a long story," she said and held him up.

In his hands, the lockets began to spark, and with a growl, Sebastien flung them away. They bounced and clattered their way across the floor, becoming little more than gems in a starry corner.

He took Mumford from her, squeezing the brown wool with blackened fingers. At that moment, there was a click, and Seventh's door opened inward. In one swift motion, Sebastien pulled the tri-barrelled pistol from his back and swung it toward a figure in the doorway.

"I won't shoot if you don't," said Christien, and he lowered his rifle-arm. "Where are the lockets? And what the bloody hell is going on with this House?"

Chapter 20
The Other Side of Everything

"The whole series of my life appeared to me as a dream; I sometimes doubted if indeed it were all true, for it never presented itself to my mind with the force of reality."
- Mary Shelley, Frankenstein: The Modern Prometheus

The vanguard rifle was a brilliant piece of work, Rupert thought to himself. The trigger was sensitive, the projectiles not-quite-bullets, and the scope was an oscillating lens that practically did the aiming for you. He was aiming now as a pair of thugs rushed out of Second and into the courtyard.

He squeezed the trigger, ever so gently changing his angle, and the two men went down, convulsing and twitching as the not-quite-bullets sent voltage throughout their bodies. After a long moment, they lay still.

"Some pumpkins, luv," said Mary Jane. "Two in one go."

"Bloody lethal, this is," he muttered.

The Vanguard dreadnought continued to burn fiercely, sparks spilling over the cobbled yard. A mechanical alarm had sounded as flames caught the dry winter ivy to race up the estate's stone walls. VINCE the automaton rolled out from the stores and his head popped open to produce a hose. In vain, he began to spray the walls, but it was a thin stream and did little to stop the rushing flames.

Servants began to file out from all exits, and St. John squinted, waiting for the telltale black uniforms to present themselves. He had just taken out two, along with the three that he and Mary Jane had dispatched earlier. That left perhaps twelve, along with their goggled leader, and he wondered if the sweepers had managed to dispatch any others.

He wiped his brow and frowned. The smoke from the airship was clearly blowing their way.

"Ruby," said Mary Jane. "Ruby, luv. Look."

He turned.

"Damnations."

The workshop was on fire.

***

"What the bloody hell?" asked Christien as he stepped into the house. He gazed around with wide eyes. "Has Seventh always looked like this?"

Ivy looked up at the ceiling/sky. Rafters flickered into planets, beams became nebulae, which became coffers which became trusses. The floor swirled its surfaces, black pool alternating between stone, wood, tile, dirt and gaping chasm to a lava-ringed hell. The tables, chairs, vials and staircase blinked from blackness to solid. But perhaps most terrifying were the wraiths that threatened with smoke and fury as they crawled between the spaces with ashen hands.

"Sometimes," said Sebastien. "When I'm releasing the women, yes, it looks like this. It can't make up its mind."

"The outside is bloody bursting," said Christien. "It looks like an explosion that's happening yet not happening at the same time."

"Arclight?" said Ivy. "She controls time and place. Perhaps she can freeze it as well."

"How did you get here?" asked Sebastien.

"It's a very long story," said Christien. "Bertie's been in the thick of it all along, but I think he's trying to clean up the mess."

"The Ghost Club," said Frankow in a feeble voice. He was struggling to stand, and Ivy rushed to his side to help him. "The Ghost Club and the War Office and the Crown. That is an unholy alliance, and they would stop at nothing to get the lockets for themselves."

He squinted at Christien.

"Is that deWinter's journal?"

"It is, indeed," Christien said, and he held it up. "And it says the lockets can't touch each other otherwise some sort of devastating reaction is unleashed."

Ivy looked at Sebastien, and they both looked to the dark corner where he had flung them. Sparks flew as two dots of light now circled each other inches above the floor. In fact, they were orbiting each other, spinning rings with celestial tails, creating a hole of absolute blackness between them. The hole was about the size of an apple, but as the lockets spun, it began to grow.

"Blast," said Sebastien.

"My God," breathed Christien. "Arclight *was* a White Hole…"

"I think she's a black hole, now," said the Mad Lord.

On one of the many tables, a tray of glass tubes shook and whipped from its place across the room. It disappeared inside the hole without even a flash. A chair began to slide across the floor next.

"Not again," said Ivy, remembering the horror of St. Katharine's Docks, when Ghostlight turned the engine house into gold and sunk the entire pier into the Thames.

"A Black Hole," said Christien, as he flipped through the pages of the journal. "deWinter says it's like an invisible star…"

"Ah, that's from Michell," said Frankow. "John Michell's writings from 1783. He was a pioneer in the astronomical realm, a true mathematician and theologian."

"But what does it mean?" asked Ivy. The winds had picked up again and the hole was now the size of a pumpkin. Bits of paper and glass whipped into it, to disappear entirely from sight.

"From what I understand," said Frankow, "Whatever goes in, never comes out. Not even light."

"According to deWinter, the lockets are triggered or activated by antimony," said Christien.

"Is that why Laury is the key?" asked Ivy. "Because you injected him with antimony as a child?"

"Well, yes," said Frankow. "That and…"

All eyes fell upon him.

"And?" said Sebastien.

"And well, your skull."

"My skull."

"But that's aluminium," said Christien.

"Not exactly," said Frankow.

"My skull is antimony?" Sebastien croaked. "Another lie?"

"Laced with antimony, yes," Frankow said. "You had an affinity for it, and I hoped your body would not reject the metal."

Seventh House shuddered as paintings were sucked from the walls to disappear into vortex caused by the spinning orbs. Electricity arced from surface to surface, and the wind howled like a thousand banshees.

"Bastien, can you close it?" shouted Christien.

Sebastien glanced at him and released a breath. He flexed his hands and turned to the corner. His hair and great coat whipped as he crossed the now wooden floor toward it.

"Wait," said Ivy. "Laury, give me Mumford."

"Mumford?" asked Christien. "Why the hell is Mumford here?"

Ivy swung around and glared at him, eyes wide and intense.

"Oh God," said Christien.

"Laury, I need Mumford," she said firmly.

She crossed the floor toward the Mad Lord, careful not to lose her footing. The spinning orb was the size of a sheep now, a fat round black sheep, and the bookcases tipped as their contents were plucked from the shelves.

Sebastien turned, holding out the knitted dog, but Mumford jerked in his grip toward the orb.

"Don't let go!" shouted Christien. "Bastien, it's truly the end if you let go."

"I don't understand!" Sebastien shouted back. "What's happening to

Mumford? Why do the lockets want him?"

"Laury, just give him to me."

"He's just Mumford."

"He's not," Ivy cried now, desperate to be heard over the growling wind. "Give him to me, Laury! Please, I'll keep him safe!"

White light beamed from Mumford's lost eye as the stuffing began to fray.

"Lostlight?" asked Sebastien and he cocked his head. "Is Mumford…Lostlight?"

"Give him to me," shouted Ivy.

"Give him to Ivy," shouted Christien. "Bastien, get him away from that black hole!"

But the Mad Lord didn't hear him. He was lost in the shock and the light of a locket.

"Everything in my life is a lie," he said. "Even a stuffed dog. Everything."

Seventh shrieked now, as a beam from the ceiling swung down, slicing between them all. Ivy and Christien threw themselves to the floor, but Sebastien didn't move. The beam barely missed him as it snapped from its nails, swooped through the air like a pendulum and was swallowed whole by the star. Ghostlight and Arclight were brilliant and blinding, and electricity flashed like lightning in a storm.

"I should let it go," said the Mad Lord in a loud voice. "I should let it all go. Everything. Everyone. It's all a lie."

Slowly, Sebastien raised his arm, held Mumford out toward the hole. He was holding on by a tattered paw, and the wool was quickly unravelling.

"Love it not a lie, Laury!" Ivy shouted. "We love you, Laury. I love you and I know you love me. Don't let that go!"

The hole was the size of a window now, large enough for the tables and bookcases to hurtle through. The dismembered automaton slid across the floor and disappeared in a rush of wires and springs. Papers, glass, beakers, paintings; everything in Seventh was being swallowed in the lockets' gravity. Even the shadow wraiths who had been skulking in the timbers and beams of the building were pulled in, their gaping mouths wide, their smoky fingers clawing as they dissolved into the void.

The gravity of the lockets was pulling her toward the dark corner, and she struggled to her feet, hair wild in the vortex, arms flailing for balance. She turned to look at him and raised her quivering chin.

"If this is how the world is ending, then let me be the first to go," she said. "Goodbye, Laury. I'm sorry I wasn't enough for you. I couldn't reach high enough or write your story to a happier ending. I love you and I hope I'll see you on the other side. If not, well…this was your choice, not mine, and I'm afraid you'll have to carry that always. I can't carry it anymore."

He looked like he would shatter at another word, so she took a deep breath and turned back to the void.

"The end of the world starts with me," she breathed, and she took the first step.

Stones, tile, and wood from the floor were peeling up in layers, and she began to slide along with them toward the orb. There was nothing to stop her – no planks or seams, no furniture or edge. It was only dirt and sand and dust and terror. Her hair was whipping like a cat 'o nine, stinging her eyes and biting her cheeks. The void was freezing and black and her very breath was being sucked out of her body. She was going to die horribly, and the world was going to die horribly, and she covered her face with her arms to stifle the sobs. She wasn't enough. She'd never been enough. She'd been foolish to ever think otherwise. Hope was a pathetic illusion. A lie, like he'd said. She'd been a fool to believe.

Something stopped her.

She opened her eyes.

The void was still raging, bits of wood and tile whipping past her to disappear into its endless depths. She looked down. Sebastien's arm was around her waist, his boots securely planted on the mindless floor. The raging chaos that was Seventh House seemed to escape him entirely, and he drew her away from the black star, pulled her to stand at his side. She looked up at him but did not smile. He didn't fight as she took Mumford from his other hand.

"I don't want you to go," he said. "Please don't go."

"Stop this," she said.

He nodded.

"Christien," he said over the howls of the raging house. "How do I stop this?"

"I—I don't know," said his brother. "I haven't found that yet."

And he flipped the yellowed pages to the end, struggling to make it out in the darkness, while trying to keep a grip on the book.

"May I see?" asked Frankow.

Christien slid over to the psychiatrist, passed him the journal, and twisted his wrist. A pocket torch popped out, and he shone it on the parchment pages. Frankow began to read.

"I'm sorry, Ivy," Sebastien said after a moment. "I wish I hadn't gone to Vienna."

"Me too," she said.

"I wish I hadn't felt Arclight," he said.

"Me too," she said.

"Can you still love me, monster that I am?"

"You're not a monster," she said. "And I do still love you. I always will. But I want to stop taking care of someone. I want to be a partner, an equal, not a mother."

He nodded.

"I don't want to be chasing you anymore. I want to have you and trust you and be safe with you. Maybe go on an adventure that I lead for a change. And most of all, I want to live. Really live. Does that make sense?"

"I think I understand."

"Remember, every day spent living is a good day," she said. "I need you to remember that."

"I can't promise it will be easy," he said. "But I will try my very best."

"I can live with that," she said, and she wrapped her arms around his waist. "Remember in the gorse bushes, when you asked me what I wanted?

He nodded again, his eyes filling with tears. It seemed hard for him to speak. Perhaps it was hard for him to be human.

"Do you know?" he asked.

"I do," she said. "And here it is. *When* we find a way to stop this, I want to leave Lasingstoke. You and I. We leave it to Rupert and Mary Jane, and their new heir, whomever that will be. I want Christien to take up his calling in London, and live a happy settled life in Hollbrook House, maybe go on adventures from time to time with a certain Black Swan in Vienna. But you and I will leave here and go north. I'm not sure where. The

Orkneys, the Hebrides? Anywhere, just north—"

"Skye?" he asked.

She smiled now.

"Skye is perfect. And we have a little cottage and live together with sheep and horses—"

"Ponies are better in the north," he said.

"Ponies, then."

"And…" His voice caught. "And dogs?"

"As many as you'd like." She furrowed her brow. "It's more a wish than a want, really."

"It's a lovely wish," he said.

"Yes," she said. "It really is."

And she leaned her forehead against his. Despite the howling, raging Seventh House, it was nice.

"Ivy! Bastien!" called Christien. "We've found it!"

They turned and pushed their way through the winds to the side of the house. Christien looked up at them, his dark hair lifting, blue eyes bright.

"But it's not good."

"Someone needs to take the third locket through," said Frankow. "Close this hole from the other side."

"But what's on the other side?" asked Ivy.

"No one knows," said Frankow. "It's a mystery."

Sebastien looked down at her.

"It was a lovely wish," he said. "I will carry it always."

"No," said Ivy. "You can't go. You can't do it. It's not fair."

"I'm the only one who can," he said.

"I won't let you," she said. "I won't let go. Not now. Not anymore."

"There's no escaping it, Ivy," he said. "I must finish what I started."

"This started long before you were born, Sebastien," said Frankow. "Long before even I was born. But of the four of us, I believe it is I who must finish that which was started. I created you, but I will not see you ended. This is on me, and me alone."

"You can't do it," said Sebastien. "You don't know how."

"Do you?"

There was no answer to that.

"There is only one way to find out. Besides," he pushed away from the wall, tugged down his vest and smoothed his great coat. It was a futile gesture, given the wind. "I would very much like to explore this new place. Imagine the scientific possibilities. Why, I may even meet my Jelena and Bohdan again…"

"Arvin, no." The Mad Lord put his hands on the doctor's shoulders. "I'm sorry, but no. I won't allow it."

"Sebastien, you may sit in the House of Lords," he said, "But I regret to say that you are not the boss of me."

And his lips quirked. As close to a smile as he ever came, Ivy thought.

The man turned.

"Miss Savage, I believe you have the last locket?"

"Wait," said Sebastien. "I need him, one last time."

She looked up at him. At some point, she had to trust.

She held Mumford up, and he took it in his hands, squeezed the tattered belly, stroked the nubby nose.

"He was my anchor," he said after a moment. "A beacon of light in my horrible dark world. He taught me to speak, to think, to be. He was the last piece of my mother that I would ever know, and I was safe when he was near. It's only fitting that Mumford saves my world once again."

He leaned his forehead against the curve of brown wool, held him as though he'd never let him go. Tears brimmed in his eyes as, finally, he passed the stuffed dog to Frankow.

"I will take good care of him, Sebastien. I promise."

"Please be safe, Arvin."

"As safe as a man can be on the other side of everything."

And the two men embraced. It was an entire lifetime in a matter of moments, until Frankow pulled away.

"I loved you like my own son," he said. He stood on tiptoe to kiss the Mad Lord on the forehead. "Live and be happy and make others so."

"Memento vivere," said Sebastien.

"Ano," said Frankow. "My boy."

He stepped away then and took a deep breath, and another. Then, he turned and crossed the sliding dirt floor toward the orb. It was the size of a carriage now, swimming with inky colour like the surface of a stagnant pond, and the electrical arcs spun around it the same way the rings spun around the lockets. Light beamed from Mumford's button eyes and the criss-cross thread that was his mouth. The light was so brilliant, spilling from the stuffed toy that Arvin Frankow was little more than an outline in front of the gaping darkness that was the orb. The stripped ceiling and walls of Seventh shuddered as he neared and the arcs crackled into emptiness, nowhere to go.

Ghostlight and Arclight slowed their orbits as they prepared to welcome their sister home.

Through the blinding Lostlight, Ivy could see Frankow square his shoulders, and she held her breath as the sister lockets ceased their spinning. He clutched Mumford to his chest and stepped through. He was swallowed immediately in darkness.

All sound ceased.

All wind died.

All light faded, dimmed, flickered as the orb at the centre of the Seventh House died.

It shrank to a pinprick within the blink of an eye, bringing Ghostlight and Arclight with it. They slammed together and buzzed for a moment, before clattering to the ground and rolling on the floor until they stopped in a corner of the room. One.

One locket made from two. Or was it three?

There was silence for a long moment as the rings adjusted their orbits, growing tighter and faster until they too popped out of existence. Ivy gazed up and around at what was left of Seventh House. Most of the rafters were gone, and she could see an eerie green sky above them. The floor was earth and stone, save where tiles pushed up between, and the staircase hung like a ladder from post and board and beam. Entire walls were gone, peeled away like orange rinds, and she could see shattered rooms behind the boards. Trees waved their bare branches through ghostly walls.

But then again, this was Seventh, the House that could not make up its mind. She didn't know what was real and what was illusion, but perhaps, that was just the nature of Seventh. It was a house in-between.

She looked up at the Mad Lord. He hadn't moved his eyes from where the black hole had been. In fact, he hadn't moved. It was as if he was frozen, a statue carved from lifelike wax.

"Laury?" she asked.

He said nothing.

"Laury, are you alright?"

"It's so quiet," he said, his voice little more than a whisper. "I daren't believe it."

She slipped her hand in his.

"I'm so afraid," he said, "That if I move, I'll shatter like glass."

"We don't have to move," she said.

"I'm afraid we do," said Christien and they looked over at him. "There are six of Bertie's Sentinels coming to blow Seventh House out of existence and us with it, if we're still inside."

Sebastien looked down at his hands.

"I don't think I can stop them anymore."

"Then we should leave and let them do it, then."

There was a sound.

As one, they turned their heads.

In the corner, the lone locket began to move.

"What the hell?" asked Christien.

The locket began to dart across the stony ground, scraping the dirt and stone and sending sparks into the air above it.

"What the bloody hell?" asked Christien again.

"Is that a letter?" asked Ivy. "Two, three…"

"It's spelling something," said Christien. "But what the hell is it?"

Sparks leapt into the air as the locket scratched five letters into the stone, spun for a moment on its axis, then stopped.

E X I R E

"It's Latin," said Sebastien. "It's from Arvin."

"Can you read it?" asked Ivy.

"Yes," said Sebastien.

"What does it say?"

"Exire."

"Good God, Bastien," groaned Christien. "What the bloody hell does it *mean?"*

"Oh."

The Mad Lord cocked his head, furrowed his brow.

"Get out."

"Get out? It means 'Get out'?"

"Yes. It means 'Get out'."

Slowly now, the locket began to spin once more, familiar black tendrils escaping from its singular gem. The wraiths rose into the air once again, swirling like a twister, reaching for them with ghostly hands. Christien took a step back.

"I think we should listen to Arvin Frankow," he said.

Together, they turned and rushed to the entryway. Sebastien flung open the door to see a Sentinel, raising its rocket arm. There was a deafening roar, a blinding flash, and Seventh House shattered under the blast.

Chapter 21

Of Rockets, Wraiths, and the Horses of Seventh

"Thus, strangely are our souls constructed, and by slight ligaments are we bound to prosperity and ruin."
– Mary Shelley, Frankenstein: The Modern Prometheus

St. John and Mary Jane stumbled out of the workshop as black smoke billowed out from the gaping geared doorway. He immediately slowed, hiking the rifle up as the goggled man stepped out from the opposite door and into the courtyard. Servants rushed toward the stables and away from the two men.

"You're stranded," St. John barked across the cobbles. "Your men are dispatched, and your airship is…"

He sent a glance over the sizzling smoking hulk, convulsing and deflated on the estate's low wall.

"…similarly inclined."

"Then I will kill all of you," said the man. "And my thirst for vengeance will be satisfied."

"Or you could just head to the pub in Over Milling," said Rupert. "And satisfy a very different kind of thirst. Slip away from this life of killing, find a plucky woman, settle down and be content. No one will ever find you."

"Where is the locket?"

"It's not worth it."

"Where is the locket?"

And he hiked his rifle.

"Not on this estate," said Rupert, and he hiked his. "It's likely in Lonsdale Abbey on Wharcombe Bay."

The smoke was stinging his eyes, and he noticed VINCE's head spin slowly on its copper body.

"Unless it's buried with Jane in the cemetery in the northwest corner."

VINCE sprayed water on the walls, the storeroom door, the cobbled ground.

"But it's just as likely in London or Paris or Eccleston, for that matter. You'll have no luck searching six hundred acres on your own now that your men are gone."

VINCE spun once again, his hose spraying water across the man's shoe. The man gritted his teeth, tightened his grip on the rifle. Water sprayed up his leg now, and he kicked to the side. VINCE clanked but continued to spray.

"Make your machine stop," he growled. "Or I'll shoot your woman."

Mary Jane slipped behind him, tucked herself behind his back.

"You'll have to shoot her through me and then you'll have absolutely nothing to go on. Besides…"

He glanced at VINCE, innocently spraying water in all the wrong places.

"I don't control him," said Rupert. "He's been malfunctioning for years."

Higher and higher, until soaking the man's arms and shoulder. He stepped back. VINCE spun toward him, aimed higher and sprayed water onto the face. He snarled at St. John.

"Robot," said Rupert with a shrug, and his eyes narrowed.

The man swung his rifle and shot VINCE's faceplate from point blank range. VINCE toppled backwards, sparks zapping and gears springing out of his head. At the same moment, there was another shot, and the man was flung in the opposite direction, hitting the cobbles with a thud. His goggles smoked as currents raced along his body and Mary Jane strode up to hit him again and again with the cane until his struggles ceased. Blood mixed with water between the cobbled stones and for a long moment, there was silence in the courtyard, save the crackle of flames and the sputter of dying machines.

It was then that they heard the rockets.

***

Rafters sliced down from the ceiling, and falling beams smashed everything in their paths. The ancient chandelier, unseen for most of the morning, swung wildly before crashing onto the floor and spraying glass in all directions like arrows. Wallpaper burned like tinder and flames raced up the walls. The paintings that remained melted under the heat and the last furnishings collapsed into ashen piles before being picked up in the wind.

Ivy rolled to her knees and wiped the soot out of her eyes. She glanced around to see both brothers unmoving on the ground, and she crawled over toward them. Christien's sleeve was on fire, and she batted it with her hands, ignoring the heat and the pain caused by the flames. He groaned and opened his eyes.

"Oh god," he moaned.

Alive.

She left him and crawled over to Sebastien, but the Sentinels boomed, and she threw herself over him as another rocket slammed into the house. Slabs of wood crashed all around, striking her back and head and hip, and she closed her eyes against the pain.

"Ivy!"

Her head was pounding, the world was swimming, but she pushed herself up. The wraiths were back, their smoky claws grabbing everything and pulling them towards the locket that spun in the centre of the room. Shattered tables, broken chairs, bits of stone, chunks of charred wood. Whatever was left of Seventh was a target. Just like the earlier 'black star,' everything the wraiths touched disappeared into the void.

"Ivy, move!"

Inky fingers were creeping her way, rolling like smoke, writhing like a snake.

"Laury, wake up," she moaned, and she shook his shoulders. "Laury."

The tendrils were almost at his boot.

Another boom and she threw herself over him once again, feeling the air burn as the rocket hurtled over her spine. But then there was silence.

"Bloody hell," she heard Christien say, and she risked a glance over her shoulder.

The tendrils had caught the rocket, and they held it, sputtering and hissing, in midair. Smoke coiled all around it until it was completely hidden, and they began to shrink back to the locket, taking the projectile with them.

It disappeared inside it with barely a puff.

"*Cor*," she whispered.

Beneath her, the Mad Lord stirred, pulled a bloody hand over his eyes. Christien knelt beside them both.

"Stay down," he said. "It's about to get ugly."

"Welcome to Seventh," muttered Sebastien.

She could hear the rumble of many Sentinels, so when he wrapped an arm around her, she buried her face in his great coat. Seventh shrieked and thundered under a rain of rockets. But there was no crash, no boom, no shattering of stone, but rather, something else, something utterly otherworldly. It was a sound of a very different sort, and she released an incredulous breath. The lockets were singing a song for their lost sister newly home. It was a shrill, piercing sound at three distinct but dissonant frequencies and contrasting pitch. It was a symphony, as one after the other, the wraith tendrils caught and swallowed each rocket, feeding the sisters with unfathomable power.

Surely, that did not bode well, she thought, and sure enough, the foundations of Seventh itself began to tremble.

She risked a glance up to see great, gaping holes in the fabric of the house. The walls were mere timbers, the ceiling mere planks, and through them, she could see flashes of iron and copper and steel of the Sentinels surrounding the house. There was no way they could survive if they stayed, but getting out would require supernatural effort.

Then again, this was Seventh.

The tremble birthed a roar and smoke burst forth from the locket like a giant arm, rushing out the shattered door into the metal chest of a Sentinel.

"Damnations," said Christien. "To the wall."

They rolled to their feet and scrambled across the floor as the fingers wrapped the Sentinel in black smoke and dragged it, screeching and smashing, through the very front of the house. Timber and window glass shattered in its path, before it was spun around and around and around. Ivy swore it was shrinking when suddenly, the locket swallowed it whole.

A second massive twister burst from the locket and out of the house, catching and dragging another mecha-man into the house and the crushing void of blackness. The very air wavered and the ground beneath their feet began to pulse like a heartbeat.

So very much like St. Katharine's Docks.

"I'd like to leave now," said Sebastien.

"Crackerjack," said Ivy.

They scrambled to their feet and rushed out the gaping doorway to the once silent wood. All around, trees had been felled and flattened and three Sentinels towered over them all, their red eyes locked on the black timbers of Seventh. Only one iron helm tracked them as they raced past them down the path, but a wild ribbon of smoke snagged its thorax and dragged it into the house.

She could hear barking as they approached the edge of the wood.

"The dogs!" shouted Sebastien, and he skidded to a stop at a thick ring of ice. He leapt over the Deadwall fence, and dropped to his knees, finally able to be smothered in the kisses he'd so long missed. Ivy grabbed Rue's reins and spun on Christien.

"What the bloody hell?" he barked. "Forget the horse. We have to go, or those things will suck us up next!"

She shoved the reins into his hand.

"Well, get on and ride off, then," he growled. "At least one of us can live."

She pulled the saddle off and tossed it to the grass. She unbuckled the bridle and slipped the mare free.

"Go," she said, and slapped the bay backside. The horse needed no encouragement and bolted off into the field.

"Oh god," grumbled Christien, as his brother shoved a dog into his arms. "I'm not carrying a bloody wolfhound next. Just a moment."

He dropped Dickie to the grass.

"Stand back, Bastien. Watch the bloody dogs."

With a roll of his shoulder, a rifle popped out. He aimed the muzzle at the base of the ice wall and fired. It cracked, split and fell away into a hundred pieces, and the dogs rushed out like a wagging wave.

"I didn't kill them," Sebastien said. "Look! They're still alive."

"You're free," said Ivy.

"Am I?"

"I'm sure of it."

And he smiled like the sun.

"Let's run, shall we?" asked Christien.

The screech of a fourth Sentinel announced its demise as they raced out of the trees and onto the field, followed by the pack of five. Finally, they slowed at the base of an old oak to catch their breath. Ivy turned to watch as red beams sliced the sky, then were silenced as a fifth Sentinel was pulled into nothingness.

"I thought you said six?" she panted, hands on knees, breaths coming in ragged gasps.

"You think I'm bloody well counting?" Christien asked. "There were six. Now there's five. I have no idea what's going on."

"Welcome to Seventh," Sebastien said again.

The sky itself was collapsing, now, funnelling like a green twister through what was left of the roof of Seventh, and the timber walls pulsated as if made of rubber. It was a heartbeat now, the heartbeat of lockets, of black holes and white holes and antimony and angels. Of time and place and Latin and life. The roar was deafening, and Ivy clapped her hands over her ears, stunned to watch as the great black tendrils moved like fingers, grabbing the very walls of Seventh House and pulling them inward. They burst out to clutch the remaining roof tiles and draw them in upon itself. Rafters, beams, planks and stone, tile, tables, chairs and tubes became a quivering pile of rubble on the ground. Still, the tendrils worked, plucking and sucking all remnants into the locket pit, until even that was gone. Soon, all that was left was a few pieces of cold stone, ivy, and an eerie green mist hovering over it all.

A lone wraith snaked out of the pit. It slipped through the trees and rolled across the grass and reached its smoky fingers across the field toward them like a serpent. Ivy had no strength to move, no will to run. Her legs were shaking, her breathing ragged. She watched numbly as it paused, mouth gaping, eyes hollow. Slowly, it rose like a cobra before them.

"What does it want?" she whispered.

"Me," said Sebastien.

***

They had piled the eleven Vanguardsmen into the courtyard, alongside the body of the lead man. Three had been dispatched by Rupert's walking stick, two from the vanguard rifle, four from the sweepers in the house and one from Cookie's frying pan. Apparently, there were three others locked in the gold cellar. It seemed like it added up but then again, he wasn't certain how many had originally marched down the ramp.

Several of those laying in the courtyard were, in fact, dead. Those that weren't, were bound securely with copper wire and butcher's twine. It surprised him at how well they had rallied, how fiercely they had defended this place, and he felt a wave of pride as he watched the staff rush to collect buckets and hoses in attempt to put out the many, many fires.

The chaos from Seventh echoed from a mile away, over the fields and pastures of the estate. The sun was burning away the fog, and he knew that, while it would bring a new day, nothing would ever be the same again. His heart broke for his nephews, praying that at least one of them would survive this morning. In fact, the roars from Seventh were growing louder, and it was a dread symphony with the crackle, thunder and hiss of the fires still raging at the Hall. But now, over it all, he heard another sound, this one distinct and maddening and it filled him with furious dread.

The *whup-whup-whup* of an airship.

Mary Jane looked over at him from across the courtyard. She looked exhausted as she pitched the water buckets onto the machine shed. She was covered in soot, but not deterred, and she nodded swiftly before turning back to the flames.

The underbelly of an airship came into view over the gothic rooftops of Second and with a deep breath, Rupert raised the rifle, prepared to send a shot into yet another canvas. He froze, however, when he saw the double eagles on the Gilded sails.

"Habsburgs," he growled and lowered his weapon. "Always so bloody dramatic."

The propellers *whup-whup-whupped* like a heartbeat as a powerful spray of water struck the machine shed. A lone Sentinel loomed beyond the courtyard wall, water hoses reticulating from its iron chest, and an eight-wheeled steamcar roared into the courtyard.

***

"Me," said Sebastien.

"No," she said. "Not after all this."

She was so very pretty, he thought to himself. Even after all she'd been through in London, Vienna, Strasbourg, and here. Pretty and plucky and proud. He'd been a fool to think it could have worked.

"It was a good wish," he said quietly.

"No, I refuse," she growled. "This time, I refuse. I won't lose you again. No."

"Live, Ivy Savage," he said, feeling the tears sting behind his eyes once more. "Really live."

He released a deep breath and this time, he felt it.

"It's not fair!" she shouted.

He turned to the wraith.

"Laury, please no!" She lunged for him, but Christien grabbed her and hauled her back. She flailed in his arms, kicking and twisting but the clockwork grip was like a vice. "Laury, don't! Please God, don't! It's not fair!"

He offered his hand, freely and the shadows closed in.

At the wraith's touch, the shock rattled his teeth. The cold shot up through his bones, froze his throat and brain, and he staggered under the pain. His breathing grew ragged as the inky tendrils wrapped around his palm, between his fingers, and along his wrist, bringing wave after wave of agony along with them. The wraiths were pulling his insides out, pulsing his veins, flooding his very core with pestilence and disease, famine and decay. He cried out as a shadow was ripped from his very flesh. A shadow of black hooves and red eyes and a mane like a thousand stinging scorpions. The Black Horse of Melk leapt from him and hit the ground running.

"My god," breathed Christien.

The horse thundered toward Seventh, leaving sooty hoofprints in its wake.

The wraiths advanced up his arm, this time bringing the heat, scorching his skin and flaying flesh from bone. Flames raged behind his eyes and boiled his blood. His knees buckled and he cried out as it seared his very heart inside his chest. A shadow ripped from him once again, this time red as fire and passion and rage, eyes like embers in a hearth, tail of blood and blaze, madness and war. The Red Horse of Strasbourg reared on its fiery legs and leapt from his body, bolting across the field and setting fire to the grass as it went.

He sank to his knees.

"One more," he panted. "Just one more."

The wraith held him still, didn't advance, didn't retreat, smoke and soot lifting from his body and falling from his eyes like ash.

"Do it," he said.

Lifting, falling, waiting, waiting.

"Do it!" he cried.

 It did, sending the blackness up his chest, his throat, his brain. He closed his eyes as lights flashed and stars exploded, and the very sun burst him in two. White heat, white frost, cold like space and the Deadspace and everything in between. Lies, deceit, false peace, delusion. Flashing swords and smiling teeth and beauty that lures to death. Cold heart, icy thoughts, and a shadow was crystallized, beautiful beyond all others, white as the moon, shining, waning, proud, vain. The White Horse of Vienna rippled to life, eyes of lust, mane of arrows, sharp and deadly and torn from him. The Spanish horse from an Austrian school, now racing toward the trees of Seventh.

He wanted to sleep. Sleep and never wake up or die and never rise. His body was done, spent, all of his bones broken, all of his tendons frayed, but the wraith surged onward, turning his shoulders black and coiling like a serpent down his other arm. Suddenly, it was heavy. *He* was heavy, weighted like an anchor and he dropped to his hands and knees on the icy grass. The smoky tendril crawled down the other arm to his wrist, then his fingers, until they sank deep into the ground, and the earth beneath them boomed.

"Oh god," said Christien.

Sebastien closed his eyes, feeling his thoughts sink down, down, down into the earth, through the dirt and the frost and the little squiggly roots, and a shape rippled from below. A pale shape of unformed things, of possible life and definite death and decay and tissue and maggots and bone.

Behind him, Ivy gasped as the pale horse emerged from the frosty earth, each hoof beat higher and higher until he was on level ground. There was no spectacle with Ash, no pretence or display. The horse simply did what it did, for reasons as deep and unfathomable as the sea.

The horse circled around and stood before the Mad Lord. He lowered his pale head and Sebastien leaned his forehead against the long nose.

"I'm sorry, Ash," he said. "I don't hate you. You were a good horse. A very good horse. I hope you find a better rider one day."

The horse grumbled and turned, strode away toward Seventh before disappearing into the trees.

With an unnatural sigh, the wraith withdrew its tendrils, releasing Sebastien and coiling back on itself like a cobra once again. Wisps of smoke floated from its amorphous shape, and it hovered, waiting, before them all.

"More?" asked Sebastien. "What more do you need? There's nothing left of me."

The wraith turned its snakelike body toward Christien.

The physician sighed.

"Well," he said. "I suppose it's time the bill comes due."

And he held out his hand of flesh.

The tendrils smoked and floated, hovered and waited.

"No?"

He offered the other one, the miracle of clockwork and steam.

Nothing.

"I don't understand…"

Ivy turned to Christien.

"Remy, do you still have that journal?"

He blinked at her for a long moment but reached into his coat and drew it out.

"I didn't know I still had that thing."

He swallowed and tentatively held out the journal. Inky fingers took it, engulfed it completely, and began to slip away, back the way they had come, flowing between the trees, rumbling through the wood, back to the House of Seventh. Then, there was silence.

They waited for what seemed like forever, before helping the Mad Lord to his feet. Slowly, dreadfully, they made their way back through the felled trees and torn earth toward Seventh.

In the place where the house had stood, there was only a blackened pit, and in the centre, a small, knitted dog with buttons for eyes.

And that was the last anyone ever saw of the Seventh House of Lasingstoke.

Chapter 22
Of Tea, Claret, and a Very Good Wish

"The world to me was a secret, which I desired to discover; to her it was a vacancy, which she sought to people with imaginations of her own."
– Mary Shelley, Frankenstein: The Modern Prometheus

House of Lords, Westminster Palace, London
1894

"And another thing!"

A fist thumped on the oaken banister and Christien jolted awake.. Late afternoon sunlight beamed in through the stained glass, and the air was heavy with cigar smoke and fatigue. He rubbed is eyes and leaned to the mutton-chopped gentleman sitting next to him.

"Is he almost done?"

"Bloody hell, I hope so," said the man. "On and on and on about this damned society."

"Society?"

"Some infernal clandestine group set to bring the Crown to task, expose their intrigues, 'keep 'em accountable' bollocks. Some say it's a splinter group from the MoD. The House is calling it *MI:Nought*."

"*MI:Nought*," Christien repeated. "That's bloody brilliant."

"So you say now," said the man. "Until they decide that Guy Fawkes had a point and endeavour to blow up Parliament."

Christien grunted under his breath.

"Our esteemed Crown Prince needs our loyalty and our support," continued the original speaker. "Not scuttlebutt and investigations. Why, this is contemptible, sirs. Contemptible, unconscionable, and simply put, bad form."

Shouts of *hear hear* mingled with catcalls and jeers.

"So, why are *we* discussing this?" asked Christien.

The man shrugged and puffed his cigar.

"One of them's supposed to be in the House."

"The House," said Christien, blinking slowly. "*This* House? The House of Lords?"

"That's the word, de Lacey. But honestly, it's more likely a couple of Jacobites getting together for night of whist and juicy."

Christien sighed and sat back, wishing he could go back to sleep.

"We are the Peerage of Steam," continued the speaker. "The Right Honourable Lords Spiritual and Temporal. All the Empire is in our hands, and therefore, her fate is on our heads…"

Christien grinned to himself. *Lords Spiritual and Temporal.* How high they sounded. How little they knew. There had only ever been one Lord both Spiritual and Temporal, and he'd been Mad as a Hatter. After this latest session spent discussing the rogue division, *MI:Nought*, he could fully understand Sebastien's choice of blankets over the head.

At some point, the session ended, and the House of Lords adjourned for the day. As Christien pushed through the great halls of Westminster, he spied a trio of Lords conversing beside the statue of John Earl Russell. He caught the eye of one, Lord Hadrian Yardley. *Fine man,* thought Christien, with a beautiful wife from Calcutta and three wild, clever, talented children. Yardley nodded slightly, raised a hand as if to beckon, but Christien walked by. He was too tired for pleasantries, although the House of Lords was rarely pleasant.

It was raining in the city, so he hailed a steamcab, which chugged him noisily back to Kensington and Hollbrook House. He paid the man, trotted up the steps, threw a wave to Jekyll, the Ghost Club's man who was always spying at the door, and slipped inside without saying a word. He was happy at Hollbrook now. It was truly a home to him, and he smiled when Pomfrey popped into the hall.

"Welcome home, sir," said the man. "Will you be taking tea before your company tonight?"

"I believe they're coming early, Pomfrey," he said. "So tea will be in order very soon."

He pulled at his necktie as he made for the stair.

"And sandwiches, sir?"

"That would be wonderful."

"And dainties? I was in Covent Garden this morning and found some delightful lemon tarts."

"Yes, Pomfrey. Lemon tarts too."

"And I found some lovely watercress—"

"Yes! Please! All of it!"

He made sure he was up the stair before Pomfrey could add to the menu, heading down the hall and pushing open the door to his room. From the cage at the window, a gold finch sang to him.

Odd how much had changed in five years, he thought, as he pulled off his jacket and rolled up his sleeves. And yet, how many things had stayed the same. He crossed the room to the cage at the window and peered in.

"Oh, look at you," he said quietly. "You do like those new seeds, don't you? I'll make sure Pomfrey picks up some more."

The bird chirped and sang, and he smiled again.

Life was a marvellous thing.

"Mr. Christien!" called Pomfrey from the bottom of the stair. "Your guests are here already! And I haven't readied the tarts!"

"Hm. Quite early," he muttered to himself. He quickly changed his waistcoat and necktie but decided against an evening jacket. This was an entirely different order of guests. Formality was not required.

He headed back down the steps and pushed into the drawing room. Five figures sat around the flickering fire, and he moved to claim a wingback chair.

"Mr. Cracker, Mrs. Broom, Miss Candymore," and he nodded his head. "Lord Yardley."

"Tosh," said Yardley but he smiled. "Where's Miss Swan?"

"Running late, I expect," he said. "Mrs. Broom, what's the news on Kewe?"

The older woman sat forward.

"It's ours if we want," she said. "Practically in ruins at the moment, but it's solid. All it needs is a bit of Housekeeping."

"That's all any of us need, really," said the man called Cracker.

The group fell quiet as Pomfrey brought in the tea.

"Tarts in a moment," he promised, before slipping out again.

"So," said Yardley. He picked up the pot and began to pour. "*MI:Nought?*"

"The MoD will love that," said Candymore, voice dripping with sarcasm. She lifted the teacup to her deep red lips. "The Met, too."

"And the Yard," said Cracker.

"It's certainly more ominous than Housekeeping, I suppose," said Christien. "We'll need to stay in the shadows as much as possible. The Crown gets messy, and the War Office operates with impunity. They need both a check rein and a clean-up crew. We will be their very own Guy Fawkes."

"There you go, Remy," said Yardley. "You're Mr. Fox."

"Mr. Fox."

They all drank to that.

There was a knock at the door.

"Ah, that must be Miss Swan."

He rose and went to the door, swung it open to reveal a woman under a black umbrella. She lifted it from her face, to reveal smooth skin, delicate lips and eyes as sharp as steel.

"Hello, Remy," said Valerie.

"Do come in, Miss Swan," he said. "Housekeeping is waiting."

She smiled and he closed the door behind her.

***

My dearest and most northern Ivy,

I am delighted to hear that you are well and truly settled into that feral home of yours so far away. It sounds truly wretched, with the cold and the wind and the very rude townsfolk, but I know you will triumph in spite of them all. While I attempt to fill you in on the latest news and gossip, I do hope you are impressed with the general appearance of this letter, being that it is typed on a brand-new finger press, given to me by my Liddle Ninny to test it out for the Ministry of Defense. I do adore it so.

On to the gossip!

Lonsdale Abbey (which was, as you know, an arm of the War Office and the MoD) has been ceded in title to the Barony of Lasingstoke! The Scourge himself has made it official, reallocating both the Abbey proper and the grounds to our own dear cause. The old Lonsdale Abbey has been renamed The Lonsdale Academy for Willful Women, *with the incomparable Agnes Tidy as headmatron! My dear Franny will join operations as schoolmistress and her bosom friend, Lizzie Borden, has accepted a position as both instructor in Drills and Pigeon Studies. For her part, Franny is doing quite well with the assist of your brother Davis. He has been more than helpful in designing her a wheeled-chair that can navigate the many dreadful steps at Lonsdale, which, as you know, can be most intimidating. She will be teaching Languages, Maths, Puzzles, Science and Sleuthing.*

You will remember that, during her recovery at Balmoral, she did in fact meet her childhood sweetheart, Prince Albert Victor of Clarence and

Avondale. He was so dreadfully ill with the influenza last year and subsequently spent several months at Lonsdale at the point of death! But Franny, Lizzie and Agnes Tidy nursed him back to health, and he has agreed to stay on as teacher and chief botanist. Apparently, he has no desire for the throne, so naturally, he will not be teaching under his proper name. I believe 'Albert Edwards' will be the name he has chosen, but I am not at liberty to disclose any more. MoD and all that rot. I am a Ministry wife now and must be mindful of my conversations.

My dear mother's sister's husband's sister's cousin's daughter, Mary Jane, and I have become chuckaboos, and she is expecting yet again. Her son, Jean-Marc, is playfellows with my own Lyle-Lindon. I do swing round the Barony from time to time. It is considerably more difficult without a steamcar, and I do miss Franny's enthusiasm at the stick.

We still have heard nothing from our dear Grigori; however, my Liddle Ninny is convinced that he is back in Russia stirring up all manner of trouble. I say tosh. Grigori was an able sport and I'm certain he is flying high with Mr. Home in the Clouds of Heaven. He always seemed a spiritual sort.

Have you heard back from the Sorbonne, dearest? I'm quite convinced that you have taken the egg, utterly aced your exams, and will be announced as the finest student ever to graduate from the Criminology course! Do let me know, and we shall raise a glass to your success! Unless, of course, you fail, and we will raise a glass at the attempt!

Well, dearest, little Lyle-Lindon Liddell will be awake soon and needing his afternoon tea. Granny spoils him so, being her first great-grandchild. He does run her ragged, but boys will be boys, and he is as precocious as they come! I'm quite convinced you shall find yourself in the family way sooner or later, so don't fret! Children are a blessing, but indeed, much work, and your life in the very far north has its own share of troubles. But then again, a life of childless freedom is not to be sniffed at, and you'll not suffer for lack with the Mad Lord at your side.

Adieu, and give yourself a peck from me!

Yours for eternity and beyond,

Fanny Helmsly-Wimpoll-Liddell, et al

***

To

Mr. Albee Thistle

Penny Thistle Press

Cecil Court, Westminster,

Lond ●

The address ended with a blob.

Ivy growled and laid down the fountain pen, cursed her fingers that were now covered in ink. She knew she needed try out the finger press her father had sent her. It would take a while to get used to it, but surely, it had to be a cleaner proposition than fountain pens and blobs and countless wells of Indigo Ink.

She blew across the ink until she was certain the address was dry. She had wrapped the manuscript in brown paper, so now she reached for the twine. Around and around and around she wrapped, twisting it to make a T in the centre, before wrapping it the other way. She grabbed the scissors and cut the string, tying the manuscript up in a tidy bow.

"How's that?" she asked.

The old postmaster looked up and adjusted his goggles.

"Looks braw," he said after a moment. "What's this'un called?"

"Penny Dreadful and a Heist in the Highlands," she said.

He grunted.

"Same as last time?"

"Aye," she said. "I'll come in and settle up at the end of the month."

He nodded and took the package.

"Hold fer yer post, hen."

He disappeared into the back, and she glanced around the tiny postmaster's shop. On Skye, it was a hub for all manner of mail and communications. There was a Teslagraph on one desk next to a very old PHAX machine, and a set of pneumatic tubes running the length of the ceiling. Outside the window, she could see the whitewashed buildings of the High Street and beyond them, the harbour. It was an overcast day, and the wind was sharp. The wind was always sharp on Skye. The wind and the clouds and sighing of the sea.

The man returned with several letters and three small packages. One was tied up in brown paper much like the one she'd given him, and she held it up.

"Tha's the newest one, then?"

She grinned and ripped open the paper.

Penny Dreadful and the Creature in the Craigs.

It was her third novel from Albee Thistle and his new publishing house, Penny Thistle Press. After her book, *Penny Dreadful and the End of the World,* had become a runaway success, he'd novelized all of her broadsheet series in book form, creating six volumes of her work. With the three finished novels, that made nine. While part of her missed the simplicity of the broadsheets, the challenge of sitting down and writing a novel was both rewarding and industrious. Besides, the isolation was good for plotting, and here, on the Isle of Skye, there was isolation galore.

"It's beautiful," she breathed, and she held the book up. "My brother did the cover illustration. Isn't it wonderful?"

"If ye say so," the man said, and he disappeared once again into the back.

Ivy slipped the book into her leather school bag, hiked the shawl over her shoulders, and tugged her woollen cap down on her head.

"See you in two weeks, Mr. Budge!"

"Aye, hen," he called from the back. "See ye in two weeks."

She stepped out of the shop and breathed the cold salt air. A very woolly Rue stood, not tied, beside an iron post, and she patted the mare's neck before flinging the bag across the saddle. She hitched her tweed skirt and swung up, revealing the breeches and boots beneath. She turned the mare onto the street and set her homeward, ignoring the glances from the townspeople on the road. She was used to it by now. They were a funny folk. They didn't care that she wore boys' caps or breeches beneath her skirts. They didn't care that she was an unmarried woman, living with an unmarried man in the rugged hills of the island. Nor did they care that she was gainfully employed as a writer of fantastical novels, whereas her man was not employed in any field of note. They thought him a lazy crofter, rather than the holder of the titles and landlord of a significant acreage by the sea. No. Even after four years of living here on Skye, they were still considered strangers and that drew stares and whispers, rumours and tales.

She didn't mind. Every day spent living was a good day.

Rue knew the way home, so Ivy sat idly in the saddle, peeling open the letters one by one. One from Rupert reporting on the year's new foals. No mention of Mary Jane or young Jean-Marc, but Rupert was not one for letters. They'd have to travel to get any family news. They had a trip planned for the end of the summer. It would be sweet to be back at Lasingstoke again.

There was a letter from her mother with old recipes that she'd forgotten and recently discovered, and new novels that she'd read and recently forgotten. A postcard from Davis on his honeymoon in Bristol. A delightfully long treatise from Fanny, married to Ninian and mother to a young son, Lyle-Lindon. Ivy shook her head. Lyle-Lindon Liddell. How perfectly, utterly Wimpoll.

Nothing from Christien, but he was a busy man. Part of her was convinced he was a spy.

Rue ambled contentedly as the High Road became the only road, heading deeper and higher into the wild countryside. The wind never ceased, and Ivy was grateful for the tweeds and woollens that wrapped her in warmth. But the view as she rode was spectacular, and she never grew weary of the endless panorama of sea and sky, rock cuts and craigs. The fields were vast and filled with ling heather and sedge, avens and sorrel. Sheep grazed everywhere, eagles soared, and ponies ran wild across the moors.

She looked back down at the last letter and her heart skipped a beat. *Dossiers Universitaires* from *La Sorbonne, Paris, IRF.*

She shuddered at the thought, shoved the letter into the school bag and urged Rue into a trot.

It was an hour and a half later when she rounded the craig to see the small crofter's holding in the distance. It was low with whitewashed stone, a thatched roof and wooden shutters that braced in the storms. The stables were also stone, as were the dry fences, sheep folds and chicken coops. Northern ivy covered everything.

Like many of the island's remote homes, it, this small crofter's house had a name. They were all uniquely suited to their namesakes, whether it was Highland Wood, or Deer Tree Head or Foot of the Stream. All in Scots Gaelic, of course. Theirs was engraved on a plaque at the front gate, and she smiled as she pushed the gate open with her very fine boot.

Eidheann Cloiche Fuar.

Cold Stone & Ivy.

It suited the house perfectly.

She heard the thunder of hoofs and glanced over the wall to the hilly paddock beyond. A small herd of ponies burst out of the trees, thick and woolly like leggy bears. There was one taller, however, a lean grey without saddle or bridle, and on his bare back, her man.

Rue began to prance as the small herd raced toward her, slowing as they neared the dry stone fence. Even at his age, Gus could have taken it, she reckoned, but Sebastien swung off and hopped the fence on his own, jogging up to walk beside her horse and smiling like the sun.

"You got the post?"

"I did," she said.

"And?"

She reached into the schoolbag and pulled out one of the packages. She checked the name and handed it to him.

Without hesitation, he ripped it open, tossing the papers and box to the side. The dogs would get it, she knew. Nothing went to waste here in

Skye. He pulled out a pair of large dark lensed spectacles and slid them over his nose.

"Well?" he asked.

"Fantastical," she said. "Did you need them today?"

"One, but I told him I couldn't help, and he left," he said. "Sometimes, I can't believe how quiet it is in my own head."

"That's a good thing," she said.

"Oh, I caught a salmon today," he said as they made their way up the path toward the cottage, she on the horse, he on foot. "Made a skink with the leftover potatoes."

"Jolly good. I'm ravenous."

"Anything else?"

She reached in and dug out the book, held it up to flash in the light. He grinned.

"I'm going to need to build a bigger bookcase. Anything else?"

She pulled out the last unopened package.

"This?"

It was addressed only to *Cold Stone and Ivy, Skye.*

"No return address?"

"None."

"Strange," he said. "Well, we'll open it after supper. Anything *else?"*

"All right, all right," she laughed, and she pulled out the letter from the Sorbonne.

"Ah hah!" he said. "Have you opened it?"

"I haven't," she said. "I'm terrified. What if I failed?"

"Unlikely," he said. "You're too clever. Ivy Savage, Girl

Criminologist. It's in the books."

"You won't let me forget."

"I suppose we'll need a crime soon, then."

"There's always crime," she said. "We'll know when it's time."

"Yes," he said. "We'll know. Something will tell us."

"Something, sometime, I expect."

He grinned, and she thought it a very good thing.

They were at the cottage now and he reached up to swing her from her horse. A pack of dogs burst out of the barn, barking and leaping and wagging with all their might.

"I'll get Rue settled," he said. "Then let her out with the others. Tea's almost ready and I need to feed the dogs."

He spun and turned to the dogs, clapped his hands and they burst with happy energy. She watched him bound toward the stable along with them, snatching sticks and tossing them across the fields. Rue followed on her own, reins swinging against her shaggy neck.

It had been a very good wish, after all.

She pushed open the door to the little crofter's house, breathed deep the smell of wood smoke and salmon. A kitchen hearth crackled, and a kettle swung over it, hissing with water already at the boil. The housekeeping was a calamity, however, with papers and notebooks, journals and clippings piled on the floors, strewn across every table and pinned to every wall. Their mutual pursuits were exhaustive and thorough. Good thing the War Office kept them in paper.

She pulled the post out of the school bag and tossed it on the table next to some wildflowers and a bottle of claret.

Claret? They never had claret. It was always Scotch in this house, and she had developed quite the palate. Beside the bottle, were two glasses and a note.

Dearest Ivy,

I may not remember all things, but I do remember some. One of the first things you said to me was that you would likely never go to Paris or study in a proper school or be a Criminologist or solve crimes or wear breeches or drink claret, but that you would always write your own story. It seems to me that you have done all that and more, with the exception of the claret. That one is on me.

With all my love,

Laury

She glanced out the window. He was leading Rue to the pasture, seven happy dogs in tow. It had been five years. Five long, remarkable, uneventful years. She had studied, he had healed. The dead still came to call, but that was a matter for the War Office now that there was no three-barreled pistol or haunted house nearby. Between the two of them, they'd figure out what they could, and send recommendations to Whitehall every few weeks. It was a fair compromise, and for the most part, most days his eyes were brown.

As Fanny had been quick to point out, they had no children yet, but truth be told, she didn't mind. She'd been a mother at eleven, saved the world at nineteen. She deserved a bit of respite, as did he. No, they had horses and ponies, sheep and dogs. The two of them sharing their stories, their lives, their bed, was enough.

But the world was big and needing of help, and the War Office had been making inquiries. A clairvoyant and a criminologist could be of great use, they'd said, if a case proved too much for the Met or the Yard. But Sebastien was right. They would know when it was time.

She grinned.

Ivy Savage, Criminologist.

They'd pop the cork tonight, regardless of her grade.

She pulled the book from the school bag, and crossed the floor to a wall of shelves, full to overflowing with books. She tucked *Penny Dreadful and a Heist in the Highlands* next to the others and stood back to admire them all.

Stories, she thought. What a marvel. Stories were everywhere, everything and always available if one only had the eyes to see. She saw with the eyes of a cat now, in a home filled with dogs. She'd once thought Sebastien would be the greatest story ever told – the Mad Lord of Lasingstoke who talked to ghosts and ran with wild horses in the night. But he was neither mad, nor a lord, and currently not at Lasingstoke. No, he was here, and he was hers and she was glad she'd kept that story to herself.

All in all, not a bad chapter for a girl from Stepney.

Hm, she thought. One was missing. Perhaps Laury had taken it. He so loved to read in the hayloft, or in the bed late at night. They were both avid readers, hence the tragedy of housekeeping.

She turned back to the table and pulled the last package from the bag. It was wrapped in twine and brown paper and it seemed familiar, the size, the shape, the peculiar soft, cold feel. She frowned.

"Sod it, Laury," she said and she pulled the twine and the paper fell away. Out of the paper rolled an object, dark brown in colour, the size of a fist.

In her hands was a human heart.

"Well," she said. "I suppose it's time for another story."

She grinned wryly and reached for the pen.

The End

***

"Why, she's gone!" barked Chief Inspector Charles Dreadful. "I reckon that rascal, Alexander Dunn, has absconded with her! Call the Met! Summon the Yard! I must have my dear Penny back, at all costs! The criminals will have a heyday with Penny missing in action!"

Meanwhile, somewhere in the Mediterranean on a private sailing ship named the Ruffian, *Penny Dreadful pressed her marvellously large sun hat onto her head. The breeze was strong, and the ship was clipping.*

She whirled.

"Where are you taking me?" she said. "I demand to know."

"Isla Nessos," said international jewel thief, Alexander Dunn. "I bought it last year and have yet to visit."

And he handed her a fluted glass.

"Claret," she sniffed. "How predictable."

"Only the best for you, Penny," he said. His eyes twinkled in the sunlight.

"Is this island inhabited?"

"It will be," he said. "Once we dock."

He cocked his head and grinned at her. She turned her body to face him.

"And that's all this is about, sir? Docking?"

"Docking, mooring, tying the knots..."

"Bringing her in..." She stepped closer to him.

"Filling your berth..." He stepped closer to her.

"Rocking the boat..."

"Shivering me timber..."

"Alexander Dunn," she said. "You are a rogue."

"A scallywag."

"A pirate."

"International jewel thief, remember?"

"You have stolen my heart quite away."

"Guilty as charged, Detective Dreadful."

And as she kissed him, the **Ruffian** *sailed into safe harbours and, coincidentally, the sunset.*

The End

Of Penny Dreadful and the Fantastical Felon

Epilogue

"He was soon borne away by the waves and lost in darkness and distance."

    — Mary Shelley, Frankenstein: The Modern Prometheus

It was fitting, he thought, that de Lacey would end up in the north. Like him, creatures did not fare well with common folk, their tempers to wild, their humours unpredictable. And yet, he had found himself a woman, and in that, he was rare. Blessed. Lucky. Whatever name for Fate one would assign for the monsters it redeemed.

He looked down at the book in his grey hand. He had slipped into the cottage and be amazed at the sheer number of books on the many, many shelves. He knew the woman was a writer, for the ink was on full display. He had snatched one from its place, hoped she would not notice. He did so love to read.

Their animals had sensed him, though, so he would not stay. As much as he would enjoy kindling her acquaintance and rekindling his, he knew by now it was not to be. He would not end the happiness of yet another family. How injurious his face. How miserable his fate. A smile from either would have filled him with love, and yet, it was not to be.

And yet, the child of the sun had not, in fact, brought about the end of the world. Perhaps his words had produced some good, after all.

So, he turned once again to the north, to the snow and the ice, the cold sea and the darkness.

ABOUT THE AUTHOR

H. Leighton Dickson grew up in the wilds of the Canadian Shield, where her neighbours were wolves, moose, deer and lynx. She studied Zoology at the University of Guelph and worked in the Edinburgh Zoological Gardens in Scotland, where she was chased by lions, wrestled deaf tigers and fed antibiotics to Polar Bears by baby bottle. She has been writing since she was thirteen and pencilled her way through university for DC Comics New Talent Showcase.

Now repped by Looking Glass Literary & Media's Desiree Wilson, Heather got her start as an indie author writing the Sci/Fi fantasy series, RISE OF THE UPPER KINGDOM, along with Gothic thriller series, COLD STONE & IVY. Next came the award-winning Dragons of Solunas series, with DRAGON OF ASH & STARS and DRAGON OF SAND & STORM. She also writes for Bayview Magazine, speaks at book conventions and is a wizard when it comes to book covers.

OTHER BOOKS BY H. LEIGHTON DICKSON

Rise of the Upper Kingdom

To Journey in the Year of the Tiger

To Walk in the Way of Lions

Songs in the Year of the Cat

Swallowtail & Sword

Snow in the Year of the Dragon

The Empire of Steam

Cold Stone & Ivy: The Ghost Club

Cold Stone & Ivy: The Crown Prince

Cold Stone & Ivy: The Seventh House

The Dragons of Solunas

Dragon of Ash & Stars: Autobiography of a Night Dragon

Dragon of Sand & Storm: Autobiography of a Goddess

Coming Soon

Ship of Spells: A Runechaser Novel

Dragon of Salt & Bone: Autobiography of an Ice Dragon

To Fall From the Roof of the World

331

www.ingramcontent.com/pod-product-compliance
Lightning Source LLC
Chambersburg PA
CBHW072204130726
47910CB00011B/1806

9 780099 388655 53